LADY LOBO

by
KRISTEN GARRETT

New Victoria Publishers Inc.

Published by New Victoria Publishers Inc., a feminist, literary and cultural organization, PO Box 27 Norwich, Vermont 05055

Cover Design Ginger Brown

First printing

Library of Congress Cataloging-in-Publication Data

Garrett, Kristen,
     Lady Lobo / by Kristen Garrett.
         p. cm.
     ISBN 0-934678-49-9 : $9.95
     1. Women basketball player--United States--Fiction. 2. Young women--United States--Fiction. 3. Lesbians--United States--Fiction.
I. Title.
PS3557. A7232L3   1993
813 ' . 54 -- dc20   93-11797
                                              CIP

H.B., this one's for you. Your skill as my 'unofficial editor' and your prowess with economy of words and your counsel of moderation when I lose my temper are invaluable. I couldn't put anything into workable form if it wasn't for you. You are a true creative genius and a big crutch in my life. Your time is on the horizon. I can see it. I love you.

One game for herself.

She figured she'd earned it. After four years as a starter. Four years of varsity letters. Four years as a team player. Four years of playing point guard and feeding the ball to other players to make them look good. Four years and she didn't have a scholarship she cared about.

One game for herself.

Casey checked the laces on her Reebok Pumps. Tight. Maybe too tight, but she didn't loosen them. She walked into the bathroom. She sometimes threw up before a game. The need wasn't there tonight. She splashed cold water on her face, looking at her reflection in the mirror as she toweled off. Mousy brown hair, pulled back in a ponytail. Her 'game-tail' as she called it. Green eyes. Freckled face. Strong chin. She looked tight.

Walking back to the locker room, she pulled her wristbands to her elbows, then lowered them again. God, she was jazzed.

The rest of the girls in the locker room looked tight, too. Scared. Girls she'd played with for four years. Girls she'd fed the ball to for four years. All familiar faces. Jenny Kendall, the five-nine center. A solid player. Be a good power forward in college. Had a scholarship to Memphis State.

Jenny turned from her locker and made eye contact. "Give 'em hell, Ellison!" she shouted.

Casey nodded.

She'd seen the scouting reports. Casey Ellison, guard, St. Elmo High School, Chatsworth, Tennessee. Five-feet-four. One hundred twenty-two pounds. A natural leader. Excellent strength. Excellent speed. Good passer. Good ball-handler. Good defense. Good classroom grades. No scoring punch. Long shot for major-college ball.

No scoring punch.

One game for herself.

Casey checked her laces again. God, she was jazzed. Maybe too jazzed. She took a few deep breaths to calm down. There was a fine line you had to walk to keep yourself on the razor's edge.

Beth walked up. She was smiling, but her eyes looked afraid. Pretty blue eyes. Full-lipped mouth that was fun to kiss. "I'm scared spitless," she said, squeezing Casey's shoulder. "Pike County. God, Case, Pike County."

Casey took a few more deep breaths.

"I wish we were in bed somewhere," Beth whispered.

"Leave me alone," Casey said, turning away. She didn't have time for other people tonight. Not even for Beth.

Someone fired up a boom box. A Janet Jackson song started thumping. The team gathered in the locker room, slapping hands and butts, a colorful sight of blue and gold uniforms and matching wristbands and white Pumps. And scared, familiar faces.

Coach Jarboe came into the locker room, hands stuffed into the pockets of his slacks, whistling 'Mairzy Doats.' "If we could win it would be the greatest night in the history of St. Elmo, girls," he said. He laughed. "Nobody expects that. We know who you're playing. Keep it close and we'll be proud of you."

"In your nose," Casey said. The players cracked up. Coach Jarboe pretended he hadn't heard.

Then they were out the door, into the din, the pounding band, the excited people. A big banner on one wall of the gym said, *Welcome To The Pike County Invitational Tournament.*

The fifty or so people, mostly families, who'd made the trip from Chatsworth looked small, underwhelming, in one corner of the stands. Casey saw her own family. Dad with his camcorder glued to his face. Mom clapping and jumping up-and-down. Zit-faced Jimmy eating popcorn and looking bored like any normal fourteen year old boy at a girls basketball game.

Casey grabbed a ball and started her warm-ups. She missed her first three shots, all from two feet behind the three-point line. She moved up a foot, found her groove and nailed her next four.

No scoring punch.

Long shot for major-college ball.

Two scholarship offers. One from the University of Tennessee at Chatsworth, the other from East Tennessee State. Both were schools in the same small conference with no national exposure, no publicity to get a good coaching job after graduation, no chance for a National Championship.

One game for herself.

The gym exploded when Pike County came out, wearing their home whites. Pike County. Defending National High School Champions as voted by 'USA Today.' Three-time defending Tennessee State Champions. Unbeaten the last three years. Tall and fast and arrogant.

Everyone on St. Elmo faltered in their warm-ups to eye Pike County. Casey did, too, eyeing Number Four. Her assignment. Rhonda Flemish. Five-seven. One hundred thirty pounds. Brown hair, nice butt, great legs. Twenty-seven points per game scoring average. Already signed a letter of intent with Tennessee.

The horn blared.

Casey gathered with her teammates at the St. Elmo bench, not really paying attention to the pregame instructions from Coach Jarboe, instead studying Number Four. Casey was going to be on Number Four like a second skin. God, she was jazzed.

One game for herself.

Both teams gathered at half-court for the tip-off. Number Four started her intimidation game first thing. Butting with a hip, jabbing with an elbow, trying to move Casey out. Casey stood her ground, jabbing with her own elbow, butting with her own hip, realizing she was stronger than Number Four.

Jenny got the tip. Beth snatched it. Casey was gone, filling the lane, a step ahead of Number Four. Here came the pass, pounding feet, grunts, roaring students, families and townspeople.

Nothing there.

Casey pulled out, dribbling the ball with her right hand, holding two fingers in the air with her left hand. Jenny broke for the basket, elbows flying. Beth dropped off on the wing, hands held out because she was open. Casey ignored both of them. She pump-faked, Number Four went airborne, Casey slid underneath, squared to the basket and shot. Swish! The referee held both hands in the air to signal a three-point shot.

No scoring punch.

"Playground fake," Number Four hissed, looking hot.

Casey didn't say anything, thinking, 'You sucked it down.'

She jumped into a full-court press. In Number Four's face with hands, elbows, feet, knees, anything. Here came the inbound. Too low. Casey soared, got a hand on it, scrambled, feeling Number Four tugging on her jersey, the cheating bitch. Casey jerked free, tipped the ball again, to Beth on the wing. Back to Casey, behind the back dribble, left-handed lay-up, just like on the playground. Around the rim and in.

"Runt bitch," Number Four hissed. "Nobody makes me look bad."

Casey didn't say anything.

No scoring punch.

One game for herself.

The locker room was steamy from the postgame showers. Casey squirmed into her jeans, sat down to lace her tennis shoes.

St. Elmo had jumped to a ten point lead after one quarter, sparked by Casey's quick start. They'd trailed by five at halftime. By ten after three quarters. Pike County's height and speed and depth broke the game open in the fourth quarter and they won going away.

Pike County 89, St. Elmo 63.

Casey felt a shadow. She looked up from her lacing. A good-looking woman in a grey skirt and a black sweater was standing there. Lady Lobos and a snarling wolf's head were monogrammed in orange on the left breast of her sweater. The woman had shoulder-length brown hair and huge brown eyes. She looked like she was in her late-twenties. Maybe early thirties from the crow's feet around the corners of her mouth and eyes. Probing, evaluating, analyzing eyes.

"Hello," the woman said. Smooth, arrogant voice, like she was a big shot used to getting treated with respect. She offered her hand. A sexy hand. Pink fingernails.

"Hi," Casey said, shaking hands.

"Good game."

Casey shrugged. "We got smoked."

"You scored thirty-two," the woman said, sitting down beside Casey. She crossed her legs, smoothing her skirt over her knees, folding her hands in her laps.

"I usually don't score that much. I'm more of a ball-handler."

The woman said, "I'm Brenda Murphy. Head coach at Oklahoma Institute of Technology."

"Oklahoma Tech," Casey said. "Brookfield, Oklahoma. Won eighteen, lost nine last year. Received an at-large bid to the NCAA

Tournament. Advanced to the second round and lost to Stanford. Big Seven Conference. Major-college ball."

Coach Murphy laughed, a calm, sexy laugh, making her face prettier. Her eyes didn't laugh. Probing, evaluating, analyzing. "I'm impressed," she said.

"I read the papers," Casey said. "From what I read, you and four other head coaches came to the tournament to look at Pike County's center. You're in the wrong locker room."

"I'm more impressed by you," Coach Murphy said. "No offense, but the Pike County center wasn't going against quality competition tonight. You're a different story. You went against a quality player tonight and chewed her up." A pause. "Have you signed a letter of intent with anyone? I'll leave you alone if you have."

"I haven't picked a college yet."

"Perhaps I can save us both some time," Coach Murphy said. "Oklahoma Tech offers the complete package. Academics and athletics. Our admission standards are strict. Can you hack it?"

"St. Elmo is a private prep school in Chatsworth," Casey said, figuring that said it all.

Coach Murphy arched her eyebrows. "I also read the papers," she said. "I asked about you."

"Four years of math," Casey said. "Four English, three lab sciences, three computer science, two Spanish, B-minus average."

"Do you have any tapes I could look at?" Coach Murphy asked. She looked excited. Or maybe Casey just wished she did.

"Are you kidding?" Casey laughed. "Dad's got about a hundred. He has a packet on me. Tapes, transcripts, SAT scores. The works."

Coach Murphy dug in her purse, handed over a business card. "Could you mail your packet to me at this address? The sooner, the better."

"Okay-fine," Casey said, tucking the card into her gym bag.

One game for herself.

Lookout Mountain was twelve hundred some feet above sea level. There was a great view of Chatsworth from the top, especially at night. Casey and Beth had a special place they parked at on top of the mountain, not far from a pile of boulders and an old Civil War cannon. They'd talk and admire the view and drink a beer sometimes if they had any and make love always.

Casey felt the same thrill, the same sense of power, she always did when Beth climaxed with her sobbing moan and clawed at Casey's shoulder and squeezed her thighs around Casey's hand.

"I love you," Beth whispered, nuzzling Casey's neck, ears, chin, slipping a hand inside Casey's jeans. Casey pulled away, back to her side of the car. She zipped her jeans and buttoned her blouse.

"What's wrong?" Beth asked. She took Casey's hand and pressed it against one of her naked breasts.

"I'm not in the mood," Casey said, taking back her hand. She picked up her beer from the dash and took a sip.

"I feel guilty," Beth said, nuzzling Casey's neck.

"Don't." Casey pulled away. "I mean don't feel guilty."

"You've been in the ozone all night," Beth said, looking quizzically at Casey.

"I'm signing a letter of intent with Oklahoma Tech tomorrow," Casey said. "Coach Jarboe has called a press conference at the school in the afternoon. It's a big deal to him to send a player to a Big Seven college."

The car was quiet. Casey looked at Beth. Beth was squeezed against the passenger door, holding her blouse closed with both hands. Her head was cocked, her mouth was hanging open. She had a hurt look on her face.

"Remember three weeks ago when I went out of town with my folks?" Casey asked. "I went to Oklahoma to visit the university. They've offered me a scholarship. I'm taking it."

"But we're going to college here next year," Beth said. Her face was changing from hurt to mad.

"I'm not."

"Why haven't you told me all this?"

"I'm telling you now."

"I want to go home," Beth said, dropping her eyes, fastening her clothes.

"Okay-fine," Casey said. She started the car and headed down the winding mountain road toward Beth's house. She glanced at Beth. Beth's head was lowered, her cheeks looked wet.

"I'm excited," Casey said. "About getting a shot at major-college ball."

"We're through, aren't we?" Beth asked. She looked up, bit her bottom lip and looked back down.

Casey laughed. "We've got the rest of senior year and the summer. I'll be back to visit, too."

"But you'll find a lover out there and I'll be here. We'll drift apart."

Casey didn't say anything. She didn't tell Beth about the blond recruit she'd met during her visit. The recruit she'd made love with three times. The recruit who told Casey she was beautiful. She pulled into Beth's driveway. The driveway was jammed with cars, the house was all lit up, music blared. Beth's brother was having another party.

Beth jumped out. "I love you, Case," she said. "I never thought you'd hurt me this way."

"I have to do what's best for me."

"I guess that's exactly what you're doing," Beth said bitterly. "You've never really loved me. All you care about is yourself."

"I care about the game," Casey corrected, reaching for Beth's hand. Beth pulled back. "Can't you see things my way?" Casey asked. "I can't help it if I'm ambitious. I can't help it if I want to go away to college, to a place where the game is played the way it was meant to be played."

"So I'm not ambitious," Beth said, still sounding bitter.

"I didn't say that," Casey said. "I'm trying to explain to you how I feel. I'm trying to tell you about the things I saw at Oklahoma Tech, the people I met. And you should see the arena. It has a feel and a smell I just can't shake."

"You can go to hell for all I care," Beth said. She added, "And don't bother about finding time to spend with me before you leave. I'm not interested." The car door slammed. Beth ran into the house.

"Okay-fine," Casey said to herself. She started her car and went home.

The first thing she saw when she got to school Monday morning was Beth sitting in a blue Mazda Miata in the parking lot with red-haired Lena Malone, laughing and talking and acting cuddly.

It was humiliating.

Casey walked into the school keeping her back stiff and not looking at Beth and Lena because she had some pride. She knew everyone would see Beth and Lena together and Casey by herself, and they'd all think Beth had dumped Casey instead of the other way around.

It was a small victory to allow Beth. Casey had an exciting four years ahead of her at Oklahoma Tech while all Beth had was Chatsworth and a career at a university that got a two paragraph article in the middle of the sports section once a week if they were lucky.

But she was going to miss Beth, and seeing her with Lee made her jealous. They'd had some good times together. Casey hated that it had to end with them disliking each other and hurting each other.

CHAPTER 2

Casey had a fist fight with a cheerleader when she was a sophomore in high school. At the bus stop before school one crisp fall morning. Casey was standing with her friends, waiting for the school bus, when a car full of girls drove by.

The car screeched to a stop and backed up to the bus stop. The cheerleader, a senior named Kandi Bannon wearing a short red dress, white hose and black heels, jumped out. Kandi Bannon was beautiful, with long black hair and big brown eyes and dimples. Casey was more or less in love with her.

Kandi walked up to Casey and started ragging on her, saying things like Casey never wore any makeup and if she did it was only a little eye shadow and some lipstick and Casey's eyebrows were too bushy, her eyes too small, her nose too freckled to ever be beautiful.

"You never do anything with your hair," Kandi said. "It's always in a ponytail or flopped onto your shoulders. I bet you don't even own a blow-dryer. You're always in jeans and tennis shoes. At best you're only cute."

"Get a life," Casey said.

"You always smell like a gym," Kandi said.

"Your boyfriend is the captain of the football team. What's he always smell like?"

"That's why I'm here," Kandi said. "I heard you've been coming on to my boyfriend. Stay away from him if you know what's good for you."

Casey cracked up.

"You heard me, bitch," Kandi said, putting on what she probably thought was a vicious expression.

"Leave me alone before you get punched-out," Casey said, throwing her books on the ground, deciding maybe she wasn't more or less in love with Kandi Bannon after all.

Kandi jumped on her, shouting and slapping and pinching, fighting like a typical cheerleader. Everyone at the bus stop crowded around to watch, the boys shouting, "Girl-fight! Girl-fight! Rip each other's bras off!"

Casey kept her promise and punched-out Kandi, beginning with an uppercut to the chin. Kandi grunted in a way most cheerleaders normally don't and hit the deck. Casey jumped on top of her, rolling her around in the dirt, grinding her face in the ground, copping a feel of a great butt while she did. Kandi squealed cuss words the whole time.

When Casey got tired of rolling Kandi around in the dirt and grinding her face in the ground, she straddled her, ran a hand under her dress and copped a feel of some sleek thighs.

"Say you're a bitch and I'm beautiful," Casey ordered.

"I'm a bitch," Kandi said in a muffled, weepy-sounding voice. "You're beautiful."

"Say I can have your boyfriend if I want him," Casey ordered.

"You can have my boyfriend if you want him."

"Wear jeans next time," Casey said. "Nobody can fight in a dress." She slapped Kandi's great butt and let her up.

Kandi ran off towards the car full of girls, black tears rolling down her dirty cheeks, sobbing, "I'm going to kill you."

"Okay-fine," Casey said, feeling jazzed. It was a point in her life when she enjoyed punching-out cheerleaders when she wasn't trying to sleep with them. Everyone was laughing and pounding her on the back.

A boy held her hand in the air and shouted, "And still World Champion!"

Casey knew for a fact she wasn't beautiful in the face. Her body was a different matter. She had an athlete's body and she was proud of it. Not one of those pencil-thin, fragile, big-breasted bodies like cheerleaders had. Her breasts were hard and compact, like the rest of her. Her shoulders were husky, her biceps and forearms as muscular as most of the nerdy boys at school from hitting the Nautilus equipment and free weights three times a week. Toe raises, half squats, military presses, bench presses, arm curls, all the Nautilus routines. Her stomach was hard and well-defined, also from hitting the weights; her waist was almost nonexistent. Her legs were thick—what the cheerleaders called 'thunder thighs'—and strong.

She ran ten miles a day, seven days a week. She also did wind sprints at the gym three times a week, after she finished pumping iron.

Casey had always been a tomboy. Climbing trees, throwing rocks, punching-out cheerleaders and nerdy boys, playing sports—basketball, softball, field hockey, track, going fishing with Dad, doing yard work with Dad. The thought of sitting around waiting for a boy to call, or prancing around with so much makeup on she was afraid to move for fear of sweating, was one of the worst thoughts in the world to her. The thought of spending time in the kitchen with Mom was just as bad.

Dad and Mom were okay parents. Dad had always encouraged Casey's tomboyishness. Mom, too, although she always said she was disappointed in not having a frilly little girl to give cooking and housecleaning lessons. Dad and Mom always fit Casey's games into their schedules and sacrificed to buy whatever equipment she needed. Shoes, ball gloves, sports bras. Whatever.

The only real fight she ever had with her parents was when they found out she wasn't going to the Senior Prom. She told them she wasn't going because she didn't want to wear a goofy dress and long gloves and a corsage, and that's what the three of them argued about. Instead of arguing about the real reason.

Casey wasn't sure when she first knew she was a dyke. She'd always thought playing games against girls was exciting. The feel of a breast against her arm while playing defense in basketball, a hard collision in field hockey and the feminine grunt and muttered 'bitch' from the girl she'd collided with, the musky smell of a sweaty girl when she barreled into second base in softball, knocking the other girl down and rolling in the dust with her.

Those things were exciting to Casey, as well as the thrill of competing against other girls, seeing if her body and talent were better than theirs. Casey thought boys were like stray dogs. She'd take note of them if they crossed her path. Otherwise she ignored them because they had no connection to the things in life that excited her.

When Casey reached eighth grade she'd moved far enough up the sports scene where she started showering with the other girls after games instead of going home to shower. The showering excited her as much as the competing and the other things. She had to fight to keep her hands off the other girls in the showers.

One day after basketball practice she stayed late to run an extra set of wind sprints. Everyone else had gone by the time she finished.

Or she'd thought everyone else had gone. She heard whimpering in the showers, peeked around a corner and saw two older girls making love. Touching, kissing, moaning, doing all the things with each other Casey had thought had to be done with boys and she'd made up her mind to do without in her life since they involved boys. The two older girls seemed to be having a lot of fun. They seemed to have even more fun when they climaxed and staggered weak-kneed and panting out of the showers.

A few days later, Casey managed to find herself alone in the showers with one of the older girls she'd seen making love. She stepped over to the other girl, touched her breasts with one hand and squeezed her butt with the other hand. The other girl kissed Casey, slipped a hand between Casey's legs and Casey was soon having fun of her own and staggering weak-kneed and panting out of the showers, gladly leaving her virginity spinning down the drain. All without saying a word. Casey had never been much for talking. She was more for doing.

Casey's goals in life weren't the least bit complicated. After college graduation she wanted to find a coaching job, hopefully on a college level, but she'd settle for high school to start with, and be the best coach she could possibly be. She wanted to find a lover she really and truly loved and settle down in a nice house. In the meantime she wanted to go to college and make good grades, play major-college ball, experience the thrill of playing in the NCAA Tournament and have fun.

Any long-lasting attachment was something in her future. Until the future arrived she wanted to stay unattached and make love to anyone she felt like making love to, because she adored females and she especially adored the first few times she made love with a new lover. It was never as good as it was the first few times. At least it hadn't yet been for Casey—unless there was a lot of variety thrown in.

Brookfield was in north-central Oklahoma. It was about fifty miles from Tulsa and a hundred miles from Oklahoma City. The land was a lot different from the mountains and trees and kudzu of Chatsworth. Brookfield was pretty much flat. It had plains of waving wheat and oil wells and cattle ranches. It was a kicked-back college town, population forty thousand. Most of the stores and shops were named things like Lobo Laundry and Lobo Barbecue and Lobo Car Wash.

Casey drove her red Nissan 240 all the way from Chatsworth to Brookfield by herself, over her parents' wishes. Dad wanted to drive with her and then fly back. Casey slammed that idea. She told her parents she was eighteen, mature, responsible and fully able to drive nine hundred miles by herself.

Dad heaved a sigh and said, "Okay-fine," but only after taking her car to the shop for new tires and a tune-up and an oil change and new brakes. She thought that was okay, although she would rather have had a new stereo system with a CD player instead of new tires.

Casey got to Brookfield late on a Wednesday afternoon. The Tech campus was nearly deserted since classes weren't starting until the following week. She had gotten there early because she had to go through the freshman orientation, which she thought was a waste of time. But, hey, someone on an athletic scholarship didn't have too much to complain about.

She grabbed a salad and an iced tea at a place called Lobo Joe's, then drove around campus. The football stadium was on one edge of campus. Next to the stadium was Mitchell Arena, where Tech played basketball games. Casey didn't even look at Mitchell. She'd get more than familiar with the place once basketball practice started in October.

There were eight or ten main streets running through campus. Classroom buildings crowded all the streets. Most of the buildings were red brick with white trim, although there were a few high-tech buildings made of glass and steel. In front of the library was the prettiest part of campus. There was a fountain and a long lawn leading to the Student Union, a fancy garden and a duck pond. It was a big campus—four hundred acres, seventy major buildings, twenty thousand students.

Casey's dorm room was in East Gundersen. The university didn't have separate facilities for the jocks. She'd live with the other students and eat her meals in the dorm cafeteria just like everyone else. East Gundersen was a gigantic building, made of red brick with white trim.

She unloaded her car, lugged her stuff inside and called the athletic department to say she'd gotten there okay. Her room was on the fifteenth floor. It took three trips up the elevator with her things.

Her room was square, painted white and had a beige throw rug on the floor. There were two beds, two study desks, two bookcases, two dressers and two closets. The room was unoccupied, although one of the beds was piled with boxes and clothes.

Casey dumped her last load on the other bed about the time a lanky brunette came through the door, sipping a diet Coke. The brunette was all arms and legs and breasts. She was wearing pink shorts, a white crop top, white sandals and maybe a pound of makeup.

"Hi," Casey said, feeling a little nervous over meeting her roommate. "I'm Casey Ellison."

"Kim Chapman." The brunette flopped onto her bed, on top of the clothes and stuff. She leaned back on an elbow and eyed Casey. "I'm a slob," Kim said.

"What?"

"I'm about as neat as a pig."

"Who cares? Just keep your mess on your side of the room and we'll get along fine."

Casey unloaded her athletic supplies first. Four pairs of Pumps, one pair close to worn-out, two pairs perfectly broken-in, one pair she was just starting to break-in to replace the almost worn-out pair. Two pairs of New Balance running shoes, two pairs of leather Cons for everyday wear, Atomic Balm analgesic for sore spots, sports bras, prewrap, tape, four dozen white socks, a women's basketball, of course, which she tossed onto her bed.

"What's all that junk?" Kim asked. She sat up and curled her legs under her butt. She had a great pair of legs. Tanned and silky-looking. Delicate ankles.

"My gear." Casey started throwing jeans and blouses into one of the dressers, the one closest to her bed. Panties, a box of beige eye shadow, a tube of pink lipstick, a box of Tampons, Secret anti-perspirant, toothbrush, Colgate, floss, a few non-athletic bras, nylon running shorts, nylon mesh running tops, grey sweats for colder weather, more white socks. She hung her coat and four jackets in the closet, tossed her three ski caps and mittens onto the shelf and her nest was built.

"Don't you have any dresses?" Kim asked, looking wide-eyed. "Hose? Heels? Perfume?"

"Nope."

"How do you live?"

"I'm a jock," Casey said. "I have what I need."

"Huh?" Kim asked, looking more wide-eyed. Her eyes were a

14

sexy liquid brown.

"I play basketball."

"For real? You're lying."

"Nope." Casey set her alarm for five-thirty and plunked it down on the nightstand.

"I have to get up at eight," Kim groaned, acting like eight o'clock was unbearably early. "The first freshman session is at nine-thirty, you know."

"I'm getting up at five-thirty."

"Huh?" Kim started twisting a strand of hair around a finger. "What for?"

"To go running. I run ten miles every morning."

"For real? You're lying."

"Nope. Want to run with me?"

Kim giggled. "No way, dude."

Casey grabbed a towel. "I'm going to shower. Want to join me?"

"Huh?" Kim asked, still twisting on her hair.

"Nothing. Just teasing." Casey wound her way down the hall to the showers, through the crowd of giggling women jamming the hall. So her roomie wasn't a dyke. No big deal. If Kim had been a dyke, that would have made problems in the long run. After Casey took her for a lover and then moved on. It would probably be hard sharing a room with someone after the fling was over.

The showers were packed. Women taking off makeup and chattering about boyfriends and such. Casey didn't notice anybody eyeing her in the shower. No big deal. She'd find a lover sooner or later. All she had to do was be patient.

Kim was still sitting on her bed twisting on her hair when Casey got back. "You really getting up at five-thirty?" Kim asked.

"Yep. I do every morning."

"I don't know if I can take it," Kim said, rolling her eyes. "I might ask for a new roommate."

"Okay-fine." Casey dropped her towel, switched off the lamp on her nightstand and crawled into bed.

"You going to bed?" Kim asked. She was obviously a rocket scientist. "It's only nine-thirty."

Casey didn't say anything. Kim asked, "Do you always sleep naked?"

"Yep. I feel choked in pajamas."

"You have more muscles than my brother," Kim said. "How'd

you get all those muscles? From steroids or something?"

"I worked for them. Good night." Casey went to sleep wondering if she'd get in trouble if Kim asked for another roommate. Or if she'd get stuck with the worst roommate in the world. Kim was nothing spectacular, but she could be worse.

Five-thirty was the best part of the day. Cool and quiet with a few stars still showing. The sky was just beginning to lighten to the east. Casey did her stretches in front of the dorm. Yawning, the blond receptionist in the lobby watched in disbelief.

Casey started down Lobo Road, past the married student housing buildings which were all darkened. She ran slow for the first two miles until she completely loosened up and felt the sweat popping, before she dropped into her rhythm. She went to her kick for the middle five miles, pushing herself to the wall, loving the way her body strained to do what she demanded, the blood throbbing in her ears, the burning in her legs and chest, thinking about nothing except the next step, the next time her foot contacted pavement. The mind-lessness of running was the best part, not worrying about classes or lovers or ball games or anything. It was a great stress reliever.

She looped around campus, out Highway 15 for a ways, past all the billboards and motels and gas stations, before circling back around campus. She dropped back into her easy lope for the last two miles, cooling down gradually, checking her pedometer every so often.

The campus was showing signs of life when she got back. A few other runners were out. Cars passed occasionally, probably locals who commuted to Tulsa or Oklahoma City. The campus was pretty, birds singing, just light enough you could enjoy all the flowers and bushes. She stopped by the campus dairy and bought some yogurt to carry back to the dorm for breakfast.

Kim was sitting up in bed, scratching her head and yawning, when Casey came back from showering.

"Morning," Casey called cheerfully, willing to forget the rough beginning the night before and start over.

Kim grunted. She obviously wasn't a morning person. Casey dropped her towel and picked out a pair of jeans and a red blouse and a pair of Cons to wear.

"You go around naked a lot," Kim said.

"We're roommates. How can we miss seeing each other naked?"

"I think you're just conceited about your body."

"Okay-fine," Casey said, appreciating the cheap shot. "My body is paying for my college. I plan to take care of it." She sat down at her desk and opened her yogurt.

"What's that?"

"Yogurt," Casey said, showing the container to Kim. "I'll bring you some tomorrow if you want."

"Mega-yuck," Kim said, frowning. "My Mom eats that when she's dieting. Do you know what they're having in the cafeteria?"

"It smelled great when I came by." Casey laughed. "It's probably bad for you. Bacon, eggs, that kind of stuff."

"I was told the dorms provide a well-balanced diet." Kim looked like someone had insulted her dog. "The brochures I got said so."

"Just teasing," Casey said, wondering why people in Oklahoma didn't have a sense of humor. She stirred her yogurt. It was good yogurt, smooth with lots of strawberries. Not being sure if she could get along with a straight non-jock, she was about to change her mind and encourage Kim to ask for another roommate. Even a straight jock would be better. They could talk about sports if nothing else.

"Where you from?" she asked after a few moments of silence. She supposed she should say something even if she didn't know what..

"Tulsa," Kim said. "I've lived there my whole life. Until I moved here." She switched on her boom box. A Mary-Chapin Carpenter song started playing.

"I'm from Chatsworth, Tennessee," Casey said, bobbing her head and tapping her feet. She liked Mary-Chapin Carpenter. At least they had music in common.

"Oh," Kim said, looking uninterested. "I've never been there." She crawled out of bed, keeping her sheet wrapped around her, even while she dressed. Her modesty seemed stupid since she dressed in a white halter and orange shorts that showed everything she had.

Freshman orientation was nothing spectacular. Casey registered for sociology, kinesiology, English, algebra and geology. Then she went to the bookstore and got her textbooks, paper, pencils and other academic trappings. A graduate assistant was hanging around to make sure all the jocks got through with no problem.

College was no big deal, Casey decided. All she had to do was be calm and patient and a little conservative in her actions, and she'd end up chewing Tech up and spitting it out in little pieces.

She hoped.

CHAPTER 3

Mitchell Arena was built of reddish brick like most of the buildings on campus. It was bracketed by the football stadium on one side and a hundred year old building on the other side. The football offices separated Mitchell from the football stadium. The complex also had the athletic ticket offices, locker rooms, showers, a weight room with all the shiny machines and oily weights and grunting, straining men and women, and trainers rooms for taping and medical treatments and so forth.

Casey pinched her arm to convince herself she wasn't dreaming, she was really and truly a jock at a program that was so big-time.

She introduced herself slowly to Mitchell. It was a dignified, old, old gym, filled with memories she could almost reach out and touch. Memories of when Oklahoma Tech had been a power in men's basketball. Memories of the two National Championships Tech had won in men's basketball. Memories of lots of big games since then, lots of great athletes who'd walked the halls.

Inside the doors was a lobby filled with rows and rows of glass cases holding pictures and trophies: Big Seven Conference Championships. Bowl-game Championships—Orange, Sugar, Gator, Fiesta. National Championship trophies in basketball, football, baseball, wrestling, tennis and golf.

Beyond the rows of trophies was the basketball arena. It was fairly small, seating eight thousand or so. It had been built when basketball arenas were small and intimate. Before the days of huge, sterile arenas. Casey had fallen in love with Mitchell at first sight and it was one of the major reasons she'd been so hot for Tech. You didn't find tradition-rich arenas like Mitchell anymore.

The playing floor was brown wood, trimmed in orange, with a huge grey snarling wolf's head at center court. An orange banner hung across one side of the arena, at the top of the stands. 'Wolves

Lair' was printed in black on the banner. On one end of the arena was the 'Circle of Honor,' names and retired numbers of the great jocks who'd played basketball for Tech in the past; all the names were men's names. 'LOBOS' was printed in black along each baseline. A high-tech scoreboard hung from the ceiling. The backboards were glass, shiny and glistening in the lights, and hung with new nets. There was a pile of trash in one corner beside a trash can and a broom. A ball rack in the center of the floor was jammed full of basketballs, old and dark and slick-looking. Practice balls.

Casey had to fight not to grab a ball and dribble around the floor and pretend she was driving for the winning score in the National Championship game.

The smells in the place almost drove her wild. Smells of popcorn and floor wax and sweat and dirty uniforms and analgesic and steamy locker rooms and the adrenaline of competition, of fear over being good enough to win a starting position or ending up just one of the dregs. The atmosphere was as familiar to her as the curve of her own hip or the feel of her bed at home in Chatsworth.

It was Jock Valhalla.

Casey stood on the edge of the court, looking into the stands, looking at the shiny glass backboards and white nets and high-tech scoreboard, and pictured the place jammed with screaming students and families and townspeople. She pictured the day when she would stand in the very same spot, moments before a crucial game, and listen to the public address announcer say, "Starting at the point, from Chatsworth, Tennessee, Caseeeey Elllliiiisonnnn!" like public address announcers always did, all long and drawn out.

That moment was in the future. In the meantime she had work to do—like winning a spot on the traveling squad. She sure didn't want to practice and sweat and bust her butt only to be left behind with the dregs when the real team went on the road for tournaments and conference games.

First she checked into the academic advisor's office.

The academic advisor was named Mrs. Manders. She was a motherly woman in her mid-forties, with brown hair turning grey in a few places. A picture of the husband and three kids sat on her desk. A copy of the Serenity Prayer hung on the wall behind her desk. Two other jocks were already there.

Casey sat down to wait her turn. One of the jocks, a blond maybe six-four with gorgeous legs, got a butt-chewing for making a D on a chemistry test.

"I'll be sending Coach Murphy a memo about your chemistry grade," Mrs. Manders said after the butt-chewing.

"Damn," the blond muttered, slapping a hip and rolling her eyes. Huge blue eyes.

"What kind of language is that for a young lady?" Mrs. Manders asked, arching her eyebrows.

The blond walked out. When she was out in the hall she shouted, "God-damn mother-fucking chemistry bull-shit!" A clang and a crash followed. It sounded like the blond had kicked over a trash can.

Mrs. Manders looked impassive, pretending she hadn't heard what the blond shouted.

Casey stepped to the desk and said, "Hi, Mrs. Manders."

"Hi, Casey," Mrs. Manders smiled, pulling out a file. "How did your algebra test go?" she asked, studying the file.

"Got it right here." Casey laid her test on the desk.

"You made a B!" Mrs. Manders said. "Super! How about geology?"

"Going good. I already did my homework for this week. Want to see it?"

"No. I trust you, Casey. You're no problem at all."

"I don't need grade trouble."

"Good luck in practice," Mrs. Manders said. "I know the first practice is scary for the freshmen."

Casey gathered up her stuff and went into the locker room. The locker room was almost empty, telling her she was running late. She dressed pronto-quick in the grey sweat pants and grey tee shirt that said, 'Lady Lobos Basketball' in black. God, she was jazzed. First practice at a major college. She silently asked God to please not let her fall on her butt.

There were thirty-five or forty women on the gym floor the second time Casey saw it. Six were the six-plus feet variety, three looking as graceful as hippos on land. Probably walk-ons, women who didn't have scholarship offers but enrolled in college anyway and walked onto the basketball court and tried out for the team. There was a bunch of the five-seven to five-eleven variety of women, and a handful of the Casey-sized variety. Casey didn't see the blond recruit she'd made love with during her visit. She didn't know if the blond had picked another college or failed entrance requirements or what, but she wasn't on the floor.

There were maybe fifty people loafing around waiting to watch practice. A reporter with a camera from the local newspaper. A writer with a camera from the college newspaper. The rest looked like family members, except for the dozen or so men jocks, wearing grey sweats with towels wrapped around their necks, holding their crotches and eyeing the women and crowing about what studs they were.

Casey had to fight not to walk over to them and say, "Listen, ass-holes, I get more loving in a week than you get in a year because I know how to relate to women better than you do." It was something she wanted to say to men every time she heard them crowing about what studs they were, but she never did. She didn't have the nerve.

There was no sense of the group of players being a team, even if everyone was dressed the same. A group was gathered here. Another group over there. People hanging close to people they knew and ignoring everyone else. One group seemed to be people who banded together because they didn't know anybody else so they at least had that in common. Nobody was doing much talking in that group.

Casey stayed by herself, doing her stretches, cutting her eyes all around. She felt a little intimidated by the size of the women she saw. The number, too. She'd never been to a basketball practice with so many players.

Was she grabbing for more than she could hold?

Everyone stopped screwing around to watch when a humongous black woman, maybe six-five by two hundred pounds, grabbed a basketball at half-court, went barreling toward a basket like a runaway train and made a thunderous slamma-jamma, hanging on the rim, vibrating the backboard before dropping back to the floor.

Everyone whooped. Casey did, too. It was the first time she'd seen a woman do a slamma-jamma. The tall blond Casey had seen getting a butt-chewing in the academic office grabbed a ball and went loping toward the basket, long hair and elbows flying. She almost dunked but not quite. The ball slammed off the front of the rim and ricochetted maybe a mile into the air.

The blond hit the deck, legs splayed out, looking like a giraffe on drugs. Everyone ragged her. She waved a hand and limped off with an embarrassed grin.

Coach Murphy and Coach DeFoe, the assistant, came out on the floor, carrying clipboards, whistles and stopwatches dangling around their necks. A pack of women graduate assistants was with them. All the coaches were wearing black three-button shirts with 'Oklahoma Tech Coaching Staff' printed on them and orange shorts showing lots of tanned, shapely legs. The mood of the players changed, got tenser, everyone moved toward the coaches, the women who'd be judging everyone and handing out the brass rings.

The women with the power.

Coach Murphy blew her whistle.

"Time to start Boot Camp!" one of the grad assistants shouted. "Give me a line! Ten across, four deep! You! In the back! Shut your god-damn mouth! We talk, you listen!"

Everyone lined up, arm's length apart. The grad assistants led a round of exercises. Stretches, jumping jacks, more stretches, a groaning set of fingertip push-ups. Jump ropes were passed out and they did that for five minutes. Casey hot-dogged a little, spinning the rope until it whistled and making everyone cut their eyes at her. She liked jumping rope.

Everyone was good and sweaty at the end of the exercises.

Coach Murphy blew her whistle.

"Seniors!" a grad assistant shouted. "You know the routine! Lead us off!"

A group of women took off running, up the steps to the top of the stands, across to the next aisle, back down, across to the next aisle, back up. Repeat the whole thing. Up-across-down-across.

Casey fell into step at the back of the pack. Running didn't bother her. It was only to separate the chaff, only to see who'd stayed in shape and who'd sucked down too much pizza and beer in the off-season.

It didn't take much up-across-down-across to start the separating. In-between the pounding feet came the sounds of strained panting. Some women started dropping out, wheezing, coughing, holding their chests.

The grad assistants were all over the drop-outs, screaming, "What are you doing? It's not nap time! Don't quit! Don't ever quit! What's going to happen when we go into Columbia, Missouri on a Saturday afternoon and you want to lie down in the second half because you're tired? You think Missouri will stop playing so you can nap? Nobody runs the Tech-ettes into the ground! If you can be run into the ground you don't belong here!"

The women would lurch to their feet, stagger along a little ways before flopping down again and the screaming started all over again.

Coach Murphy and Coach DeFoe stood in the center of the court the whole time, watching the running, listening to the screaming, pointing at players, exchanging comments and making notes on their clipboards.

The second time around the gym, Casey almost ran over the blond giraffe who'd gotten a butt-chewing and then missed her slamma-jamma. The blond was sinking fast, crab-walking up the steps on her hands and feet, and wheezing like an old steam locomotive. Casey grabbed her waist, feeling a definite set of love handles, and pushed her out of the way. The blond giraffe was probably a walk-on. No serious jock grew a set of love handles in the off-season.

"Too much pizza and beer," Casey hissed.

"Fuck you," the blond gasped. "My knee hurts." She sprawled down to rest. Hair was glued all over her face by sweat.

A red-faced grad assistant was on the blond in a flash, screaming, "Let's fuck this off and go out for some Whoppers and Big Macs and chocolate shakes! Does that sound good to you? It looks like something you have a lot of experience with! Is that your butt you're dragging around or a semi-truck?"

Coach Murphy blew her whistle after three laps.

"That's enough!" one of the grad assistants shouted. "We don't want to kill you! And, believe me, you look like you're dying!"

Everyone gathered on the floor. They divided into groups of five and did wind sprints. Casey was in the next to last group. Start at the base line, full-speed to the free throw line, pivot on a hand before full-speed back to the base line—pivot, full-speed to the half-court stripe—pivot, back to the base line—pivot, full-speed to the opposite free throw line—pivot, back to the base line—pivot, full-speed to the opposite base line—pivot, back to the starting point and out.

Casey finished first in her group by ten feet. She walked around behind the basket after she finished, flexing her muscles, staying loose for the next round. Heaving. Wind sprints were hell no matter how good of shape you were in.

After the last group finished, the first group started again. They went through the rotation three times. Most of the women were crawling by the end. Casey finished first in her group by fifty feet the third time. No big deal. She was the only one in her group who wasn't crab-walking.

Coach Murphy blew her whistle.

"Let's hit the stands again!" one of the grad assistants shouted. "Get your knees high this time! You should be lubricated by now!"

Everyone groaned and went staggering toward the stands.

Practice ended two hours later. Casey hadn't touched a basketball the whole time. Run-run-run. She headed to the locker room with everyone else. Everyone was bitching and cussing Coach Murphy like she was a stray dog.

The blond giraffe sprawled on the bench in front of the locker next to Casey's. The giraffe didn't even take off her shoes. She just sat on the bench with her eyes closed and her hands squeezed between her legs, looking like she was ready to deposit her lunch on the floor.

"You need some conditioning," Casey said, flopping onto the bench, unlacing her shoes. "I run every morning. You're welcome to join me. I leave from in front of East Gundersen at five-thirty more or less."

The blond giraffe didn't say anything. She didn't even open her eyes. Casey pulled off her socks and worriedly studied a sore spot on her heel before finally deciding it wasn't turning into a blister.

A grad assistant came into the locker room. She was holding a clipboard. "All you walk-ons listen up!" she shouted.

A group of about twenty women in a corner of the locker room started squirming on the bench and swallowing hard, waiting to see who was lousy enough to be a first-day-cut.

"The following people are invited back tomorrow," the grad assistant said. She read a list of five names. "Thanks to the rest of you for coming out. Join the intramural league and try again next fall."

The five walk-ons who'd been invited back started pounding fists on their thighs and murmuring, "Yeah-yeah-yeah." The rest of the group slammed their shoes to the floor, looking hot. Two started crying.

One woman said, "Why does Murphy always send a flunky to do her dirty work? Doesn't she know how to talk? I've tried-out three years in a row and all I've heard out of her is that god-damn whistle she blows."

Another said, "It's fine with me. I'm quitting, anyway. I can't take this much running."

"You scholarship people listen up!" the grad assistant shouted. "The following people owe me five extra laps tomorrow for dogging it today." She studied her clipboard for a few seconds before she snapped, "Daniels."

The blond giraffe next to Casey flinched.

Casey eyed the blond.

Tobie Daniels. Freshman center. Six-four by one hundred fifty-five pounds. From Dallas, Texas. First-Team All-State in high school. A *Street and Smith's* All-American. A definite stud. A serious jock. So why was she in such rotten shape? Probably a combination of poor training habits and laziness, luxuries Casey couldn't afford.

"The following people report to Coach Murphy's office after you shower and dress!" the grad assistant shouted. She read off a list of ten names. Casey did her own flinching when 'Ellison' was the last name called. What had she done?

"That's the first rule!" the grad assistant shouted. "Never-never-never go into Coach Murphy's office until after you shower. That shows disrespect, considering what you people smell like after practicing for two hours." She held her nose and added, "Rule number two is never-never-never go into Coach Murphy's office unless you're fully dressed."

Casey peeled off her soggy clothes and dumped them in the clothes hamper. She grabbed two white towels from the huge pile of clean ones stacked on a table, one for her body and one for her hair, and headed to the showers. Her muscles had the kind of warm ache that came from pushing her stamina to the wall and holding it there for a while. A hot shower was going to feel good.

She noticed everyone eyeing her on the way. No big deal. Everybody always eyed everybody else in a women's locker room. Even straight women eyed other women, scoping out the competition. A group of women were gathered around a locker at the end of the room, listening to a boom box, talking among themselves and relaxing. The group was all seniors. Casey knew their names, heights, weights, points per game averages. Everything.

The guards in the group looked extra-close at her. She looked back just as close, looking for athletic things. Muscled legs, upper-body strength, the certain cock of a hip or tilt to a head that meant someone was a stud and knew it.

"Hi," Casey said when she got close enough to speak.

Most of the seniors ignored her. A few nodded. Alysa Johnson, the black six-five center, rumbled, "Ellison," in a voice like a bass drum.

Casey thought about that in the showers. She knew all the scholarship player's names, especially the ones she'd be competing with for a position, but why would they know her name? Especially the seniors? The Gods of the basketball team?

Between her shampoo and rinse, Casey noticed a willowy black woman doing more than the usual eyeing. The woman was maybe five-four and weighed maybe one-ten and had short hair shiny with drops of water trapped in the curls. She had small, pointed breasts, and a plump, firm butt. She was shaving her legs in-between eyeing Casey.

A dyke on the prowl if Casey had ever seen one.

Casey turned to face her, put her hands on top of her head and tilted her head back to show what she had to offer. When she lowered her head and wiped the water from her eyes she noticed the woman was still watching. Her eyes had more than a spark of interest. Casey knew her own eyes probably had the same spark because, truth be known, she was a little lonely. She hadn't really found any friends at Tech yet, and definitely no lovers.

The black woman grabbed a towel and walked over, breasts jiggling, thighs rippling, eyes dancing all over Casey's body. "Hi,"she said in a buttery voice. "I'm Sharika."

Casey shut off her water and introduced herself. Sharika seemed older, early twenties, maybe. She wasn't a basketball player; she hadn't been at practice, Casey was sure of that.

"You look tired," Sharika said.

"I am a little."

"I was in the stands watching you practice," Sharika said. "You're in excellent condition. I'm an athlete, too. That's why I can shower with the basketball team."

"I can tell. You have a great body," Casey said, tracing a fingernail along the side of Sharika's breast down to her hip. "Your muscle tone is excellent. Could we get together later and discuss training techniques?"

Sharika laughed, her eyes shined. "I was fixing to ask you that. I have a friend who lets me use her apartment sometimes. Why don't you come over? I'll cook us dinner."

"God, that sounds great," Casey said, touching Sharika's arm. "What's the address?"

"The Orient Apartments on Block Avenue, apartment one-twelve."

"Give me about an hour and a half," Casey said. "I have to see Coach and then run by my dorm room."

"Hurry every chance you get. I'll be waiting." Sharika walked out, butt swaying. The back view looked as good as the front. She left the showers on the opposite side from the basketball locker room, through the door that was labeled, Tennis-Volleyball.

Casey was the last one to line up outside Coach Murphy's office. The other women didn't stay inside long so the line moved fast. Casey relaxed when she noticed everyone was smiling when they came out.

When it was her turn, she went inside and said, "Hi, Coach."

Coach Murphy had a nice office, the kind of quietly professional office Casey wanted someday. It was decorated with an orange carpet, leather chairs, college diplomas and certificates from coaching clinics on the walls, and a picture of the husband and two kids and a steaming mug of coffee on her big wooden desk.

Casey didn't sit down. She wasn't about to waltz into the head coach's office and flop down in a chair without an invitation.

"Everything okay?" Coach Murphy asked, looking up from some papers she was working on.

"Fine, Coach."

"Classes okay?"

"Yes, ma'am."

"You're everything I was told you are," Coach Murphy said, leaning back and tossing a pencil onto her desk. "Your high-school coach told me you have outstanding work habits and you do. You're in mid-season condition right now. I'm also pleased by your speed. You're possibly the fastest woman on the team." A pause. "Were you holding back a little today?"

"Yes, ma'am," Casey said. "I was taught to never run as fast as I can unless I absolutely have to."

"You have to tomorrow."

"Yes, ma'am," Casey said, hoping Coach Murphy didn't think she was lazy. She timidly said, "I didn't think anyone was paying attention to me today. I didn't think anyone even knew my name, except you."

"Oh, we know who you are," Coach Murphy said. "We had an eye or a stopwatch on you all during practice. You're our prize recruit. All the other scholarship women out there are ones we recruited heavily and expected to get. You dropped into our laps like a Christmas present. The people in Tennessee made a mistake by letting you get away."

"Thanks," Casey said, shuffling her feet.

"We're starting scrimmages in two weeks," Coach Murphy said. "You'll be working with the second-team."

Casey felt a ripple of excitement jump up her back. And then just a trace of fear over scrimmaging with the second-team. "I don't understand," she said slowly. "You're saying I made second-team on the first day? The traveling squad on the first day?"

"The traveling squad will fluctuate before the season begins, but you'll be on it," Coach Murphy said. "How do you feel about that?" Her eyes were probing, evaluating, analyzing, saying, 'Does second-team please you? Is that all you hope to be?"

Casey wanted to jump around and pound her fists on her thighs and scream, 'I feel great about second-team! I feel great about anything above water girl on this team!' Actually she stood still and said, cockily, "I've been a starter on every team I've played for. Ask me how I feel when I'm a starter on this team."

Coach Murphy laughed. Her eyes softened. "I heard you caused quite a stir in the weight room last week," she said, looking curiously at Casey. "I heard you bench pressed more than everyone on the men's baseball team, except for one catcher."

"Baseball players aren't very strong," Casey said, feeling self-conscious. "They spend all their time chewing tobacco and scratching themselves. It only took two-twenty to beat them."

Coach Murphy laughed again. "That's all, Casey," she said. "I have an open door policy with my players. Helping them is an integral part of my job. If you need anything don't hesitate to come to me."

"Yes, ma'am." Casey was doing her own smiling when she left Coach Murphy's office. She noticed Tobie Daniels still sitting in front of her locker, holding one shoe in her lap.

"Better hustle," Casey called. "You'll miss dinner at your dorm."

"I'm working on it," Tobie groaned without opening her eyes. She sounded half-dead.

Casey did her own groaning when she noticed a grad assistant tacking a sign on the locker room wall. The sign said:

ROAD TRIP RULES FOR TRAVELING SQUAD

1. All players/coaches will wear:

a) Dress or top/skirt with no hems higher than the knee (note this does not say jeans, shorts, culottes, pantsuits or Spandex).

b) Bra, panties, slip.

c) Hose.

d) Lipstick, eye shadow, mascara, perfume (note this does not say eyeliner, foundation/base or rouge).

2. Hair will be clean at all times and worn in the natural color (no multicolored styles, nothing outrageous).

3. Fingernails will be clean at all times and trimmed as neatly as possible considering we are athletes.

4. Body hair will be removed semiweekly (at a minimum).

5. Any player/coach caught using profanity in public places (elevators, restaurants, airports, etc.) will be disciplined.

Casey wrote the letter in her mind as she drove to meet Sharika for dinner and conversation and hopefully a little more:

Dear Dad and Mom,

I'm doing good, starting to adjust and make friends. I miss you both. I even miss Jimmy, believe it or not. It seems strange not to have him around to bug me every five minutes about loaning him money or driving him and his friends to the mall. We had first practice today. Coach Murphy told me I'll be on the traveling squad so I'm feeling pretty excited right now. She wants us to look wholesome when we travel so please send money for clothes. Why didn't someone tell me she's a dictator with breasts before I got here? Mom, why didn't you spend more time with me, teaching me how to wash dresses and crap like that? Or how to use mascara? Ha! Seriously, I can't believe I'm here, playing for someone like Coach Murphy. I've waited my whole life to have a coach like her.

P.S. College is so different from high school. The women in college are bigger, stronger, faster, smarter. And they're meaner—more intense—than high-school players.

CHAPTER 4

One day before practice when everyone was hot-dogging and doing slamma-jammas, Casey did her own trick. Spinning a basketball on each index finger. It was her equivalent of a slamma-jamma. A photographer from the college newspaper was hanging around and snapped Casey's picture.

After the picture was snapped Casey bounced one of the balls off her head and the other off her knee. Both spun off the backboard and dropped through the basket. Everyone whooped like she'd cured unemployment. Casey didn't tell them it was pure luck making the trick shots.

The next day the picture of Casey spinning a basketball on each index finger was on the front page of the college paper. Below the picture was a foolish caption that said, 'Freshman Casey Ellison and Lady Lobos hope to spin web around Big Seven foes this year,' or something like that.

A few days later word came down the memo chain that Casey was scheduled for an interview with a reporter from the college paper for an in-depth story. The head memo writer, a.k.a. Coach Murphy, thought it would be great publicity for the team.

The reporter was a senior journalism student named Toni Denson. She was about five-five and real skinny, maybe one hundred pounds. She had blond hair, cut short and moussed back, and blue eyes and dimples.

The interview lasted for about an hour, questions about home and family and career ambitions and so forth. When the interview was finished, Toni closed her notebook and turned off her recorder and put her pen in her purse.

"Do you want me to print you're a lesbian?" she asked, leaning close, resting a hand on Casey's knee.

"Uh," Casey said, caught by surprise. She hadn't thought she was advertising what she was. "Do you want to print that?" she asked when she regained her poise.

"Yes," Toni said. "But I feel it should be your decision."

"I think I've got enough to deal with already," Casey said. "What with being a freshman and all."

"Okay," Toni said, standing, slinging her purse over a shoulder, picking up her recorder. "You know the women will crawl out of the woodwork after they read my article. I'm jealous of the good times in front of you."

"What do you mean?"

"You'll see," Toni said, laughing.

The first woman to crawl out of the woodwork was a junior named Kristy Neapope. She was about five-six and had jet black hair and brown eyes and a pointed nose and a great complexion. She was skinny like Toni. They met on the third floor of the library one evening. Casey was doing algebra homework at a study desk. She looked up and saw Kristy was standing there, dressed in a black blouse and a tan skirt and white sandals.

A dyke on the prowl if Casey had ever seen one.

"I read about you in the school paper," Kristy said after they exchanged introductions.

"You have one of the most beautiful complexions I've ever seen," Casey said, touching Kristy's hand. Her skin had a warm, light-brown glow.

"I'm a Fox," Kristy murmured, dropping her head slightly.

"I know. You're beautiful," Casey agreed, thinking it was a conceited thing for Kristy to say even if it was the truth.

Kristy's face flushed. "I mean I'm a full-blooded Native American," she said. "A Muskwaki. The white man calls us Sac and Fox."

"Oh." Casey studied Kristy. There were some Native Americans in and around Tennessee, Cherokees mostly, but Casey didn't think she'd ever actually met one. Except for the one she met the time she went to Cherokee, North Carolina with her parents. The Native American she met that day had been wearing a costume like Sitting Bull wore in cowboy movies. He made his living by charging tourists five dollars to take his picture.

"I've never met a Muskwaki," Casey said, not stumbling over the odd word too much.

"But you've heard of us," Kristy said proudly, lifting her head.

"We had a great leader who fought the white man for many years. His name was Black Hawk. The white man put him on a reservation after they captured him. He died there."

"Are there many Native Americans in Oklahoma?"

Kristy nodded. "About three hundred thousand."

"Doing anything later?" Casey asked, making her move.

"What do you mean?" Kristy's eyelids flickered, she looked confused.

"Let's go somewhere and have fun. I hear there's a lake west of town that's supposed to be pretty. We could drive out there and talk."

"Lake Osage," Kristy said, still looking confused.

After Casey had parked her car under a tree beside Lake Osage, she maneuvered Kristy into the back seat. Kristy was hesitant the whole time.

"What's wrong?" Casey asked.

"Nothing. I don't know." Kristy closed her eyes like she was waiting to get a shot from the dentist.

Casey leaned over and probed Kristy's mouth with her tongue. Unbuttoning Kristy's blouse, she cupped Kristy's full, warm breasts in her hands, sighing happily when Kristy's nipples crinkled with excitement.

"What are doing?" Kristy asked, sounding as confused as she had in the library.

"Having fun," Casey said, slipping a hand under Kristy's skirt, running her hand lightly up Kristy's trim, golden thighs, tugging gently at Kristy's panties, eagerly stroking Kristy's damp crotch.

Kristy didn't help with any of the undressing or take part in any of the fun-having. She just kind of lay there like a limp fish. Casey didn't care. She had both of them naked in a few seconds and pretty much started going for it with Kristy's body as fast as her mouth and hands could go.

"This doesn't feel right," Kristy whispered. Her eyes were still squeezed shut, a tear was running from each corner. "It feels wrong."

"It feels great to me. You're beautiful."

"I'm a virgin," Kristy whispered. "Please don't hurt me."

"Want me to stop?"

"Yes," Kristy whispered.

"Okay-fine," Casey said. "I don't want you to do anything you're uncomfortable doing." She squirmed into her jeans, glancing around to make sure no cops were around. It would be less than funny to suddenly look up and see a cop shining a flashlight into the back seat where two dykes had almost done their thing. It would be worse getting slapped with a Crime Against Nature felony and losing her scholarship, especially when nothing had happened.

Casey heaved a sigh after she was dressed. Kristy had a gorgeous body. She was sorry to see it slip through her fingers. But she really didn't want to force herself on anybody.

Was she losing her touch? Was she going to have trouble spotting a dyke on the prowl for the rest of her life?

"This was wrong," Kristy said. She started crying. "I should have a boyfriend who can give me a home and kids. You can't give me any of that."

"Not hardly."

"Please drive me to the Catholic Center on campus." Kristy said.

"Are you Catholic?"

"Yes."

"A Catholic Muskwaki?"

"I'm sorry," Kristy wailed. "Is there something wrong with that?"

"No, I didn't mean it that way," Casey said, rubbing Kristy's head soothingly. "How did you happen to become Catholic?"

"My grandfather was badly wounded in Korea," Kristy whimpered. "A Catholic priest stayed with him until the doctors came. When my grandfather came home, he made everyone in the family convert. He thought he lived because of the Catholic priest."

"That makes sense," Casey said. "I guess."

"Please take me to the Catholic Center," Kristy wailed. "I need to confess."

"About what? All we did was kiss."

"I don't know. Something," Kristy said. "I don't want to see you again."

"Well, just jump right up and hurt my feelings," Casey said. She dropped Kristy off at the Catholic Center and went to her dorm.

When she walked in the door, she noticed Kim wearing a filmy white wrap and wiping at something in the center of her bed with a wad of paper towels.

Kim jumped about ten feet when she saw Casey. "I spilled

something on my bed," Kim said. Her face was bright red.

"Was your boyfriend here tonight?"

"Kenny's best friend Mike came by tonight," Kim said, dropping her face, looking exposed. "I swear I didn't give it up for him. Don't tell Kenny. Please."

"Okay-fine." Casey grabbed her books and went to the study lounge, assuming Kim wanted to be alone while she cleaned her bed. She did her homework for the next two weeks.

Kristy called a few days later. "I have to see you," she said.

"You know what I want."

"I'll give it," Kristy whispered.

"Okay-fine." Casey picked Kristy up and they drove to Lake Osage again. Kristy started crying after they were naked, covering her face with her hands.

"I can't," Kristy said. "I thought I could, but I can't."

Casey didn't say anything, looking around for a bus or train to jump in front of.

"Take me to the Catholic Center, please," Kristy said through her fingers. "I need to confess." She started crying harder. "I've applied to become a nun."

"What?" Casey blurted, feeling as dumfounded as she sounded.

"I don't want to see you again."

"Okay-fine." Casey dropped Kristy off and went back to her dorm. Kim was flailing away at her bed with a wad of paper towels. "Was your boyfriend here tonight?" Casey asked.

Kim dropped her face. "Kenny's other best friend Roger came by tonight," she said. "We didn't do anything. Don't tell Kenny. Please."

"This figuring-out-sexuality thing is a bitch, ain't it," Casey said, only half-kidding. She grabbed her books and went to the study lounge.

Kristy called a few days later and the whole screwball situation repeated itself. Casey wanted to pound her head against a tree or a rock after she took Kristy to the Catholic Center for the third time. The only good thing about the whole deal was being caught up on her homework for the next ten years or so.

Sharika, the willowy black tennis player, was a regular lover. As regular as Casey wanted it to be, about once a week or so. Sharika seemed to live for sex. She made a big production out of it. Every time Casey saw her, Sharika was wearing a filmy something that exposed most of what she had to offer. The apartment was always dark except for a few burning candles.

Sharika usually fixed a meal of pasta or a seafood salad and they shared a bottle of wine. Sharika always fed Casey, sitting on Casey's lap, purring and caressing. Once Casey was good and seduced, Sharika led the way to the bedroom and gave Casey a long massage and a strong climax. Casey always fought her climaxes with Sharika, holding them back for as long as she could until finally letting them wash over her in stronger and stronger waves.

Casey enjoyed the flip side of Sharika, too. It was fun to burrow along Sharika's body until finally reaching a sopping wet woman, nudging Sharika over the edge until she started sobbing and thrashing around on the bed like she always did.

Afterwards, Sharika always snuggled in Casey's arms and started talking about love and attachments and so forth. "There's more to life than casual sex, sugar," she always said in her buttery voice.

"Casual sex is fine with me right now," Casey always said.

"You'll never find a better lover than me," Sharika always said.

Casey always laughed.

Tobie Daniels started running with Casey after a week of getting her butt run into the ground at practice. Tobie sure added a lot of pleasant scenery to Casey's morning run, with her gorgeous legs and long blond hair and huge blue eyes. Tobie was close to being model/movie star beautiful.

Tobie's high-school team won the Texas State Championship her senior year. She picked Tech after being approached by six hundred colleges and universities and receiving scholarship offers from most of them. She picked Tech because of academics and because she wanted to go to a college away from home and because she thought so much of Coach Murphy.

At first.

She had since changed her mind and decided she hated Coach Murphy's guts and she talked about transferring to another college sometimes. Mostly because she thought practice was humiliating. She came to Tech expecting to be treated like a star and instead she was treated like any other player. She didn't understand why a star of her caliber had to run and practice instead of just being allowed to show up for the games and kick ass.

Casey thought Tobie was more or less conceited.

The first day of running, Tobie barely made a mile before she stopped running and started walking, hands on her hips and her head lowered. Casey kept going. Tobie walked a ways, then went back to her loping gait that ate up ground. She dropped out after two miles of walking/running. A few days later she made it to the two mile mark. The three mile mark a few days after that. Before long, she was right beside Casey, loping and panting at the ten mile mark. She gradually lost the love handles around her waist from sucking down too much pizza and beer in the off-season and went beyond model/movie star beautiful.

It became a routine Casey looked forward to. They'd meet in front of the dorm at five-thirty, do their stretches and go for their run. Tobie didn't interfere with Casey the least little bit. She loped and panted and wiped at her sweat and didn't flap her mouth, seeming to enjoy the mindless release of running as much as Casey did.

After their run, they'd stop for yogurt at the campus dairy. They'd sit on the bench outside the dairy and eat their yogurt and talk while the sun came up and the campus started buzzing.

One morning, after they finished eating, Tobie said, "I've been feeling homesick lately. It's embarrassing."

"I feel that way sometimes, too. I miss Krystal hamburgers so bad I could scream. What's so embarrassing about it?"

Tobie stared into the distance, a wistful look on her face. "You should've heard the way I bragged to my family and friends in Dallas before I came here," she said softly. "About how I'd be the starting center my freshman year. If I don't at least make the traveling squad I can't go home again. I'll probably kill myself."

"Maybe you should see a counselor," Casey said. "Suicide is serious stuff. I'll go with you if you're afraid to go by yourself."

"I'll be okay," Tobie said. She loped off, leaving Casey feeling helpless and confused because it seemed like Tobie sometimes hinted about wanting a friend, but when you tried to be her friend and get her to open up, she loped away.

One day Casey left her dorm and noticed a woman with long, permed/moussed blond hair. The blond was lounging on a bike and studying Casey with a tight smile on her face. The blond followed her to class, was waiting outside the door when class ended and followed Casey to her next class. The blond was waiting again when Casey's class ended.

Casey walked up to her and asked, "Are you following me?"

"Like, yeah," the blond said. She was close to being as gorgeous as Tobie and was maybe an inch shorter than Casey. She had green eyes and a turned-up nose and perfect teeth. She was definitely full-bodied, with breasts to next week and a butt to match.

"What do you want?"

The blond put her hands on her hips and cocked her head. "Duh," she said, rolling her eyes. "What do you, like, think I want?"

"The Catholic Center is that direction," Casey said, pointing, not trusting herself to read any signals from any woman anymore.

"Like, so?" the blond asked, looking confused. "I'm, like, a Methodist," she added. "When did we start talking about religion? I must've, like, missed something."

"Sorry," Casey mumbled, feeling embarrassed.

The blond said, "I saw you the other day. I thought you might, like, want to come over to my place and let me read you poetry."

"You thought that just from seeing me?"

The blond laughed. "What can I, like, say? That I fell in love with you from afar. It was like a tree falling on my head."

"How can I refuse a romantic proposition like that?" Casey grinned."Give me your address. I'll come over later. This evening."

The blond's name was Katie Catcher. She shared an off-campus apartment with two other women. Katie answered the door wearing a white tee shirt and red spandex shorts. She was sucking on an orange popsicle and held a book in her hand.

"Yo," she said, handing Casey an orange popsicle, and leading her to the couch, motioned for her to sit down beside her. "Come here."

Katie open the book and started to read a poem. She read it with enthusiasm, putting passion and tension in her voice, waving her popsicle in the air theatrically. The poem was about love and happiness, crashing ocean waves, brilliant moons hanging in the dark sky and heated bodies thrusting , rolling, embracing on the sand.

Casey noticed she was licking her own popsicle vigorously.

When the poem was finished, Katie threw down the book and cried, "Doesn't that just, like, turn you on?"

Casey nodded weakly.

"Your mouth is orange."

"So is yours."

"Let's get you cleaned up," Katie said softly, taking Casey's hand and leading her back to the bedroom.

Casey really enjoyed Katie's body. It was soft and rounded and smooth. Katie was good in bed, eagerly giving all she had, greedily taking all Casey had.

"Don't you just, like, *love* poetry!" Katie said afterwards, holding Casey close.

Casey sighed.

The next time Casey went to Katie's a spidery woman, maybe five-seven by one-fifteen, with cropped brown hair and huge brown eyes answered, wearing black Capri pants, a white blouse and holding a light bulb.

"Hi," Casey said hesitantly.

"Yo," the woman said. "I'm Carla. Katie had to, like, leave, but told me you might come by. Could you help me with the bulb in the bathroom?" she asked. "It's, like, history and I can't reach it."

Casey followed Carla into the bathroom. "Why don't you get a chair so you can reach it?"

Carla sucked a knuckle, explaining pitifully, "I tried to but I banged my hand on the door and it hurt."

"Okay-fine." Casey said, going to the kitchen for a chair, carrying it back to the bathroom. She jumped onto the chair, twisted out the old bulb, exchanging it for the new one Carla held up to her, their hands touching. Casey twisted in the new one.

"You're so brave and strong!" Carla said admiringly, clasping her hands under her chin and batting her eyelashes.

Casey laughed and hopped off the chair. When she hit the floor, she was only inches away from Carla. She inhaled Carla's spicy perfume. Carla's eyes sparkled. Her lips parted slightly.

"You femmes are totally helpless, aren't you?"

"I'm not femme, I'm butch." Carla said, kissing Casey. "I'll make it, like, worthwhile for you. Come on."

Casey hesitated, confused, but Carla pulled on her arm gently, saying softly, "Katie isn't possessive, like, you didn't make promises, right? You can be with me, if you want to. Do you?"

Casey nodded. She did want to, and decided she would worry over her confusion later.

Carla's breasts were firm and rounded, her thighs long and sleek, her stomach flat and hard. They spent maybe ninety minutes going for it and worked up a great sweat. Carla was one of the best lovers Casey had ever had. Also the hairiest. She didn't shave anything.

"God, you've got gorgeous legs," Casey said, running a hand along Carla's thigh, tugging gently at the silky brown hair.

"You have, like, gorgeous everything." Carla sighed, snuggling in Casey's arms.

The next time Casey went to Katie's, Carla was there again, wearing black Capri pants and a white blouse. "Hi, Carla," Casey said.

"I'm, like, Darla," Carla said. "Carla's twin."

"Oh." Casey said, feeling off-balance. Carla hadn't said anything about having a twin.

Darla was holding a computer keyboard and a screwdriver. She flopped onto the floor, unscrewed the back of the keyboard and spilled its guts all over the floor. "Do you know anything about keyboards? My fucking keys are, like, sticking."

"Really?" Casey sat on the floor and peered inside the keyboard too, but she didn't know much about keyboards. She asked, "When will Carla be back?"

"Later," Darla said.

"I called earlier and she said she's be here."

"So? I'm here." Darla threw aside the keyboard and screwdriver, gently pushing Casey down on the floor, kissing her.

"You're a dyke, too?" Casey stammered.

"Why would you, like, think that?" Darla said, pretending to be amazed.

"How did identical twin sisters get to both be dykes?"

"Duh," Darla said, rolling her eyes. "Do you wanna analyze it or do you wanna, like, have fun?"

"I'm not much for analyzing," Casey said.

"Bitchin'!"

"Is there a moral dilemma in this?" Casey babbled.

"How do you, like, spell that?" Darla asked, helping Casey to her feet, leading the way to her bedroom.

Casey went nuts when she got Darla into bed, giggling and running her hands all over Darla's body. Darla shaved herself bald. Legs, pits, even her crotch. It was the first time Casey had ever been to bed with a completely bald woman. Darla was as good a lover as Carla. Casey couldn't tell the difference between them except for the amount of hair

"I can't figure this out," Casey said, lying in Darla's arms.

"Poor baby." Darla patted Casey's hand.

The next time Casey went to Katie/Carla/Darla's, Katie answered the door sucking on an orange popsicle, and said, "You must have, like, one bitchin' time when you come here. You come here a lot."

Casey dropped her eyes guiltily, then took a deep breath. "I don't like sneaking around. I've...uh...spent time with both your roomies."

"Bitchin'!" Katie said, giggling. "Like, simultaneously? I get both of them in bed two or three times a week and make a twin sandwich out of myself. It's, like, a multiorgasmic bitchin' good time."

"This is like quicksand," Casey groaned. "I stepped into it and now I can't get out. The harder I struggle, the deeper I sink."

"Do you want out?" Katie asked.

Casey dropped her eyes, shook her head.

"Like, that's what I thought," Katie purred, taking Casey's hand.

"Duh," Casey said.

Then, the next time she went to Katie/Carla/Darla's she almost had a heart attack. Carla/Darla both were waiting. Both were wearing black Capri pants and white blouses. They looked at Casey with that certain spark in their eyes.

"I think the water in Oklahoma does things to people's minds," Casey said.

Carla/Darla giggled, flashing their eyes at Casey.

"I'd better go," Casey said, fumbling for the doorknob. "This is a little weird for me."

Carla/Darla walked to Casey and held her by the shoulders, begging her not to leave.

"Don't you, like, want us together?" Carla breathed. "Everybody we meet wants us together. Isn't that, like, a fantasy of yours?"

"Duh," Casey said.

"You should see your face. It's, like, a combination of guilt and delight," Carla whispered. "Guilt Lite."

Casey groaned. "It can't be Guilt Lite. I'm Catholic. I get full-strength guilt." And she was getting full-strength guilt. Making love with two women was lust plain and simple, but women weren't supposed to act out of lust. Lust was offensive and tacky.

"Our whole lives we've only let Katie Ever-ready make a twin sandwich with us," Darla said, kissing Casey on the cheek. "We're offering you something special. You've already had us separately. What difference does it, like, make if you have us together?"

Casey was sure there was something wrong with that kind of logic, but she wasn't sure exactly what. She went to the bedroom and made a twin sandwich out of herself. It was a multi-orgasmic bitchin' good time.

"How did all this get started?" Casey asked afterwards while cradled between the twins. "This...you know."

"When we were younger, we, like, hurt each other a lot," Carla said.

"We fought over women, stole women from each other and we hated each other," Darla continued.

"Katie showed us, like, how wrong it was for for sisters to hurt each other," said Carla.

"She read poetry to us and made love to us, and, like, showed us how stupid it was to hurt other people because of love," Darla added. "So now we love each other and we share anything we have with anyone we love."

"I don't want to see you again," Casey said, getting out of bed. "I thought this would be a fun release from all the pressure of basketball, but it's more than I can deal with. Too kinky. Maybe. I just don't know."

The twins started crying and saying they weren't kinky, they were loving, generous women and Casey had hurt their feelings. Two crying women on her hands at the same time was more than Casey could take.

"I'm sorry," she said helplessly. Casey got out of there and drove to Mitchell.

After basketball practice, while everyone was showering, Tobie said, "College sucks. I got another D in chemistry. Coach Murphy's going to rip my ass when she finds out."

"Bull-shit," Casey crowed. "Being a major-college jock is great. We have a warm, dry place to sleep. Decent food. A quality education. Use of some of the best athletic facilities in the country. And tons of good-looking babes to rage. What more is there to life?"

"How'd a *man* get in our showers?" Tobie asked.

"What's that crack supposed to mean?" Casey asked, feeling a little hot under the collar.

"Nothing, Bruno," Tobie said. She popped Casey with a towel and walked out.

Casey went back to see the twins inside a week. Something pulled her back. She didn't know what, but she had to have another twin sandwich. She slunk out afterwards, feeling whorish and perverted and confused. She felt like Kristy, torn between becoming a nun and going for what felt natural. It hurt so good.

CHAPTER 5

The Tech-ettes were walking proud and talking loud when the preseason polls came out. They were ranked Number Fifteen in one major poll and Number Sixteen in another, the highest preseason rankings in the school's history. Three other Big Seven teams were in the Top Twenty-five. Missouri, Kansas and Texas State.

"Look at us," Casey crowed, showing the paper to Tobie, feeling cocky, arrogant, smug, every feeling she could think of.

Tobie snatched the paper out of Casey's hands. She ripped it to shreds, threw it on the floor and stomped on it. "Who cares if I'm not part of it?" she shouted, face flushed, eyes snapping. "If I don't make the traveling squad I'm transferring. That bitch Murphy hates me. I know she does."

"Okay-fine," Casey said. She walked away, refusing to let Tobie ruin her good mood. That's what it's all about, babe: Playing on a Top Twenty-five team that had a chance to go all the way, being a jock at a major college where the football team was having a miserable year, and the men's basketball team was projected to finish next-to-last in the conference, so everybody focused on the women's team.

And everybody was focused.

Women in the dorm, Kim included, started asking Casey for free tickets to the upcoming Lady Lobos Invitational Tournament. Stubble-faced men hit on her in the Student Union, in the library, in the weight room at Mitchell, cocking their eyebrows, flexing their muscles, offering phone numbers, dinners, movie dates, sex. Willing-eyed women stopped her in rest rooms, in front of the dairy, in the parking lot outside Mitchell, smiling toothy smiles, touching her arm, offering phone numbers, dinners, movie dates, sex. Her phone was ringing off the hook. This lover, that lover, Katie, Carla/Darla, Sharika-Sharika-Sharika. They were all hot, demanding, inspired in bed.

43

Between beds—classes. Classes where every professor knew your name even though he or she didn't know a third of the other students' names. Professors who thought jocks were lumps of flesh and were poised to make their contribution to the scientific community by jerking your eligibility if you screwed-up.

Algebra tests.

Geology field trips.

English reports.

A poor grade not only meant wobbly eligibility, it also meant a chat with a disgusted-looking Coach Murphy and a lot of time spent running laps while a grad assistant followed you, holding your algebra test, screaming, "Every god-damn bad grade you make means you've embarrassed all of us! You missed question twenty-one! I don't believe it! What is X-squared plus nine-X minus one equals zero? Is that so god-damn hard? Have you heard of the quadratic formula? I could teach a monkey to solve that equation!"

The whole time the other players ragged on you and, somewhere in the back of your mind, you searched and searched for an alibi until you finally offered, "Test anxiety, Coach," and the grad assistants went off on your butt because if you suffered anxiety over the quadratic formula what would you do with two seconds left, the game on the line and the ball in your hands?

Basketball practice changed. The running ended. Practice was closed to everyone except the players and coaches. The team worked hours on the fundamentals required for Coach Murphy's run-and-gun fast break offense. Footwork. Setting their plays. Passing. Dribbling. Lane positioning. Rebounding positioning. Full-court press, three-quarter-court press, half-court press, all essential to create the turnovers needed for Coach Murphy's offense. Zone defenses, man-to-man defenses, all with a 'Go get the ball!' philosophy, all designed to create turnovers just like the presses. Loudspeakers blared music and cheering constantly so the team would get used to crowd noise.

The intensity turned into something that almost had a life of its own, a King Kong that weighed on everyone's back.

Casey was no exception.

How far down the depth chart am I? Will I really make the traveling squad? If I'm only one player back from the traveling squad maybe someone will get hurt and I'll move up. God! What am I saying, what am I thinking, what have I become, if I'm wishing for one of my teammates to get hurt. But if that's what it takes...not a serious injury...just enough to help me...and, most importantly, even if I was the prize recruit have I screwed-up, has someone done better in practice, so now I'm not the prize recruit and I'm, instead, someone they're disappointed with and I've dropped from second-team to water girl and nobody has told me?

Two weeks before the tournament, Tobie started living in the gym. She could been seen two hours before practice started, shooting baskets, working on her footwork all by herself. She was a jazzed-up tornado in practice, screaming profanity, flinging elbows, skidding across the floor on her stomach and clawing for every loose ball, getting in shoving-and-shouting arguments with the trees she was competing against, the smaller players scattering while the trees roared at each other.

An hour after practice she could be seen running the stands, red-faced, panting, frustrated-looking. Later she could be seen in the showers, standing naked under a nozzle, one hand leaned against the wall, her head lowered, eyes closed, lips moving as she talked to herself.

If anyone talked to her she'd say, "She'll carry fifteen on the traveling squad. Fifteen. With all the tournaments and road games plus the conference schedule she needs a lot of depth. I need to move past a walk-on to make it. I can't believe it. That bitch hates me. I know she does."

The week before the tournament, the coaches turned into assholes. Nobody could do anything right. The grad assistants ragged on everybody, screaming themselves hoarse. "God-dammit-god-dammit-god-dammit! Ellison! You're out of position! Rotate-rotate-rotate! Who's going to stop the fast break if you don't rotate and stop it? You're on the point! Let's try it again!"

A few minutes later a head-shaking Coach Murphy shrieked her whistle.

A red-faced grad assistant screamed, "No! No! No! Ellison! Move your feet on defense! Don't shift your body! Move your god-damn feet!"

And you nodded your head, groveling like a whipped dog...but wanting the screaming in a perverted sort of way. If the coaches were screaming at you it meant they hadn't given up on you, you hadn't dropped into the sewer with the dregs. And you felt relieved...but you wished the screaming would stop...but you were thankful it didn't.

Then the whistles shrieked again and Coach DeFoe screamed, "How's it going to feel when you bring your ranking into your own tournament and get blown-out? Get your heads out of the newspapers! Get your minds off the hero-worship! Think win-win-win!"

"All of you hit the stands!" Coach Murphy screamed, taking a turn at being an in-your-face ass-hole. "I'm ashamed of you! I can't light a fire under you no matter what I do! I won't be part of a team this sloppy!"

She flung her clipboard across the floor and stomped out of the gym, pulling at her hair, screaming at everyone who got within ten feet, making you want to scream, 'Semper Fi! Semper Fi! I'm ready to die for you, Coach Murphy!' and run and run until you slammed into whoever the enemy was and exploded into nothingness because you didn't know what else to do to make Coach Murphy happy except explode into nothingness.

The rumor started in panted whispers that Coach Murphy had some phone calls to make so she'd invented an excuse to leave practice for a while.

Coach Murphy was back thirty minutes later, looking calm, sipping a cup of coffee and chatting with Coach DeFoe. The players came down from the stands, all groveling like whipped dogs, hating the groveling...but thankful Coach Murphy had consented to tolerate them for a few more minutes...had consented to give them another chance to win a curt nod of her head or a tight smile on her face.

The whistles shrieked. "Hit the showers!" a grad assistant screamed.

Everyone ran to the locker room and found shiny new uniforms and warm-ups hanging in front of some of the lockers. It was like coming downstairs at Christmas and finding Santa Claus had left the perfect present for you under the tree.

The home uniforms were white with orange and black trim and numbers. The road uniforms were orange with grey and black trim. The warm-ups were black with orange and grey trim. Oklahoma Tech and snarling wolves heads were all over everything. They were great uniforms, heavy and reeking of the smell of silk-screen paints and dyes. They were lots better than anything Casey had worn in high school. She'd been assigned number 3.

She counted the uniforms hanging around the locker room. Sixteen women on the traveling squad.

A wild celebration broke out in the far corner of the locker room.

One of the walk-ons, a Native American woman named Jodi Light-foot with long black hair, was jumping around and waving a uniform in the air. "It's mine!" she shouted. "It's really mine! I get to travel with everyone!"

The other walk-ons were crying and slapping her on the back and saying she had to be the torchbearer for them because they hadn't made the traveling squad.

Tobie sat down and held her uniform, spreading the big number fifty-five across her lap.

"You made it, you made it," Casey whispered to her. "You'll be able to go home again."

Tobie didn't say a word. She just sat there, squeezing her uniform with both hands like she was trying to convince herself it was real.

One of the grad assistants said, "I don't know what you're doing with that uniform, Daniels. As lazy as you are you don't deserve it."

Tobie jumped to her feet. "Why don't you cut me some slack!" she shouted, taking a step toward the grad assistant, hands held in fists at her sides.

The grad assistant got in Tobie's face, ten inches shorter but looking like Goliath. "Daniels," she hissed, "we're not here to stroke your ego. The only ego-stroking you need is looking at the scoreboard and seeing the Tech-ettes with the lead and no time left on the clock."

Tobie sat back down, head lowered, face flushed. The grad assistant slapped Tobie's shoulder before moving through the locker room and ragging other players about not deserving uniforms. The shot Casey got was, "You won't have that uniform long, Ellison, unless you learn to play defense. Have you heard the word before? De-fense."

"Yeah," Casey said. "De horse jumped de fence and got away."

She talked to her parents that night.

"We're flying out for the tournament," Dad said.

"I won't be able to spend much time with you."

"We know that," Dad said. "If we only get to say hi, that's fine. We wouldn't miss your first college game for anything. We're flying into Tulsa on Friday. We'll rent a car and drive to Brookfield so you don't even have to mess with us."

"Okay-fine," Casey said.

She spent Wednesday evening with Sharika, eating dinner, getting massaged and making love. She spent Thursday evening with the twins, getting Ping-Ponged around and climaxing. Friday she spent daydreaming in her classes, squirming in her chair and looking at her watch. Texas Christian was playing Southern Missouri State in the seven o'clock game. Tech was playing North Texas in the nine o'clock game. The minutes seemed to crawl.

The sound of cheering and bands playing could be heard in the locker room. Casey was taped and dressed an hour early. So was most everybody else. She sat in front of her locker, squeezing air into her Pumps, letting the air out, squeezing it back in, running her hands over her warm-up, adjusting her wristbands, undoing the ribbon around her game-tail and redoing it. God, she was jazzed. Too jazzed? For a Home Opener? She didn't think so.

Tobie came drifting in from the direction of the trainer's room thirty minutes before scheduled game time, looking nonchalant. She was naked except for a silver cross around her neck and a bra and panties. Both of her ankles and her left wrist were taped. Her panties were pink with a red bull's eye on the crotch. She probably wore the same panties for every game because of some superstitious reason.

Everyone had their stupid superstitions. Tobie's panties. The ribbon around Casey's game-tail that had to be blue and nothing but blue. Alysa's taped right thumb that wasn't injured, but she taped for games because she'd scored thirty points in high school one time with her right thumb taped.

Tobie flopped down on the bench. "Texas Christian is kicking the shit out of Southern Missouri," she said.

"I'm thinking about our game."

"I'd be pumped if I was second-team and looking at some playing time," Tobie said, punching Casey's shoulder. "Bench time doesn't really excite me. Can you believe that bitch has me listed as third-string center? I should be starting. She hates me. I know she does."

"Maybe it's your attitude."

"What fucking attitude?" Tobie asked innocently. She kissed the cross around her neck before squirming into her uniform and warm-up. Left leg first, left arm first, left foot into a sock and shoe first.

More superstition.

Casey knew. She always said a Hail Mary and an Our Father before dressing and dressed her right limbs first. Religious things you didn't know when you'd started doing, or why, since God and the Virgin Mary probably didn't care about basketball games. But you were afraid not to do them now just in case you got knocked headfirst into a goal post, snapped your neck and had to explain your side of the story to God a lot sooner than you'd expected.

"First game's over!" a grad assistant shouted. "Fifteen minutes!"

The rush to the bathroom started. Throwing up. Peeing. Splashing cold water on faces. Casey stayed where she was. She felt like her knees would give out if she moved. She was looking at maybe ten or fifteen minutes of playing time, if the game turned into a blowout. Maybe no playing time if the game was close.

"Standing room only!" a grad assistant shouted. "Here's your chance to strut your stuff, ladies!"

The seniors started going around slapping everyone's butts and bashing forearms with everyone. "Chill, babe," they kept saying. "This one's locked."

Casey took a few deep breaths. She was either hyperventilating or having a heart attack. She'd never been so jazzed in her life. Every muscle in her body was trembling. She wanted to run and jump and shoot and dribble and just generally go ape-shit and score about fifty thousand points.

"North Texas is out!" a grad assistant shouted. "Welcome to Mitchell, you Texas ass-holes! Do you know the only thing uglier than your uniforms are your faces?"

The cheering heard in the locker room got louder. The pounding from the Tech band almost rattled the walls.

Coach Murphy came into the locker room, carrying her clipboard, looking like God, looking like the definition of Semper Fi. Her hair was fixed in a bun and tied with an orange and black bow. She was wearing an orange and black tailored suit with an orange/black corsage on her breast and grey hose and two-tone orange/black open-toed heels. She went around whispering to the seniors and giving them hugs. Some of the seniors looked like they wanted to cry.

Coach Murphy walked to the door. Casey waited for the God-America-school-family-yourselves pregame speech she'd always heard in high school. "Let's go," Coach Murphy said, sounding calm. "Double-line lay-up drill."

Everyone crowded to the door, seniors first, the rest in a pack. Alysa was holding a shiny new basketball. Casey took a few more deep breaths. The excitement, the fear, the adrenaline were almost overwhelming, they were almost tangible, emotions she could almost taste.

A grad assistant standing at the door shouted, "Play with emotion! That's what it takes to be a winner! E-mo-tion! Do you know what that word means, ladies?"

Everyone screamed, "Bet your ass!"

"You're lying!" the grad assistant shouted. "I don't think you know anything! You don't give a damn if you win!"

Everyone screamed, "Kick their fucking asses!"

The grad assistant held up an orange and black hand towel, stretching it between her hands, turning it this way and that so everyone could see it. *You Done Good!* was printed on the towel above a snarling wolf's head. "We have three dozen of these to pass out this season!" the grad assistant shouted. "Who wants the first one?"

Everyone screamed, "I do! I do!"

"Earn it!" the grad assistant shouted. She swung the door open. The screaming of the crowd and pounding of the band almost knocked Casey back on her butt.

"The Tech-ies are lit tonight!" the grad assistant shouted. "This is for us, ladies! These are our people! Let's give 'em a show! Look flashy in the pregame!"

Then they were out the door, down the runway, pausing in the dim lights behind the stands, at the fringe of the screaming people and the playing band. The band swung into *Wipeout.* Probably a special request from Coach Murphy since she liked oldies. The crowd got jazzed by the song and started stomping on the stands, making it sound like the whole arena was falling down.

The traditional howling started, high-pitched, mocking, sending a chill up Casey's back, affecting everyone else the same way. Everyone started tossing their heads, prancing, pawing their feet, doing everything but whinnying like a herd of wild horses excited to the verge of a stampede by the sound of eight thousand wolf howls floating across the prairie on a cold winter night.

Everyone looked at Coach Murphy, eyes begging for relief from the emotions. "Throw us some fresh meat!" the begging eyes said.

Coach Murphy nodded.

They poured through a gap in the stands, onto the court, into the bright lights, into the explosion of cheers and popping flash bulbs, seeing North Texas in their green and white uniforms warming-up under the far basket, seeing the high-tech scoreboard flashing, *Lady Lobos! Lady Lobos!* All around and overhead, the stands jammed with stomping, howling people, close enough you could reach out and slap their hands or exchange, "Hi, how you doing's?" with them, the student section acting the wildest, looking primordial with faces painted half-orange and half-black.

In the middle of everything, gathered on the floor, were male cheerleaders shouting, "Lady Lobos! Lady Lobos!" through megaphones, and female cheerleaders in black uniforms with fluffy hair and tons of makeup, pompoms held above their heads, knees bent, feet tucked into their butts, being complete bimbos but, God, so gorgeous and totally edible-looking. Crowded around the fringes, along the base lines, were camera crews from all the newspapers, and Tulsa and Oklahoma City TV stations.

It was hot, it was deafening, it was tight, it was the last place in the world a claustrophobic would want to be.

It was like nothing Casey had ever seen or heard.

Major-college ball.

To the snarling wolf's head in two lines, the howling in the stands swelling, the starters leading the way now. Alysa passing to Weatherly. Weatherly driving for a lay-up and circling back. Deb following Weatherly, rebounding the ball, passing to Weatherly who passes to Alysa driving for a lay-up, Bonnie rebounding and passing to Alysa who passes to Penny driving for a lay-up. Movement. Action. Flash. Crowd-pleasing. All the players clapping hands, shouting encouragement, cutting glances at North Texas to see them cutting glances back, seeing them wilting in the intimate atmosphere, seeing the scared looks, the intimidation on their faces.

The twenty minute warm-up time was gone in a flash. The horn blared. The three centers lined up, loping to the backboard, taking their feeds from the guards. Six-five Alysa, black, intense-looking, soaring, reaching, flash bulbs popping, a thunderous slamma-jamma, pure, raw power, rocking the backboard, sending the crowd into a frenzy, howls echoing from one side of the stands to the other.

Six-three Weatherly, black, even more intense-looking, a combination of speed and power, soaring, slamma-jamma. Six-four Tobie, frail and pale, pure agility and finesse, soaring, blond hair glistening in the popping flash bulbs, slamma-jamma. Coach Murphy watching, frowning, shaking her head but turning away without chewing butt over the hot-dogging. The blanched faces of the North Texas players, the understanding as they realized what they were—a cupcake tune-up for a national-caliber team in a cupcake tune-up tournament hosted by a national-caliber team.

To the bench, forming part of a corridor, clapping, listening as the five starters were introduced, slapping their hands and butts when they run through the corridor, wishing, oh, God, wishing it was you getting introduced, wanting the fame, the recognition, however fleeting, however unimportant to the overall scheme of the world, bad enough to do anything to gain it, even kill. Feeling like screaming, 'I'm so proud I could explode! This is the best basketball team I've ever seen! This team will never lose, nobody's good enough to beat this team! And I'm part of it!'

Standing in front of the bench, watching Alysa get the tip, Bonnie snatching the ball, baseball pass to Penny on the wing, North Texas back-pedaling on defense, hands up but looking disorganized, alternating between crying, "Ball! Ball!" and "Help! Help!" as the Tech break exploded on them. Interior bounce pass to Deb, easy lay-up. Then sitting down on the end of the bench with the other freshmen, chewing fingernails, moaning, cussing, bitching about the referees, needing only popcorn and a Coke to be just another spectator with one of the best seats in the house.

Tech 54, North Texas 23 at halftime.

Casey trotted to the locker room with everybody else. She didn't really feel like part of things anymore because she'd done nothing to contribute. Nothing. She hadn't even broken a sweat the first half. Tech had used seven players. She hadn't been one of them.

Coach Murphy came to her right before they left to play the second half. "Deb's knee is flaring up," Coach Murphy said. "Nothing serious, but I'm not going to use her the rest of the game. You're starting the second half."

Casey went numb, thinking of Dad with his Camcorder, Mom with her moist eyes, all her lovers and friends, fear over falling on her butt in front of everybody. She dimly heard her own voice, felt her head nodding, heard Coach Murphy's voice without hearing what she was saying.

Finally she heard a distant, "Casey-Casey-Casey," through the fog. She saw Coach Murphy's face, eyes crinkled at the corners, a tight smile on her lips.

"Listen to me," Coach Murphy said. "Composure. I want to give you some time with the first-team. Then some time with the second-team. I'll empty the bench toward the end. Run the spread. Hold the lead. Okay?"

Casey managed a nod. Coach Murphy slapped Casey's butt and walked away.

"Blow 'em to next week so I can get in the game," Tobie hissed. "My parents are here from Dallas. I want to help kick the shit out of this Texas bitches in front of them."

"Okay-fine," Casey said. She went to the bathroom, threw up and trotted out to play the second half. "No turnovers, no turnovers," she said to herself over and over.

The first time she touched the ball she fumbled it, kicked it, dove for it, knocked it out of bounds with her face, all when nobody was within twenty feet of her.

Bodacious start, babe, simply bodacious.

Coach Murphy called time-out and motioned Casey to the bench. "What are you playing out there?" Coach Murphy asked when Casey reached her.

"Basketball," Casey squeaked, seeing her college career flash in front of her eyes.

"No," Coach Murphy said thoughtfully. "It looked more like soccer to me." She winked, slapped Casey's butt and said, "Let's play basketball from now on. That's what the people paid to see."

CHAPTER 6

Casey liked Associate Head Coach Maxie DeFoe because she was learning more from Coach DeFoe than any coach she'd ever had, except for Coach Murphy. Black, fortyish, tall and rangy, straightforward, a meticulous taskmaster, she'd been in coaching for twenty years, all as an assistant. Coach DeFoe also had the title of Minority Recruiter, which meant she went into the inner-cities and small, mostly black towns and recruited any black players Coach Murphy had scouted and targeted.

Coach DeFoe was The Defensive Expert. Box-and-one, triangle-and-two, one-two-two-zone. Name the defense, Coach DeFoe could coach it. And coach the offense it took to beat it. She was soft-spoken and encouraging most of the time, without being the rah-rah type. Coach DeFoe's attitude was, 'I'm here to coach ball, not baby-sit a bunch of spoiled brats.' She didn't waste her time on discipline. If you screwed-up she just sent you to Coach Murphy, and went on with her life while yours turned into squirming pain because of her referral.

The grad assistants were The Enforcers From Hell, putting the decisions from the top of the memo chain into motion, making sure the decisions were obeyed. They also did the advance scouting on future opponents and were the traveling secretaries, making sure hotel reservations, equipment logistics and such went smoothly. Energetic, aggressive, mid-twenties, a year or two from their playing days, hungry to make a name for themselves so they could get a full-time coaching job. They knew the game, knew the kind of women who played it and didn't put up with any bull-shit. If you didn't want to put in the work it took, you could haul your butt out the door as far as the grad assistants were concerned. And part of their job was to make sure you knew just how close the door was.

Casey learned a lot from the grad assistants and she knew what they did was important to the team's success—but she still hated their guts because it seemed like she was the target of an inordinate amount of their attention.

By contrast, Coach Murphy was harder to figure. Casey spent hours trying to figure out Coach Murphy. She was sure Coach Murphy spent even more hours trying to figure out her players. To start with, Coach Murphy was *The Flash:* a smooth, organized professional who dealt with the press, the school administration, the Athletic Director, the budget, the majority of the recruiting, game scheduling and serious discipline problems like dismissal from the team. She controlled the team image. How the team looked to the university, the press, the fans, other teams. And themselves. Thirty-four years old. Married for ten years to an airline pilot. Two kids. Education Doctorate. A definite overachiever.

Casey was in love with her.

Casey had played for a lot of coaches in her career but none like Coach Murphy. Coach Murphy was an intricate manipulator. Talented enough she could have been a lawyer. She juggled everything in her world and prodded and twisted and bullied until she got exactly what she wanted. For herself, for her coaches, for her players.

Each player got treated differently by Coach Murphy. Casey got the arm around the shoulder, the quietly, tirelessly explaining mother-figure who never lost her temper, who never acted upset no matter how big a bonehead screw-up Casey made. Casey was never afraid to turn to Coach Murphy for advice or instruction, and that made her learn. If Coach Murphy had screamed and gotten red-faced Casey would have closed up, kept her questions to herself and not learned anything.

The seniors got a mockingly disgusted Coach Murphy. If a senior made a bonehead mistake Coach Murphy would arch her eyebrows, give them a certain look, a tight smile and sometimes she'd applaud. The senior would drop her head and look more crushed than any words could have made her feel because Coach Murphy's approval was what everyone craved. Her disapproval was what they all feared. Because of her power.

Some of the players got an impatient Coach Murphy. A coach who put her hands on her hips and glared and questioned whether a certain player was a woman or a rock, but no, a certain player couldn't be a rock because even a rock was too smart to make the same mistake time and time again.

Other players got the hot-tempered coach who called them into her office and slammed the door and chewed their butts, the sound of muffled screaming heard in the locker room, until everything got quiet and the player came out a few minutes later, looking determined and angry and ready to get the job done.

Tobie got the cruel Coach Murphy. The coach who ragged on Tobie from the second she walked into the gym. Criticizing everything from Tobie's shoelaces to her hair to her lack of upper-body strength to her laziness-laziness-laziness. Tobie always got public butt-chewings. In the middle of the gym floor, in the middle of the locker room, in Coach Murphy's office with the door open so every word could be heard in the locker room, even in the showers, Coach Murphy fully dressed, steam soaking her hair and clothes as she chewed Tobie's naked butt, Tobie holding a bar of soap, shifting from one foot to the other, blushing from head to toe and trying to look at the floor, raising her eyes only when Coach Murphy said, "You will look at me when I'm talking to you."

Everyday after practice, Tobie would go out in the parking lot and scream and cuss and kick trash cans over and throw rocks at street signs and pull a limb off a tree and beat-beat-beat the ground.

"I'm going to kill that bitch!" Tobie would scream as she beat the ground with a limb. "What does she want? My scholarship? She can't have it!"

"Okay-fine," Casey would say, sometimes seeing Coach Murphy watching Tobie through her office window, that certain look and a tight smile on her face.

"Why does she follow me into the showers to rip my ass?" Tobie would scream. "God-damn, that's humiliating!"

"Just be glad she's not a he," Casey would say.

"She might as well be a he," Tobie would scream. "Why does she hate me?"

"Your playing time has gone up from two minutes a game to six minutes," Casey would say.

Tobie would stop beating the ground and stare at Casey. Then she'd break her limb over a knee and go loping away, kicking over trash cans, jerking college newspapers out of boxes and flinging them on the street, screaming cuss words at everyone who laughed at her. Casey would crack up because Tobie wasn't stupid, but she was blind. Too blind to see she was being manipulated. Like everyone else on the team.

Several days before each game all the coaches would rag the players, jeering and taunting. Relentlessly, profanely, loudly. In the locker room after practice, players would scream and bounce shoes off the walls and slam locker doors and cuss the coaches, always using 'them' and 'us.' The day before the game, the coaches would be excited, encouraging, complimentary, showing the players they were part of 'us,' too, and everyone would come together and at game time a stone wall of unified 'us'es' would be presented to the opponent, the point being the Lady Lobos always had someone they were fighting against, some threat, either the coaches or another team.

If that wasn't manipulation, then Casey didn't know what was.

That was all basketball-related manipulation. It didn't stop there. Coach Murphy liked poking her gorgeous, high-cheekboned face into personal things, too. Like if she saw or heard about you driving on one of the campus streets at the speed of late-for-class, you knew a butt-chewing for sure and punishment laps maybe were looming on the horizon. Or if she heard you were involved with a crowd who drank too much or did drugs and made bad grades, she'd have you doing the squat-and-squirt in a plastic cup everyday and going to counseling.

One day Casey went to see her counselor about her schedule for the next semester and found Coach Murphy there, sipping coffee, chatting with Casey's counselor and looking at a file. When Coach Murphy came out Casey asked if anything was wrong.

"You people need to learn one thing," Coach Murphy said. "You're here for college. You won't be anything in life without an education. I'd gladly lose every game every year if I could graduate all my players."

"But-but-but," Casey stammered, wondering if Coach Murphy had gotten a memo from God and knew something Casey didn't.

Coach Murphy laughed. "Good grad assistants don't grow on trees," she said. "They have to be groomed. The first step in grooming is making sure they have the grades to get into graduate school." She walked away, leaving Casey standing there with her mouth hanging open.

It seemed Coach Murphy had a Grand Scheme in her mind and if the players relaxed and trusted her everything would work out to benefit everybody. It was when you did something to screw-up her

Grand Scheme that she got mad. Of course, Casey did her best to limit the number and severity of her butt-chewings by playing as hard as she could and making as good grades as she could. She still got in trouble sometimes, anyway, and, at first, she tried to offer the alibi, "I'm just an eighteen year old freshman. I don't know what I'm doing half the time. It's a hormone thing." She dropped that lame line when it only increased the squirm-factor of her butt-chewings by adding a discussion on maturity and accepting responsibility for one's own actions.

The squirm-factor caused by maturity-and-accepting responsibility discussions was nothing compared to the way Casey squirmed the day Coach Murphy dismissed her from the team. Coach Murphy stopped practice and said, "Casey, get the hell out of my gym. I'm sick of you," sounding irritated but not mad.

"Huh?" Casey squeaked, her chin on her insteps. "You want me to leave practice?"

"I want you to clean out your locker and get out," Coach Murphy said. "You're too quiet. I want my guards to be talkers. I want my guards to be the fire on the team. You can come back when you're prepared to provide what I want."

Casey slunk out, feeling humiliated and terrified. She was back the next day, groveling, chattering a mile a minute, saying anything, screaming whatever popped into her head and trying to ignore how self-conscious she felt.

It wasn't nearly as much fun getting manipulated as it was laughing at other people for getting manipulated.

What it came down to in the end was there was no way to avoid butt-chewings from Coach Murphy, no matter what you did. If you were good enough as a player, you weren't good enough as a student. If you were good enough as a player and a student, you weren't good enough as a woman. But they weren't the kind of butt-chewings that made you say, "The hell with it. I'll never be good enough for you." They were more the kind of butt-chewings that made you say, "Oh, yeah? Well, I'll show you!"

Casey finally decided Coach Murphy was an actress definitely and a multiple-personality sociopath maybe. What role Coach Murphy would play at a particular time depended on the situation and who she was playing the role for. And there was no way to predict what role she would play. All you knew was if Coach Murphy was on you she had a reason, the most probable reason being you weren't doing what she wanted you to do, and you better get your-young-self back on track pronto-quick because you didn't know if Coach Murphy had the talent to play the role of Terminator, but you sure didn't want to find out.

As far as why she was in love with Coach Murphy, Casey had no explanation. She would've slept with Coach Murphy on demand, whenever, wherever, however Coach Murphy wanted. Not to improve her standing on the team, but because she was definitely in love. She knew Coach Murphy would never demand sex because not only was she straight, she was the ultimate professional.

Still, sometimes, at night, in her dorm room, Casey dreamed about sleeping with Coach Murphy and woke up on the edge of a climax.

Regardless of all that, Casey knew she had a relationship with Coach Murphy that would last long after she left Tech and that's what puzzled her the most. She'd never before considered the possibility of a long-term relationship with a woman without sex being involved.

Casey put her textbook on the floor. She shifted on the day bed, holding out her hands so she could enjoy the warm glow from the kerosene heater sitting on the floor.

She was in a room, a loft or whatever, on top of a hardware store in downtown Brookfield. The floor was brown hardwood, the walls painted white, the windows covered with white sheer curtains. On the far side of the loft was a stove, a refrigerator, a double sink and a curtain that shielded the bathtub and toilet. There were five easels with paintings on them sitting around the room. The place smelled like paint and kerosene and tuna fish sandwiches.

Kristy was sitting on a bar stool at the center of the loft, not far from the kerosene heater, wearing a blue sweat shirt and jeans. A leg was curled beneath her, a glass of distilled water was on the floor beneath her stool. She was reaching out and making light, delicate brush strokes on the canvas sitting in front of her. She had a pensive look on her face.

Pensive.

A word Casey had learned at college. She liked it. She never used it in conversation because it seemed like a word a nerd would use. She liked to think it, though.

Kristy had changed a lot since she embarked on her am-I-a-dyke-or-am-I-a-nun crusade. She cut her hair short, about an inch long. She put away her contacts and wore her glasses all the time, usually perched on the tip of her nose. She stopped shaving her legs and underarms. She stopped going to the Catholic Center to confess. She dropped out of college, rented the loft, took a job at Burger King and spent most of her time painting. She'd even sold some of her paintings and said she might quit her job at Burger King and work full-time on her art.

"What are you painting?" Casey asked.

"You," Kristy said, turning her head and peering over the top of her glasses.

"Let me see." Casey stood and walked toward Kristy.

"No!" Kristy took the canvas off the easel and backed away.

"Okay-fine." Casey flopped back on the day bed. Kristy returned the canvas and sat back down. "I don't know if I want you to paint me," Casey said, pointing to the paintings around the loft. "Your paintings are all black and brown and deep blue. Dark colors. Angst-ridden." Angst. Another word she'd learned at college.

"I don't have a reason to be anything except angst-ridden," Kristy said.

"Why? Because you think maybe you're a dyke?"

"I don't like that word," Kristy said, an accusing look on her face. "I think it has insulting connotations. But you're right. That's part of it. I'm also the only twenty-two year old virgin in the history of humanity. That's enough to make anyone anxious." She chewed her bottom lip.

"Come here," Casey said, patting the day bed.

"No," Kristy said stubbornly. "You'll try to fuck me if I do. All you want from me is sex."

"Right," Casey said. "That's why I keep coming around. Because of all the sex I get from you." She more or less sighed because if Kristy would only undress, Casey would take care of part of her angst. Maybe all of it. Kristy was almost as puzzling as Coach Murphy. Both were women Casey had relationships with without sex being involved. College was certainly enlightening even if it wasn't sexually entertaining all the time.

"I know you're comfortable as a lesbian," Kristy said, reaching down to pick up her glass of distilled water. "I admire that, I suppose, because I'm not comfortable as anything. No matter what I do, there's always this nagging doubt in the back of my head that I'm doing something I shouldn't be."

"Why?"

"Because my whole life I've wanted to be a good Catholic girl," Kristy said. "Going to Mass once a week. Running off to confess to Father Dumb-ass once a month. Living in the house in the suburbs with a husband and one-point-whatever kids. Good Catholic girls don't have lesbian affairs."

"We're not having an affair," Casey said. "I'm not sure what we're having, but it's not an affair."

"It's close enough to be a sin," Kristy said, face lowered. "You're a lesbian and we talk about lesbian stuff and we've been naked together in the back seat of a car."

"Okay-fine."

"You're sleeping with someone, aren't you?"

"I can't imagine a life without sex."

"There's nobody in my life but you," Kristy said. "You're the only one I've kissed my whole life."

"You haven't kissed your parents?"

"I mean in passion," Kristy said, giggling. "Thanks for spending the afternoon with me. I don't get to see you enough."

"You're welcome."

"Let's talk about sports now," she said, looking studious, adjusting her glasses. "Tell me about the tournament in Eugene last weekend. The papers here have been saying what a prestigious tournament it was."

"It was," Casey said, feeling relieved the conversation was turning to something she was more familiar with. "All the teams there were ranked in the Top Twenty-five. The Oregon papers were ragging us when we got there, saying they could tell just from watching us practice that we have more swagger and attitude than any women's team they've ever seen. We tried to blame Coach Murphy because every team reflects the personality of their coach, but she just laughed at us. The Oregon papers were calling us *The Tech Juggernaut* by the time the tournament ended and touting us as a definite contender for the National Championship."

"Are tournaments exciting?"

"Yep," Casey said, laughing. Kristy was funny even if she wasn't sexually entertaining. "One of the best parts is walking into the hotel restaurant with the rest of the Tech-ettes. It's a big ego-trip. Seeing the way the other diners stop eating to stare at us, hearing everyone whisper when they see how much food the team puts away. A six-five, two hundred pound woman doesn't exactly eat like Scarlett O'Hara."

Kristy giggled.

"We got Notre Dame in the first game," Casey said. "Get outta here, fool! We emptied the bench."

"Tech one-oh-three, Notre Dame seventy-one," Kristy said. "You made thirteen points. I felt mad because you guys beat up on a bunch of Catholic women."

"Who's telling this story?"

Kristy giggled again, tossing her head, looking tres, tres cute.

"We got Michigan State in the second game," Casey said. "They're the best team we've played this year. We were lucky to beat them by five. Tobie Daniels outdid the space shuttle when we got into the locker room because she didn't get any playing time. She hit the ozone in maybe two seconds. She screamed and screamed about Coach Murphy. She trashed the towel cart. She grabbed a ball and fired it through a window way up close to the ceiling. Crash! Glass came tinkling down on everyone's head. Coach Murphy came in and gave her a fifteen minute butt-chewing right in front of everybody, the worst butt-chewing Tobie has ever gotten. The butt-chewing ended with Tobie getting fifty punishment laps because, number one, the broken window has to come out of Coach Murphy's budget, and number two, Tobie humiliated Coach Murphy because Coach Murphy brought a team into another school's facilities and one of her players caused property damage, and if Oregon never invites Tech back again Coach Murphy will understand because who wants a bunch of thugs in their tournament."

"I don't know Tobie Daniels," Kristy said, sounding self-righteous, "but I don't think I like her. She sounds like a bitch."

"She does have a temper," Casey said.

"I assume you've done her," Kristy said. "You're good at doing people. You're so...direct."

"You got away."

Kristy didn't say anything. She lowered her face, looking as self-righteous as she sounded.

"We got the host team, Oregon, in the championship round," Casey said. "The Lady Ducks. Duck-ette soup. Roast duck-ette. See ya later, sucka."

"After the Oregon game is when Coach Murphy said you get to

be a starter because you made twenty-one points," Kristy said, sounding like a proud parent, lifting her face. "And also because you 'executed the Tech game strategy with a precision that belied your lack of experience.' That's what the papers here said."

"I am well coached," Casey said, deciding not to tell Kristy it hadn't been all that romantic/dramatic. After the Oregon game, Casey had slipped away for thirty minutes of athletic sex with a gangly brunette waitress named Traci she'd met in the hotel restaurant. Coach Murphy was waiting outside Casey's door when she got back, arms crossed, one gorgeous foot tapping, that certain look on her face.

"Where have you been?" Coach Murphy had asked.

"In the gift shop." Casey had glanced at her empty hands about the same time Coach Murphy did. "I decided not to buy anything," Casey had said.

"I see," Coach Murphy had said, looking calm although her voice was mad-sounding. "Let's try again. Where have you been?"

"Saying good-bye to a friend I made."

"Ten laps," Coach Murphy had said. "Five for lying and five for missing bed-check. Our next road trip you're restricted to your room when you're not with the team. Don't ever lie to me, Casey."

"Yes, ma'am."

"I'm pleased by your progress," Coach Murphy had said. "Deb will be moving to the second-team. You'll take her spot on the first-team as of now." She had paused to lock eyes with Casey before saying, "I expect my starters to set a good example for the other players," and walking away.

Casey had gone to bed, feeling humiliated for maybe the thousandth time because of Coach Murphy. The first-team promotion hadn't meant much compared to the disapproval she'd seen in Coach Murphy's eyes and heard in her voice. And what if she didn't, couldn't, set the kind of example Coach Murphy wanted? Truth was, Coach Murphy's mind and expectations worked on a level Casey wasn't sure she could reach.

"Don't you feel guilty?" Kristy asked. "Taking another woman's position?"

"No," Casey said. "I beat her straight-up. It's not written in stone, anyway. If I don't keep producing I'll be back to second-team."

"Did the other woman cry?"

"Not in front of the team," Casey said. "Maybe she did when she was alone. I would've cried."

"I can't picture you crying," Kristy said. "There's something about you that seems too hard to cry. I can't put my finger on it, but there's something there. Something...hard."

"I'm Catholic," Casey said. She cracked up because Kristy tumbled off the bar stool, squealing, "Whoa," soaking her face and hair and clothes with distilled water. She landed on the floor with a grunt, arms and legs splayed out, glasses crooked, mouth hanging open, distilled water dripping from her chin.

"Huh?" she gasped.

CHAPTER 7

"At guard, from Chatsworth, Tennessee, number threee, Case-eeey Elllliiiisonnnn!"

Through the corridor of players, knees weak, a lump in her throat, slapping hands, feeling slaps on her butt, into the open, bashing forearms with the other starters, cutting glances at the opponent in their purple and white road uniforms, seeing them cutting glances at her.

The first start of her college career.

She took a few seconds to glance into the howling stands. Dad and Mom were sitting three rows behind the Tech bench with the other parents. Dad with his Camcorder glued to his eye, Mom crying and wiping her cheeks with a tissue. Sharika was sitting on the bottom row of the student section with three other black women, pointing at Casey, laughing, clapping her hands. A big white poster board sign was bouncing higher up in the student section. The sign said, *We Love You, Case. Katie And A Twin Sandwich.* She thought about Kristy sitting in her loft, listening to the game on the radio, painting and struggling with her angst.

Conference Opener.

Texas State Lady Cougars. Eight wins, two losses. Ranked Number Twelve in the country. No cupcake tune-up. Oklahoma Tech Lady Lobos. Nine wins, two losses. Ranked Number Eleven in the country. No cupcake tune-up, either. Big Seven women's basketball. Big, fast, physical.

A Monday night, the first game of a smash-mouth week. Texas State tonight. On the road to Boulder, Colorado to play the Lady Buffaloes on Wednesday night in another conference game. Home against New Orleans Thursday night in a traditional game. On the road again Sunday afternoon, to Knoxville, Tennessee to take part in a nationally televised doubleheader, a CBS-orchestrated spectacle called, *The Big Seven—Southeastern Conference Challenge.* Missouri was playing Vanderbilt in the first game. Tech was playing the Number One Tennessee Lady Volunteers in the second game.

That's what it's all about, babe. The season in full-swing. Make-or-break time. Major-college ball.

Into the huddle at the bench. Coach Murphy squatting in the center of everybody, face calm, eyes on fire. "If we get the tip, look for the break," she said, shouting to be heard over the howling people and pounding band. "If the break's not there go to Three-Overload-Left. Look to the weak side. Alysa should be open. If she's not, go to Lobo-Split. Find your seams in the zone. Look for your cutters. If your cutter's not open, Alysa will be. Remember! Run-run-run! Casey! Release-and-go, quick to our basket on every shot they take, force the break, don't worry about your defensive assignment, we'll cover until you get back. Whoever comes down with the ball look for Casey on the break first. Shove their zone down their throats until they choke on it."

Out to the half-court circle, standing on the wolf's head; it was as big as her. Butting hips, feet, elbows with blond Number Four in a purple and white uniform. The referee holding the ball, blowing her whistle, tossing the ball into the air.

Casey zipped away as soon as the ball left the ref's hand. Down the court, seeing Alysa get the tip, Bonnie snatching it, baseball pass, grab it, pounding feet chasing, behind the back dribble around the State tree covering the basket, spin the ball up...and in. Two points.

Casey saw State had their fast break setup perfectly, two players streaking down the sidelines, a step ahead of the Tech players. She slapped the ball into the crowd after it dropped through the net to slow State down. The ref's whistle shrieked, followed by a pointing finger and a shouted, "Don't touch the ball after your team scores, Number Three! Next time it's a technical!"

Casey nodded, jumped into full-court press, in the blond's face with hands, elbows, feet, anything. State inbounded cleanly. Press, press, press the blond all the way down court. The blond was good, dribbling behind her back, between her legs, burst of speed, pivot, behind her back again and another burst of speed. The blond was damn good, sweating, concentrating, high-spirited will to win in her eyes. Pretty blue eyes. They reminded Casey of Beth's pretty blue eyes.

State scored, shut down the Tech break, set up their zone. They were good. Three-Overload-Left. Three players on the same side. Pass-pass-pass. Casey to Bonnie to Weatherly, back to Casey. Weak side open. Zing! pass to Alysa, pivot, spinning the ball up...and in. Two points. Coach Murphy pacing the sidelines, clapping her hands, nodding her head in approval.

Tech 29, State 29 at halftime.

Casey changed her soaking wet jersey in the locker room. Coach Murphy had given her a ninety second breather at the ten minute mark but she'd otherwise played the whole twenty minutes. It had been a rough first half. Casey's sides were sore from all the rib-shots she'd taken from State elbows. She'd also gotten cocky one time and thought she could zip in among the trees, grab a rebound and zip out before anyone noticed she was there. Fat chance. She ended up getting a knee in the face and came staggering empty-handed out of the pack holding her nose and blinking tears out of her eyes.

Ten minutes into the second half, Tech 42, State 39. State called time-out. Alysa came out for a breather. Tobie got the call. She tore off her warm-up, got instructions from Coach Murphy and loped onto the court, pointing a finger at the State players and taunting them, the State players pointing and taunting back, everyone acting like old friends, ragging about families and butt sizes and high-school games.

Five seconds after Tobie came into the game she got into a brawl with the State center. A serious brawl. The State center had a bloody nose and a swollen lip, Tobie a mouse under her left eye.

The State bench emptied. The Tech bench emptied, the Lady Lobos howling, "Let's rock-and-roll!" as they poured across the court. Casey ran into the pack, started shoving people and shouting, "Quit-quit-quit!" She got nailed on top of the head with a fist, heard someone scream, "Ouch! God-damn hardheaded Okies!"

Someone pulled her game-tail. She turned around, ready to punch someone out, and saw Coach Murphy, face flushed, hair wild all over her head. Coach Murphy pointed to the bench. Casey ran to the bench and joined the rest of the Lady Lobos, everyone milling around and shouting, "We want you!" at the State players.

Two grad assistants finally managed to pull Tobie kicking and screaming to the bench. Howls came raining down on the court along with paper cups and ice cubes. Coach Murphy walked to the bench, gave Tobie that certain look and pointed to the locker room.

"No!" Tobie shouted, stomping a foot, fingering the mouse under her eye.

Coach Murphy arched her eyebrows.

Tobie ran to the locker room, slapping her hips and screaming profanity, the State players pointing and ragging.

The referees huddled to sort things out. Tobie got ejected in absentia. The State center got ejected. The State head coach got a technical foul for arguing over her player's ejection. Then she got ejected because she wouldn't shut up. Coach Murphy looked grim the whole time.

It took thirty minutes to calm everyone down and get the court cleaned. State continued the game under a protest filed by their assistant coach. Casey stepped to the free throw line and nailed the two technical free throws. Tech got the ball, came back down and scored again to take a seven point lead. After that the game turned into an elbow-flinging, profanity-laced melee. The referee's whistles were shrieking almost constantly, a steady stream of players from both teams fouling out and going to the bench.

Tech managed to hold on and win 59-55.

The Lady Lobos ran off the court as soon as the buzzer sounded. Everyone was cussing and rubbing sore spots. Tobie was sitting in front of her locker in street clothes. The mouse under her eye had turned dark blue. Everyone asked her what happened.

She snapped, "It's my time of month, okay?"

Everyone left her alone after that.

Coach Murphy came into the locker room. She gave a speech about how well everyone played and how they deserved to win because they were the better team. She gave the You-Done-Good towel to Alysa for scoring twenty points and blocking four shots. Then she said, "Tobie," and walked into her office. Tobie followed. Coach DeFoe followed. All the grad assistants followed. The door got shut this time. Everyone waited for the screaming to start but it never did.

Nobody bothered to shower. They all sat around, talking in low voices and waiting to see what happened. Tobie was in Coach Murphy's office for thirty minutes. When she came out, her face was flushed, she wouldn't look at anybody, she grabbed her gym bag and left without saying a word.

Coach Murphy came out. Coach DeFoe came out. The grad assistants came out. Everyone looked grim. "Tobie has been suspended from the squad," Coach Murphy said. She paused while all the players murmured and exchanged looks. "She won't dress for any of our games this week. Right now she's considering whether or not she wants to transfer to another university." Coach Murphy took a deep breath. "The Commissioner for Big Seven Women's Sports was here tonight. This was supposed to be the showcase game for the start of the conference schedule. What we showcased I don't know."

Coach Murphy paused to clear her throat, making eye contact with everyone in the room. "I've asked my secretary to type a letter of apology to the Commissioner to be presented before he leaves," she finally said. "Right now Coach DeFoe and I are going to the State locker room to apologize to their coaches and players in person."

Coach Murphy started out. She stopped at the door, turned and made eye contact with everyone again. Casey dropped her eyes when Coach Murphy looked at her. Coach Murphy's eyes were ice-cold. She was ready to lay some thunder on somebody.

"I won't tolerate this type of behavior from my team," Coach Murphy snapped, sounding like she was fighting not to grit her teeth. "Anyone who doesn't understand that should be prepared to pay the consequences." She walked out. Coach DeFoe followed.

"Hit the showers!" a grad assistant shouted. "Curfew's not enforced tonight. No practice tomorrow. You've earned some time off after the way you played tonight. The bus leaves for the airport at ten sharp Wednesday morning. Don't-don't-don't be late! Goddamn, what a game! Did Daniels clock that State bitch or what?"

The rumor started in the showers that Coach Murphy had played for the State head coach in college and Tobie was lucky Coach Murphy didn't pull out a gun and execute an up-close head-shot right between Tobie's gorgeous blue eyes. The rumor also started that the State center had shoved a finger up Tobie's butt during all the shoving and jockeying for position under the basket, and Tobie had turned around and nailed the State center in the nose.

Alysa, six-feet-five, two hundred pounds of black and soapy and glistening WOMAN, rumbled, "I know that shit be right. The cracker shoved a finger up me one time. I returned the favor when we went on defense. Tobie shoulda done that instead of clocking the bitch."

Then she chuckled and rumbled, "You ladies know when we go down to Heartland to play them gals again they gonna do catch-up on our happy asses. That gonna be one wild game. Yes, ma'am, we better be taking us a passel of doctors along when we go down yonder. I be knowing my big black ass'll crawl out alive. I don't know about some of you scrawny white girls. Lower Case."

Everyone cracked up, releasing tension, pulling closer so they'd feel protected from what happened to Tobie, protected from the insecurity of maybe permanently losing a teammate. A family member. It was like Tobie had been killed, and they were laughing instead of mourning because laughing was easier.

A grad assistant poked her head into the showers to see what everyone was laughing about. They all shut up. All the coaches, even Coach Murphy, were outsiders. Outsiders who didn't understand the emotions of competition, the cheap shots, the hissed words, that you took and took until your jazzed-up mind forced you to get some revenge. And then the coaches, the outsiders, judged you and suspended you for being jazzed when they were the ones who jazzed you. They took you away from your family. They killed you.

After the grad assistant left, everyone heard her say, "Coach Murphy's right. They are wrapped too tight," to another grad assistant.

Casey grabbed a wet towel and popped Alysa a good one. Everyone cracked up again. "Go on with your bad self, Lower Case," Alysa rumbled. "I ain't had my supper yet. I might eat you for a snack."

Someone brought the mourning out in the open and asked Alysa if she thought Tobie would transfer. Alysa was a psychology major so she was everyone's guru.

"Tobie ain't going nowhere," Alysa rumbled. "She'd have to be a total fool to quit a team like this. Tobie ain't being no fool. She'll do her suspension and be back. Yes, ma'am, we got us a team this year. Only a fool'd transfer."

Everyone showered silently, thinking about what Alysa had said, until Alysa finally rumbled, "Lower Case, since we ain't got no curfew tonight, how about me and you go out and snare us some bone? I'm in the mood to bust a move on a man. Unless you're planning to get busy tonight with one of them little split-tails you're so fond of."

Everyone cracked up again.

Sharika wasn't the most talented woman in bed, but she made up for it in desire and energy. And appetite. After Sharika climaxed she was ready to start building toward another climax. She'd go on and on. Taking breaks to eat and shower but otherwise providing a non-stop pornographic experience.

The place Sharika's 'friend' let her use was a nice apartment. One bedroom, one bath. Green carpeting. Paneled walls. Heavy, plush furniture with lots of fluffy throw pillows. Great stereo and a 25-inch remote control Sony TV with cable, including all the premium channels. Ceiling fans, skylights, a miniature fireplace warming a dozing yellow-and-white alley cat and lots of potted plants. A kitchen with all built-in appliances, including a microwave. A king-sized bed in the bedroom.

Sharika shifted on the couch, pressing her naked body closer to Casey's, pressing her lips to Casey's open mouth, her tongue probing Casey's mouth, over Casey's teeth and gums, under Casey's tongue, across Casey's lips, tasting everything Casey had to offer. Casey returned the probing. Sharika's body was filmed in sweat, making her feel slick and even sleeker than she normally did.

Sharika broke off the kiss. She pulled back, looking excited. Her eyes glowed a deep brown in the light from the fire. "You really spending the night with me?" she asked softly. "Are you waking up with me in the morning?"

"Yep."

"I wish I'd known sooner. I'd of made it extra-special. You've never spent the night with me."

"I didn't know curfew would be lifted until after the game," Casey said.

Sharika cradled her head against Casey's shoulder, snuggling close, and murmured, "I was afraid for you when all the fighting started tonight. All those big women swinging and beating on each other and bloodying each other, and you right in the middle trying to break things up."

Casey laughed.

"I took my best friends to the game," Sharika said. "I showed you off to them." She lifted her head and pressed a hand to Casey's chest. "I told them we're lovers. Do you mind? I trust them."

"Okay-fine," Casey said, not caring, really, what Sharika said to her friends. "If you trust them, that's good enough for me."

Sharika laid her head back down, snuggling close again, enveloping Casey in silky brown limbs and reassuring feminine warmth and musky female smells.

Casey guessed she dozed off, replaying the game in her mind, the stupid turnovers she'd made. Like the lousy pass she zipped over Bonnie's head and into the third row of the stands, almost nailing Dad and his Camcorder, Dad grinning and shaking a fist at her, the fist no doubt appearing in his view finder. Had that been a Freudian slip? Had she wanted to nail Dad and the Camcorder he'd kept focused on her for as long as she could remember?

She was dimly aware of Sharika slipping off the couch and padding into the kitchen. She dozed and replayed the eighteen dozen rib-shots she'd taken from someone's elbows, the knee she'd gotten in the face, the sight of Tobie, red-faced and screaming, hair flying, fists flying, pounding again and again into the head of the State center, the cheap blind-side shot one of the State forwards gave Tobie that gave Tobie the mouse under her left eye, the stunned look on Tobie's face when she walked out of the locker room with her gym bag and her suspension, the cold humiliation in Coach Murphy's eyes when she left the locker room to apologize to the State coaches and players. All just fleeting events when they happened, quick flashes that she only had time to react to without thinking about, coming back in clear focus in dozing retrospect.

She opened her eyes, reached for the phone and called Tobie's dorm room. Tobie's roommate said she wasn't there.

"I don't know her number at home," the roommate said. "You can probably get it from Dallas information. I heard she got suspended. She might've gone home."

Casey hung up.

Sharika came back, padding across the floor, eyes shining. She was carrying a tray with a bottle of wine and two glasses and sliced cheese and rye bread and a bowl of strawberries. She put the tray on the coffee table. She sat on the couch, touched Casey's shoulder, murmured, "This is as special as I could make it."

"You're really the nurturing, motherly type, aren't you?" Casey asked, running her hands up Sharika's long legs.

"Am I?" Sharika's eyes looked amused.

"One hundred percent femme," Casey said, thinking how she liked Sharika's personality best of all her lovers.

"You might be surprised," Sharika laughed.

Casey pulled her onto the couch, pushed her onto her back, probed her mouth, licked and kissed and tasted every inch of Sharika's body, from the bottoms of Sharika's feet to the small drops of sweat gathered at the nape of Sharika's neck, until she was finally rewarded for her efforts by the sounds of Sharika's thrashing, sobbing climax.

"Oh, girlfriend," Sharika gasped, trembling in Casey's arms. "I could make love to you until the world ends. It feels that good."

They showered together, shampooing each other's hair, washing each other's bodies with soapy washcloths. Then they stood and held each other for a long time while the hot water squirted on them, staring into each other's eyes, trying to read each other's minds, exactly the same height so all the body parts matched, all the body parts rubbed together perfectly.

"I love you," Sharika whispered, her breath tickling Casey's cheek.

"I love you, too."

They dried each other, and then moved back to the living room. Sharika threw another log on the fire, shooed the lazy cat away, and spread a fuzzy blanket on the floor in front of the fireplace.

"Do you like Anita Baker?" she asked, kneeling in front of her stereo.

"Sure," Casey said. "I'll listen to anything if you like it."

They stretched out on the blanket in front of the fireplace and had their room temperature dinner while Anita Baker softly serenaded them. Sharika even turned eating into an erotic event. She took a strawberry, put it in Casey's mouth, took it out, licked it, slid it up-and-down between Casey's legs, licked it, ate it. A piece of cheese into her own mouth, took it out, offered it to Casey to lick, slid it up-and-down between her legs, put it in Casey's mouth.

Dipping her fingers into a glass, she dripped wine onto Casey's breast, licked it off slowly and teasingly. Repeated everything on the other breast. Repeated everything on Casey's stomach. A piece of bread in her mouth, a long kiss, sharing the bread during the probing. Casey was close to the boiling point by the time they finished eating.

Sharika rolled Casey onto her stomach. She rubbed baby oil all over her hands, all over Casey's body, massaged Casey's shoulders, arms, fingers, butt, legs, toes, going gently over sore ribs. She rubbed baby oil all over her own body, stretched out on top of Casey and wriggled up-and-down, side-to-side, on top of Casey, her breathing getting heavier.

Casey felt like groaning, 'I take it all back. You're a great lover.'

It was the truth. The better Sharika got to know her body, the better Sharika got as a lover.

Sharika rolled Casey onto her back, oiled Casey's front, repeated the massaging and wriggling, blew hot air into Casey's ear, sucked out cold air, whispered, "There are other women in your life."

"I'm not always a good girl."

"I'll never come between you and your other women," Sharika whispered. "I hate for you to cheat on me, but I'll put up with it until you get your fill." Her tongue flicked into Casey's ear. She blew in hot, sucked out cold.

"What about your 'friend?'" Casey asked. "The 'friend' who lets you use this apartment. Do you sleep with her?"

"There's no friend," Sharika whispered. "This apartment's mine, lover. Everything in it is mine. I've been playing head-games with you."

"What?"

Sharika wriggled to Casey's breasts. She blew hot, sucked cold. "Doesn't a little mystery in a lover make her more exciting?" she whispered.

"But..."

Sharika wriggled to Casey's stomach. Her tongue flicked into Casey's belly button. She blew hot, sucked cold. "I'm older than you think I am," she whispered. "A lot older. And I'm crazy about my young lover and her hunny-sweet Suh-thun accent. I want her to be mine forever."

"But..."

Sharika wriggled between Casey's legs. Her tongue flicked inside Casey. She blew hot, sucked cold. "What if I told you my name hasn't always been Sharika?" she whispered.

"But..."

"You're a user, girlfriend," Sharika whispered. "You've got a beautiful woman's body with a man inside. Women are just cheese-cake to you. Cheesecake for you to gorge yourself on."

Casey didn't say anything. She was past caring.

CHAPTER 8

"There's a nice article about you in the paper," Dad said. "Want to hear it?"

"Okay-fine," Casey said. She was stretched out on her bed, twirling the phone cord around a finger, feet propped against the wall. She pictured Dad sitting in his recliner, glasses perched on the end of his nose, the paper spread on his lap, light from his favorite lamp shining on his salt-and-pepper hair. Mom was probably sitting on the couch in her pink robe and fuzzy pink slippers, glancing up from her needle point and smiling every so often. Zit-faced Jimmy was probably in the kitchen with his face in the refrigerator. Or in the upstairs bathroom with his face in a Playboy and a hand in his underwear.

"*Area Woman Sparks Lady Lobos To Three Wins,*" Dad read. "*Former St. Elmo star Casey Ellison, a freshman at Oklahoma Tech, played a key role in three wins for the Brookfield, Oklahoma university this week.*"

The Colorado game had been a bitch. Everyone had trouble breathing because of the altitude. The crowd acted drunk and taunted the Tech-ettes from the time they stepped onto the court. The Colorado players tried to prove first thing they weren't going to be intimidated by the thugs from Tech. Every play under the basket ended in a shoving/screaming match. The worst part of everything was the flat feeling everyone on the team seemed to have. Like a piece of the machinery was missing. Everyone kept glancing at the bench, at the spot Tobie would normally have sat.

Nobody, not even her parents, had seen or heard from Tobie since she walked out of the locker room with her gym bag and her suspension.

The altitude caught up with Tech ten minutes into the second half. Colorado fought back from nine points down and took the lead with thirty seconds left. Casey drained an off-balance ten-footer at the buzzer to tie. She was fouled in the act of shooting and had a chance win with a free throw.

Colorado called time-out to freeze her.

In the huddle at the Tech bench, Coach Murphy started planning the overtime strategy like any good coach would. Her eyes said, 'I wish anyone else was shooting this free throw instead of my little freshman guard.'

After the huddle, Alysa put an arm around Casey's shoulders and rumbled, "Poor old Alysa's tired, Lower Case. I ain't got the breath for no overtime. Hit this thing and let's go to the house."

Casey stepped to the free throw line in the middle of all the taunting and screaming and band-playing and singing of The Good-Bye Song. She filled her mind with good thoughts, thinking about what a simple thing a free throw was, about the fifty in a row she'd hit one afternoon in practice.

She took a deep breath, bounced the ball once, nailed the free throw and ran to the locker room. She only scored three points in the game, but they were the three points that won it. That's what it's all about, babe. Clutch plays. Ignore your puckered butt and do what it takes to win. Major-college ball.

Tech 79, Colorado 78.

Coach Murphy gave her the You-Done-Good towel. She gave it to the team to autograph before it was put in the trophy case at Mitchell, feeling like it was the first step to adding her own special memories to Mitchell, memories that other players would feel long after she was gone.

Everyone was subdued on the plane going home. There was no crowing over a two-and-zero conference record. The only talk was a soft murmuring about playing Tennessee on Sunday on National TV instead of New Orleans on Thursday. The grad assistants started ragging on everyone to quit worrying about Tennessee and concentrate on New Orleans. Everyone shut up and turned in on themselves, thinking about Tennessee no matter what the grad assistants said. Casey knew she couldn't have stopped thinking about Tennessee if God Himself had told her to.

"Lower Case," Alysa whispered, "what's Sunday going to be like? You've been there. Tell me what it's going to be like. I have to know."

"It's a road game," Casey whispered. "Nothing more, nothing less."

"You're a liar," Alysa hissed. "Tennessee has won three National Championships in five years. It ain't no normal road game."

New Orleans was a blowout in front of another howling standing-room-only crowd at Mitchell. The starters played five minutes of the first half and five minutes of the second half. The bench mopped-up and set a new conference scoring record for women's basketball.

Tech 129, New Orleans 88.

The crowing about bringing on the high and mighty Tennessee Lady Volunteers started in the showers after the New Orleans game. They were three-and-zero in the toughest week of the season and feeling invincible.

"The article goes on and talks about the fight in the Texas State game," Dad said. "I won't read that part to you. It's not very flattering."

Casey laughed, not caring if the article wasn't very flattering. Tech had won the game and that was all that mattered.

"Do you know how proud we are of you?" Dad asked in his deep, fatherly voice. The same voice he used to use after they'd spent all day together in a boat on Lake Chick and caught eight or ten bass and cleaned and packed them in ice so Mom could have the thrill of frying them for supper. During the drive home, Casey would slide across the seat of Dad's pickup and rest her head on his shoulder. He would wrap an arm around her and talk to her about how he used to go fishing with his dad. Casey would listen to Dad's deep, fatherly voice and feel so safe and protected and loved she'd sometimes doze off and Dad would have to carry her into the house when they got home.

"I know you're proud of me," Casey said. "I'm glad. I want you to be proud of me."

"You're a good daughter," Dad said, sounding all soft and mushy. "You've always worked hard and made good grades. You've never given us a minute's trouble. No worries about drugs or drunk driving like some kids. We wouldn't trade you for any other daughter in the world."

"Okay-fine," Casey said, maybe sounding all soft and mushy herself. She was a Daddy's Girl. Always had been. Probably always would be.

"Are you thinking about Sunday afternoon?"

"I've been thinking about Sunday afternoon all my life," Casey said. That wasn't a lie.

The apartment Katie/Carla/Darla shared was huge. Beige carpeting, white walls, three bedrooms, two and a half baths. The living room had a couch, two easy chairs, a bean bag chair, a coffee table, a stereo and a dead goldfish in a bowl. No TV. The walls were bare. The kitchen had a microwave and a vegetable steamer. No frying pans or pots or anything like that. Katie and the twins were the kinds of vegetarians who ate plants, dairy products and nothing else. The refrigerator was usually stuffed with every kind of vegetable you could imagine and cottage cheese and chocolate milk and quart-sized bottles of beer. Nothing else.

Casey thought Katie/Carla/Darla were the most fascinating, exotic women in the world. Katie was a senior microbiology major. Carla/Darla were juniors. Carla was an architecture major, Darla an environmental engineering major. They weren't stupid. They were good at making a physical education/athletic coaching major like Casey feel stupid when she looked at some of their textbooks. Most of the time when Casey asked them something they said, "Duh," and rolled their eyes. Or they'd say, "Like, toe-tuh-lee wack," and slap Casey's butt. That made Casey feel stupid, too.

Katie/Carla/Darla had the most stable lesbian relationship Casey had ever seen. They'd been together for three years, living in the same apartment, sleeping in the same bed, talking in the same singsong chanting voices and using the same screwball language, making love together, doing everything together. They lived like a straight married couple, complete with gold bands on their left ring fingers like they were married, but there were three of them instead of two. Plus their 'mistress.'

Casey played the role of mistress.

At first Casey thought the relationship she had with Katie/Carla/Darla had just sort of happened. Fat chance. After seeing Casey's picture in the college paper, they decided there was 'something in her eyes and toe-tuh-lee impish grin' that made them hot for her. They looked her address up in the student directory and 'like, staked out the crib.' It took them ten minutes to figure out Casey was a dyke.

After following her around campus for a while, watching her with Toni and Kristy and Sharika, they decided Casey had a shortage of breasts in her life so Katie and her breasts were picked to initiate the seduction. The whole thing had been an intricate plan to add a mistress to their marriage. It made Casey a little mad to find out she'd been so easily manipulated by a pair of 38D's, but she didn't know what she could do about it. She comforted herself by thinking she probably wasn't the first woman in history to get blind-sided by a pair of world-class knockers.

When she told the twins how she was a little mad, they both said, "Duh," and rolled their eyes. Then Carla said, "Like, there's the door."

Casey lay on the bed, filmed in sweat and feeling satisfied. She thought about Katie with her beautiful face and huge green eyes and full body and eagerness in bed. The twins with their cropped hair and pert faces and flashing brown eyes and spidery bodies.

"You'd just replace me if I left, wouldn't you?" Casey asked.

"That's, like, a moot point," Carla said. "You're not departing."

Casey burrowed between them and didn't make a step for the door. She lay there stroking an abundance of sleek feminine appendages and listening to the twins have an argument about the dead goldfish in the bowl on the coffee table and should they or shouldn't they throw it away.

"We can't, like, prove George is brain dead," Darla said emphatically. "We haven't given him an electroencephalogram or anything. Maybe he can still think so he still is. I'm not putting him down the garbage disposal if he's, like, still."

The argument evolved into a debate on philosophy and Descartes and Socrates and Plato. It ended when the twins decided philosophy was toe-tuh-lee wack and compromised by agreeing to keep George in the bowl, but to stop feeding him since he didn't eat the food they gave him anyway and it seemed a crime to waste goldfish food because there were probably goldfish in India or somewhere who were starving.

Casey giggled. Sure it was silly and dumb and maybe even childish, but it was just the twins' way of adding their personal touch to their lives and doing things their way. A kind of deliberate eccentricity. And Carla/Darla were definitely eccentric—the shaving department, for example.

"Like, duh," Casey said. "Since your shaving habits aren't an indicator of butch/femme attitudes, then what's the reason for one of you shaving and the other not? Is it a kind of double-feminist statement on both your parts?"

"Do you like my hairy body?" Carla asked.

"Do you like my bald body?" Darla asked.

"Yes to both questions," Casey said, tugging the hair on Carla's thigh with one hand and fondling Darla's bald crotch with her other hand.

"Duh," Darla said, rolling her eyes. "We're, like, identical twins. We have to be different in bed for you and Katie Ever-ready some way."

"Okay-fine," Casey groaned as Carla sucked on her ear and Darla slipped between her legs.

Katie only added to the eccentricity. Between the three of them they didn't have even one car. They took a bus when they went home to visit their families. Otherwise they rode bikes everywhere they went. They had a two-wheel cart they tied behind their bikes and pulled to the store when they needed groceries. They took cloth sacks to the grocery store with them and put all their stuff into the cloth sacks instead of paper or plastic. They didn't have a checking account because they said checks killed trees. They rode to the bank and got cash when they needed it. They didn't have credit cards because they were plastic. They had four big trash boxes in their kitchen, one for aluminum, one for plastic, one for paper and one for glass, all of which they periodically hauled to the recycling plant.

Casey thought not having a TV was the most eccentric thing of all. One night she asked Katie why they didn't have one.

"Like, toe-tuh-lee wack," Katie said.

"But you miss Roseanne and Bart Simpson and Bill Cosby and all that stuff."

"Like, so?" Katie said mockingly. "What's a straight fat woman, a long-bucks black man and a cartoon boy got to do with my life? Would they peep a TV show about me?"

Casey didn't know if Katie/Carla/Darla were toe-tuh-lee wack themselves or the America Of The Future. She did know she was in love with them. And she meant love. Sometimes, when she was sitting in her classes, she'd get to missing them so much she couldn't stand it. She'd race to their apartment as soon as her classes ended, and when Katie or Carla/Darla saw her, they'd attack each other and start stripping and stumbling toward the bedroom.

Afterwards Casey couldn't help wondering if she loved Katie/Carla/Darla the way lovers should love each other or if she loved them the way a junkie loves cocaine.

The Saturday night after the New Orleans game Casey stopped by Katie/Carla/Darla's. Just to visit and eat a little tofu and drink a little beer and unwrap. That's what she told herself, anyway.

Carla and Darla were wearing matching blue culottes and looked so tres, tres cute it made Casey lick her lips. The twins were listening to music and drinking beer. The first thing Casey noticed, other than how tres, tres cute the twins looked, was a foosball table sitting in the middle of the living room. A nice foosball table, with leather trim and everything.

"What's this?" Casey asked, spinning one of the bars, admiring the new sheen of the game.

"Like, foosball," Carla said. "Duh."

"It's, like, a b-day present from mom-and-pop," Darla said. "Wanna play? It's, like, ten megatons of fun."

"You'll have to show me how," Casey said slyly, trying not to laugh.

"Bitchin'!"

Casey sipped on the bottle of beer while Carla and Darla gave a detailed explanation of foosball. "Got it," she said when they finished. "I'll play you two."

"Joke!"

"Like!"

"No joke," Casey said. "I'll beat the crap out of you. I can beat you two at anything with balls."

Carla and Darla cracked up.

Looking at the twins, heads lowered over the table, showing their straight white parts, twisting amateurishly on their bars, chattering between themselves how they were going to, "like, mangle the rookie at foosball," filling the air with their smells of perfume and freshly-shampooed hair and beer, Casey felt one of those soft and mushy twinges you sometimes feel when you look at someone you love. She snickered when she was through feeling soft and mushy because the twins were dead meat.

She served, poking a ball through the hole with her thumb, putting maybe a ton of english on it. The ball bit and swerved sharply. Casey snagged it with her center, clothesline pass to her forward, simple pull-shot and crack! the ball slammed into the goal.

"Duh," Carla said, lowering her face to peer into the goal. "I, like, didn't even peep it." She was playing goalie.

"Lucky shot," Casey said, serving again quickly to keep the twins off balance. English, snag, clothesline, pull, crack! "How about that!" she declared. "Two lucky shots in a row."

"Have you, like, played this before?" Darla asked.

"Like, no," Casey said.

The twins looked at her suspiciously, narrowing their eyes, pursing their lips. Casey cracked up because no matter what she said the twins automatically assumed it was a lie.

"Maybe I've played a time or two," she admitted, feeling a little guilty for bullying the twins with their own birthday present. "I might have a couple of foosball trophies at home."

"You're, like, such a conceited ass-hole!" the twins chorused. Casey shoved her bar all the way through and poked Carla in the stomach. "Like, ouch," Carla said. She grabbed a handful of Casey's hair, pulling her close so they could kiss.

"God, you taste good," Casey said.

"Like, ditto," Carla said, licking her lips.

Katie walked in the door, shouting, "Like, party time! Katie Ever-ready's here!"

She changed tapes in the stereo, putting on some kind of smash-face music, Judas Priest or Anthrax or something. Then she chug-a-lugged half a quart of beer and started dancing in the middle of the room, hopping up-and-down, waving her arms and flopping her head back-and-forth on her shoulders. Carla and Darla danced with her, doing the same hopping and waving and flopping.

"Go for it, ladies," Casey said, watching, eyes more or less bulging. It was one of the most exciting dances she'd ever seen, all the hopping and jiggling and rippling.

"Hot!" Katie shouted. She stripped off her blouse and threw it on the floor. Her bra landed on top of her blouse. Shoes. Jeans. Panties. Jiggle-jiggle-ripple-ripple.

Carla's culottes joined Katie's clothes on the floor. Darla's culottes joined the pile. "It's hot all right," Casey said, fanning her face with a hand, sipping on the beer, pushing her eyes back into place.

Katie stopped hopping and looked at Casey. "It's not any, like, fun to have a mistress around just to peep at," Katie cooed. Carla and Darla stopped hopping and eyed Casey.

They all three had wild grins on their faces.

"Oh, shit," Casey said.

The lights went off, the music kept blaring. Three pairs of hands grabbed Casey. Someone tied a blindfold around her eyes. Around-around-around she went in a circle, losing track of exactly where she was in the room. Someone shoved her, she reached out to grab something for support but got only air. She landed in two pairs of arms, was lowered to the floor.

"I have to go home," Casey offered, hoping just the offer would save her soul from eternal damnation, even if it was insincere.

"Like, your REM-cycle is talking," Carla breathed, sucking Casey's bottom lip. "No curfew tonight."

Casey's clothes melted away as fast as butter on hot grits. Hands pinned her face down to the floor. She felt a liquid dripping onto her back and butt. The liquid was cold as ice. She felt someone blowing. The liquid turned hot as fire. Then hands and liquid and blowing were all over her. She got flipped from her face onto her back and onto her face again, ice-fire-ice-fire.

She went numb, licking, tickling, massaging anything she could touch or taste, feeling helpless and overwhelmed, knew Katie and the twins felt the same. There were just too many body parts to keep up with. Katie and the twins were talking nonstop in their screwball language, bodies were shifting, ice-fire-ice-fire, Anthrax or Judas Priest blaring. And the aroma of women. God. It was thick enough to founder on.

"Like, good-bye, girls," Carla groaned and started having her usual noisy climax.

Darla giggled. "Carla, like, lost," she said. "She popped the first O."

"Like!" Katie said.

Casey was numb enough to be dead. She gave it up and started screaming at the top of her lungs. She wanted it to end. It felt too good, too intense. She'd never thought she'd hope for a climax to end, but she did. She screamed for maybe fifteen seconds.

"Toe-tuh-lee hype," Katie breathed respectfully.

"For sure," Darla breathed, equally respectful. "Like, Casey lost, but she, like, won."

"Carla, you bitch," Katie said. Then she groaned, "Geronimo," and started having her usual sobbing/crying climax.

"I, like, won," Darla groaned and started having her usual noisy climax.

Casey lay there trembling, weak, whorish-feeling. She heard bodies shifting, the music lowering. The blindfold came off. She blinked in the bright lights. Katie and Carla were holding each other, nuzzling each other's necks. Darla was propped against the couch, holding a cigarette between two fingers and puffing without inhaling. Everyone looked like crap, faces flushed, eyes bright, hair plastered to cheeks and foreheads. Casey knew she looked the same.

Casey gathered her clothes. Everyone lay there watching her curiously. "I won't be back," she said. "I just can't deal with this."

"Joke!" Carla said.

"Like!" Katie said.

"We've heard this before," Darla said, puffing on her cigarette.

"I can't take this anymore," Casey said. "It's too intense. It blows the top of my head off. I'm going to have a heart attack someday because of you three. So...bye."

"Bye."

"Bye."

"Bye."

They all three sat on the floor, sipping beer and watching Casey. They had serious looks on their faces and love in their eyes.

Love times three.

Casey dropped her clothes, snuggled down in the middle of all the hot, moist feminine bodies. The quart of beer made the rounds. Casey took a sip when it was her turn.

"We'll be in Knoxville T-N, like, tomorrow afternoon," Carla said. "To peep the be-bop-a-do-wop on the Tennessee dykes. We're, like, journeying on the friendly skies. Darla and Katie Ever-ready and me. It's going to be, like, a ten megaton hangover bitchin' good time."

"How are you, like, getting there?" Darla asked.

"We're taking a bus to Tulsa," Casey explained. "Then we're flying to Columbia, Missouri to pick up the Missouri team. We're all flying together to Knoxville. Same thing coming back. It saves money for both teams to travel together."

Everyone nodded, satisfied.

Then Casey said, "I've been, like, pondering; what do you do if, like, Carla and Darla are in the mood but Katie's not?"

"Katie Ever-ready not in the mood?"

"Joke!"

"No joke! Like, remember two weeks ago when she was, like, toe-tuh-lee wack with the ten-day-common? She was, like, Katie Never-ready for a week."

"Do you two make love?" Casey asked.

Carla and Darla acted like they were poking fingers down their throats and gagging. Katie said, "I've been, like, pondering. Malibu and a tofu shop after we take the walk with the mortar boards."

"Toe-tuh-lee gnarly, dude-ette!"

"Joke!"

"Like!

They all three acted like they were poking fingers down their throats and gagging. Katie leaned around, opened a drawer in the coffee table, clicked something that made a buzzing sound and turned around with a big grin. She was holding a grey dildo that turned around-and-around and went in-and-out. Everyone cracked up and rolled around on the floor laughing at Katie.

"It's, like, a Big Four-O present for my mom," Katie explained.

Everyone laughed harder. Then they took a group shower and went to bed together. Casey could say Katie/Carla/Darla were fascinating and exotic and eccentric, and they were all those things, but she knew why she was in love with them. And she couldn't help it.

CHAPTER 9

The warm-ups ended with a flurry of slamma-jammas from both teams, both backboards rocking, each team trying to show they were bigger and stronger and meaner than the other, both teams with three wins in the week, knowing only one would finish the week with four wins. Both head coaches were at the scorer's table, pointing fingers, talking nonstop, working on the refs, wanting every call to go their way, working on each other, too, laying the mental groundwork in case they met again in the National Tournament at the end of the year.

The public address announcer said the CBS cameras were coming on the air and for everyone to make noise, but nothing changed because the noise was already deafening, in the hundred decibel range, everyone screaming their heads off, the band pounding out Rocky Top.

Knoxville, Tennessee. In the mountains of east Tennessee. Fifty miles north of Chatsworth.

Home.

Thompson-Boling Arena was huge, seating almost twenty-five thousand. It was one of the new sanitary basketball arenas. It was sold out for the doubleheader.

When Casey was a kid it was a big treat, the biggest thrill of her life, the times Dad and Mom took her to Knoxville to watch the Lady Vols play. She couldn't count the number of nights she'd lain in her bed, smiling and thinking about growing up and playing for the Lady Vols, wearing the Big Orange, playing in front of twenty-five thousand screaming fans. When she fell asleep she'd dream it was all true, she was wearing the Big Orange, hearing her name over the public address system, running through the corridor of players while the twenty-five thousand people screamed and the band played Rocky Top.

All those thoughts and dreams had come true. She was playing in Thompson-Boling Arena, she was hearing twenty-five thousand people screaming, she would hear her name over the public address system, she would run through the corridor of players in an orange uniform.

But it wasn't Tennessee orange she was wearing.

"At guard, from Chatsworth, Tennessee, number three—"

She didn't hear anything else. The boos started and got louder and louder. She ran through the corridor of players, burst into the open, stood in the center of Thompson-Boling Arena and the boos rained down on her like hailstones.

She didn't know where Dad was with his Camcorder or Mom with her wet eyes or the rest of her family and friends were sitting; she couldn't see them but she knew they could see her, could hear her getting booed like a dog. The only sign of friendship she could see was a big white poster board sign bouncing way up at the top of the arena, *We Love You, Case. Katie And A Twin Sandwich.* And her teammates. Muttering to themselves, angry looks on their faces.

She wanted to cry. She wasn't the local girl done good and come home. She was a traitor, instead. She wanted to scream at all twenty-five thousand people, 'I would've picked Tennessee in a second over Tech, but Tennessee didn't want me. Tennessee didn't even come watch me play in high school. Well, screw you! I would've picked Tennessee then, but I wouldn't now. I'm an Okie now!'

But she couldn't scream. Nobody would hear her. So she waved. And the booing got louder. Alysa trotted out, threw an arm around Casey's shoulders and rumbled, "I don't think these crackers like us, Lower Case. Ain't no big thing. I don't like them, either. Do you?"

Before the tip, the Tennessee players started slapping each other's hands, ignoring the hands the Tech players were offering, and shouting, "Their fighting game won't work here! If they try it we'll give it back to 'em!"

"Go on with your bad selves," Alysa rumbled, pulling her hand back, looking furious, an awe-inspiring sight. "We left our fighter at home. We don't need her for the likes of you."

Everyone got in each other's faces, waving arms and talking trash, seeing who would back down from the intimidation first, Alysa and Weatherly exchanging, "Muh-thuh-fuck yo-selves," with the Tennessee trees, everyone's eyes feverish, jazzed half-insane by the quality of the competition and the big crowd and the CBS cameras and the national audience.

The head ref shrieked her whistle and shouted, "I'll start this game by ejecting both first-teams if I have to!"

Everyone shut up and took their positions around the circle, tight-lipped and grim-faced.

The first three times Casey got her hands on the ball, the crowd taunted her, singsonging, "Ca-sey! Ca-sey! Ca-sey!" The first three times she got her hands on the ball, she squared to the basket and fired, ignoring everyone else, ignoring Coach Murphy's game plan, ignoring everything except wanting to score and score and score and shove the booing up everyone's butt.

Her first shot was an air-ball. Her second shot bounced off the front of the rim. Her third shot was another air-ball and the taunts turned to laughs. Tennessee converted all of her missed shots into easy baskets, the third one drawing Casey a hacking foul, a toma-hawk job on one of the Lady Vols, committed from pure frustration.

"Cheap-shot bitch!" the Lady Vol shouted, picking herself up from the floor, rubbing her forehead where Casey's forearm had landed.

"The hell with you!" Casey shouted. "The hell with you and fuck you and fuck everything about this place!"

She was spitting fire, but she felt cold inside because she knew what was going to happen.

Coach Murphy benched her.

It was the most humiliating moment in Casey's life. Trotting off the court, everyone booing and laughing their heads off, everyone knowing she was getting benched for losing her grip, knowing her-self she'd lost her grip and let the crowd get to her and rattle her. And all her family and friends watching.

Two minutes into the game: Lady Vols 8, Lady Lobos 0.

Casey sat at the far end of the bench, as far away from the people and TV cameras as she could get. As far away from Coach Murphy as she could get. She grabbed a towel and covered her face because her chin was trembling and she knew in a second her face would screw up and she'd start crying. She felt someone squatting in front of her, felt a hand on her knee, heard Coach Murphy's calm voice.

"Casey, look at me."

"I can't," Casey said. She'd dug a huge hole for the Lady Lobos, a hole they wouldn't be able to crawl out of. She'd let everybody down. Let all her teammates down.

"I understand," Coach Murphy said. "Composure, Casey." She walked away.

Casey got put back in ninety seconds later.

Casey was the first one showered and dressed. She grabbed her gym bag and left the locker room, going to the players' entrance where she could be alone except for one bored-looking security guard standing around. She sat on a bench and thought of all the dreams, all the wants, all the needs. Childish dreams and wants and needs. All coming down to one shot.

One simple shot.

A shot she'd made on countless playgrounds, in countless gyms, in countless practices, in countless games. A shot she'd nailed hundreds of times in her parents' driveway on cool autumn afternoons, shooting at the regulation hoop Dad had put up, dribbling and nailing the same shot over and over again until it got dark and cold and Mom opened the front door and called for her to come inside and drink some hot chocolate and get warm.

That's what it's all about, babe. Choking in clutch plays. Succumbing to your puckered butt. Major-college ball.

A missed ten-footer.

Lady Vols 81, Lady Lobos 80.

Memories of watching a ten foot shot bounce off the front of the rim, dropping to her knees, pounding the floor with her fists, seeing the Lady Vols mobbing each other at half-court, calm-looking Coach Murphy walking to the Tennessee bench to shake hands with the Lady Vols coach, remembering where she was, remembering the booing, the TV cameras, standing, fighting through her teammates trying to console her, screaming, "Choke-choke-choke!" and running into the locker room, The Good-Bye Song echoing in her head no matter how tightly she pressed her hands against her ears.

Most of all, memories of an exhausted Alysa fouling out thirty seconds into the overtime, everyone looking down the bench, realizing their hole had been exposed, everyone thinking the same thing: Tobie. We sure could use your seventy-six pale, frail inches. Where are you?

Casey looked out the window at the parking lot. The team bus was sitting outside the door in the twilight, parking lights on, luggage compartments open, smoke puffing from the tail pipe. There were two girls standing just outside the door. One looked about ten years old, the other twelve or thirteen. They were wearing heavy coats and ski caps, breath steaming from their mouths, stomping their feet to keep warm, clutching game programs and pens in their mittened hands. Two adults, a man and a woman, huddled together in the background, talking between themselves, hands jammed in their coat pockets.

Casey remembered the times Dad and Mom brought her to Lady Vols games, how they'd waited patiently while she stood outside the players' entrance, hoping to get an autograph or a glimpse of one of her heroines. Autographs that were meaningless now, she'd misplaced them years ago. Or lost them. Or thrown them away.

She stepped to the door and opened it. "I don't know when the Tennessee players will come out. Do you want to come in and wait?"

"You're Casey," one of the girls breathed. "We're waiting to see you. We're from Chatsworth."

"Want to come in and I'll autograph your programs?"

The girls looked at their parents. "Please, Daddy," one said. "Can we? Please?"

The father nodded. Casey signed their programs. Then she opened her gym bag and gave each of the girls a pair of orange and black sweatbands and a roll of athletic tape. One of the girls said, "Is this real tape? Just like the players use?"

Casey nodded. "It's J-and-J. The same as I use."

"You're famous," one of the girls said. "We read about you in the paper all the time. The paper says you play on a mean team, but I don't believe it. I'm a guard just like you."

"I'm not," the other girl said. "I'm a center because I'm tall."

"You're not tall," the first girl said. "You're just growing faster than everyone else."

They left, walking across the parking lot, walking faster and faster until they started running, holding their hands out to show their parents what they'd gotten. Casey went outside, threw her gym bag into the luggage compartment and got on the bus. She sat in the very back, turning her back and staring out the window at the mountains and bare trees and thinking about her childish wants and needs and dreams.

After the plane took off, Coach Murphy stood up. "The way you came back to force the overtime was the most stirring moment I've ever witnessed," she said. "I'm so proud of you. As women and players. You gave it all you had today. I can't ask more of you."

She sat back down, digging in her purse, lighting the one cigarette a day she allowed herself right in front of everybody instead of sneaking away to smoke like she usually did.

Some of the players started crying, covering their faces with their hands, shoulders shaking, glad the long week was over, wishing, oh, God, wishing they could've capped it with a win over the Number One team in the country.

Wishes. They belonged in the same closet with the childish dreams and wants and needs and lost autographs. But Casey still wished she had another chance at the ten-footer, another chance to make her dreams come true. And she wished she didn't have to look at the covered faces and shaking shoulders, and listen to the stifled sobs because it was all her fault, all the sadness was her fault.

The sound of music and laughter and crowing drifted through the curtain separating the Lady Lobos on the plane from the Missouri team. Some of the Lady Tigers opened the curtain and peeked through, faces flushed and excited, expressions friendly. They saw all the covered faces, heard the crying and dropped the curtain back in place and went back to their celebrating.

It was easy for the Missouri players to look friendly, they were going home winners. They'd beaten Vanderbilt, also in overtime. It had been a great day for women's basketball, with two exciting games on National TV.

It had been an 'I want to die' day for the Lady Lobos.

Alysa started rumbling, talking about growing up in Hugo, Oklahoma, nothing but a hole in the wall place, really. About sitting on the front porch of her family's rickety one bedroom house that eight people lived in. Sitting with her grandfather, watching the rich people in their fine, fine Chevrolets and Fords drive past on the highway just outside the front door. Her grandfather always told her she was meant for better things, that she'd get out of Hugo, Oklahoma some day and see fine, fine places and make something of her life. How her grandfather passed away her senior year in high school, how he never knew she did get out of Hugo and go on to college and was going to make something of her life.

Then Alysa's story changed to one about a cottontail rabbit that used to sneak into their backyard and eat dandelions. Oh, Lordy, she wanted to catch that rabbit bad. She didn't have any use for it except maybe to eat it, but she wanted to catch it because it was so wild and free and beautiful and maybe some of the wildness and beauty and freedom would rub off on poor old Alysa. She schemed and thought and built trap after trap out of sticks and old boards and chicken wire, but she never was able to catch that cottontail because he was plain old smarter than poor old Alysa, and maybe that's why he was wild and free and beautiful and Alysa wasn't. Maybe Alysa wasn't wild and free and beautiful because she was just plain old dumb.

Next, Alysa rumbled about a possum that kept sneaking into their backyard to eat from a trash can. Alysa wanted to catch that poor old possum bad, too. Because he was ugly and slow and dumb. She didn't have any use for the possum except maybe to eat it. She sure didn't want any of his ugliness or slowness or dumbness to rub off on her because she had enough of that her own self. Still, she wanted to catch it. Maybe to put the poor old ugly and slow and dumb thing out of his misery. She schemed and thought and built trap after trap, but she could never catch that possum because he was plain old smarter than poor old Alysa, too.

Well, now, Lordy, poor old Alysa didn't know what to think at that point. Not only was a wild, free and beautiful cottontail smarter than poor old Alysa, an ugly and slow and dumb possum was smarter than poor old Alysa, too. Anyway, she finally realized maybe that poor old possum was ugly and slow and dumb in her eyes, but he wasn't in his own eyes, and didn't think he should get killed just because someone else thought he was ugly and slow and dumb.

Well, well, now, Lordy, poor old Alysa felt right proud of herself at this point. She was just as good as this William Shakespeare fellow at figuring out this beauty-is-in-the-eye-of-the-beholder thing like he'd done, but she didn't need kings and queens and other fine royalty around to figure it out. All poor old Alysa needed was a cottontail and a possum and a backyard in Hugo, Oklahoma.

In the end, poor old Alysa decided she'd had the last laugh on the cottontail and the possum because she was living at Tech and playing on a fine, fine basketball team like she'd dreamed of her whole life, and it didn't matter what happened to her, not even if she thought what happened to her was bad, at least she was going places and experiencing life while the cottontail and the possum were still stuck in Hugo eating dandelions and trash, respectively.

Casey listened to Alysa's story, even though she doubted there was any point to it. It was only a bedtime story Alysa was telling in her rumbling voice. A story to soothe a bunch of heartbroken children who needed to sleep and forget their heartbreak.

The team bus that brought them from the airport got to Brookfield at one in the morning. It was cold, twenty-five degrees, and spitting snow. The usual crowd of families and friends and lovers was congregated in the parking lot of Mitchell.

Casey stepped off the bus and saw Kristy standing beside her beat up Ford Escort, exhaust smoke puffing. Kristy was wearing a big brown coat and earmuffs and stomping her feet. Sharika was waiting beside her white Corvette, in a full-length mink coat and matching mink cap.

Casey walked to Kristy's car and threw her gym bag into the back seat. Kristy's eyes flickered behind her glasses. She ran around and got behind the wheel. Sharika drove off, tires screaming, engine roaring, over the curb, sparks flying from under her car, thudding over the speed bumps and disappearing in the snow and cold.

"Where are we going?" Kristy asked, peering through steamy glasses. She took her glasses off and wiped them on her coat.

"Your place," Casey said. A Gloria Estefan song was playing on the radio. A sad, dreamy song that put a lump in Casey's throat. She clicked the radio off.

"I wasn't putting any pressure on you," Kristy said. "I didn't expect anything. I just wanted to see you. Maybe say hello. I haven't seen you in so long."

Casey leaned her head against the seat and closed her eyes. She knew there was a lot of shit she had to deal with, but she didn't feel like it right now. She just couldn't handle it right now.

"You look nice," Kristy said. "You should wear dresses more often."

Casey tugged at her hose, ripping and jerking and tugging until she shredded them around her knees.

"Oh," Kristy squeaked. She cleared her throat. "I guess you go through a lot of hose."

Casey didn't say anything, ignoring how immature she felt for ruining a pair of new hose.

"I cried when I watched the game," Kristy said softly. "At the end when you were on your knees pounding the floor I wanted to reach into the TV and touch you. The cameras zoomed in on you and kept flashing from you pounding the floor to the Tennessee celebration. The woman announcer said, 'I don't want anyone to tell me women don't take the game as seriously as men. These are finely-tuned athletes, physically and psychologically, with a lot of pride and they compete to win.'" Kristy touched Casey's shoulder. "I hadn't thought about it like that before today. It's true, isn't it? You want to win every game you play."

Casey didn't say anything, thinking, I'm glad to hear I was used as the agony-of-defeat model.

"Both the announcers were real complimentary," Kristy said. "They said you did the right thing taking the shot. They said something about the weak side being covered and Tech's pick play failed and you had to take the shot. There wasn't time to setup anything else."

"I was there!" Casey shouted. "I don't need you telling me what happened!"

Kristy flinched. The car swerved. "I'm sorry," she said. "I'm trying my best. I don't know much about sports. I don't know what to say."

"I'm sorry." Casey touched Kristy's shoulder. "I know you're trying to help, but don't say anything, just don't."

"Okay."

In the loft, Kristy switched on a lamp and lit her kerosene heater. She stood beside it, looking at her hands. Casey flopped onto the day bed without undressing, covering herself with a blanket, hiding her head under a pillow, trying not to think, trying not to feel.

When she opened her eyes, a dim grey light was coming through the sheer curtains. She was undressed. Kristy was sitting on the edge of the day bed, wearing a blue robe. A tray with a thermometer, a jar of Vaseline and a hypodermic was on the coffee table.

"You're burning up," Kristy said, pressing a cool washcloth to Casey's forehead.

"Do you want to take my temperature?"

"I already have," Kristy said.

"I thought I dreamed that."

"Don't look so embarrassed," Kristy said, touching Casey's cheek, her eyes soft. "I took a lot of rectal temps when I did my internship. Babies and old people mostly. Your temp's one hundred." She picked up the hypodermic.

"What's that?"

"B-12," Kristy said, peering over her glasses. "Want a few seconds to prepare?"

"Shots don't bother me." Casey felt the blanket lift, her leg being

94

shifted, cool alcohol on her hip, the sting of the needle, cool alcohol again. "You're good."

"It only takes practice," Kristy said. "Being a diabetic helps." She took Casey's hand and said, "Stay with me today. It's cold and snowy outside. You don't need to be out. I had the breakfast shift at Burger King. I've already called in sick. Stay here today and let me nurse you."

"Okay-fine," Casey said, feeling drained, feeling like not doing anything. "I'm so tired," she said. "This week took a lot out of me."

"I can sense we're drifting apart," Kristy said. "Please don't hurt me right now. I feel too vulnerable. Cut the time you spend with me or do anything you want, but please don't hurt me right now."

Casey felt her chin trembling; it was just too much, the shit she had to deal with couldn't be controlled any longer.

"Do you want me?" Kristy whispered, loosening her robe. "I'll let you if that's what it takes to keep you."

Casey turned to the wall, hiding her face in a pillow. How could she face her teammates again after what she'd done? She remembered the faces, Alysa's and Weatherly's and everybody's, how hopeful they'd looked when the ball left her hands, how trusting everyone had looked, faces saying, 'We know you can do it, Lower Case. You pulled our fat out of the fire at Colorado. You can do it here, too.'

She'd never forget how the hopeful, trusting looks had instantly changed to crushed looks when the ball bounced off the front of the rim and the horn sounded.

"You're not hard," Kristy whispered, sounding awed, moving beside Casey, rubbing her back. "It's just an act. On the inside you're as confused and afraid as I am." She kissed Casey's shoulder. "Thank you for doing this in front of me. It means so much to me."

Kristy took off her robe and slipped under the blanket with Casey, pressing her naked body to Casey's, kissing Casey softly on the mouth again and again. "Make love to me, please make love to me," Kristy whispered.

Casey shook her head, hiding her face against the pillow.

Tears. They belonged in the same closet with the dreams and wants and needs and lost autographs and wishes. But she still cried.

CHAPTER 10

Coach Murphy closed the door to her office. She perched on the edge of her desk, one gorgeous leg swinging, one delicate hand tapping a pencil against her chin. Her face looked a combination of mad and worried.

"Where have you been for the last two days?" she asked.

"Sick," Casey said.

"You weren't in your dorm."

"I was staying with a friend."

Coach Murphy pursed her lips. "Why didn't you call me?"

Casey dropped her eyes.

"You will look at me when I'm talking to you," Coach Murphy said, using her talking-to-Tobie voice.

Casey raised her eyes, her butt puckering, wondering how much squirming pain her poor-loser-tantrum was going to cost.

"Do you feel okay now?" Coach Murphy asked.

"Yes, ma'am."

"Twenty laps," Coach Murphy said. "Ten for your vanishing act. Ten for cutting class without notifying the academic advisor. You can run them when you're feeling stronger."

"I feel strong as a horse," Casey said. "I'll start on them today."

Coach Murphy crossed her ankles. The pencil kept tapping her chin. She said, "I feel a great deal of responsibility for my players. The freshmen most of all. Young, impressionable, away from home for the first time. Their parents trust me to look after the welfare of their daughters. I always have, and always will, fulfill that trust."

"You've had more of an impression on me than anyone else at college," Casey said."

Coach Murphy smiled her tight smile, her eyes saying, Are you full of shit or what. The look jumped out and hurt Casey's feelings. "I'm not just saying that," she said softly.

"I believe you," Coach Murphy said. A pause. "This is what I could do. I could shorten your leash as of today. I could have a grad assistant escort you to your classes. I could ask for a list of your closest friends and their phone numbers. I could set your curfew at ten o'clock and closely monitor it. I could demand to know where you are, or how to reach you, twenty-four hours a day."

"Yes, ma'am," Casey said, groveling, riding the storm out instead of trying to fight it.

"Or," Coach Murphy said, eyes probing, analyzing, evaluating, "I could treat you as an adult and trust your vanishing act won't be repeated. Would that kind of trust in you be misplaced?"

"No, ma'am."

Coach Murphy arched her eyebrows.

Casey swallowed hard, knowing she wasn't going to be allowed to just ride things out. "I would prefer to be treated like an adult," she said, "because that's what I am. I promise you I'll act like an adult in the future so I'll be sure and be treated like one."

"Yes?" Coach Murphy said, sounding expectant.

"I acted like a child," Casey said slowly. "I deserve to be punished in some way. So my curfew will be nine o'clock for the next week. And," she took a deep breath and bit the bullet, "I'll tell my professors my absences are unexcused so I don't deserve any make-up work and I should receive zeros for the days I was gone."

"Okay," Coach Murphy said. Her eyes softened. "Do you want to talk about why you went AWOL?"

Casey hesitated. "I thought about quitting while I was gone," she finally said. "I thought about going home and getting a job at one of the Dalton carpet mills or something."

Coach Murphy frowned. "Why would you even consider that?"

"I'm no good," Casey said, wondering if she was only wanting a pat on the back, forgiveness for costing Coach Murphy the Tennessee game. "I've been playing over my head so far. It's a fluke. I'll never be good enough to play on a high level."

"Casey," Coach Murphy said, "there are two ways a team can take a loss. One way is to keep looking back and let it destroy them. The second way is to go forward, grow better and stronger, learn from it, correct the mistakes they made. I prefer the latter way of taking a loss. Believe it or not, I know what I'm doing with you. Every coach worth her salt knows it's a feast or famine with freshmen. I accept that with all my freshmen, and I'm right beside you, starving during the famine, pigging-out during the feast. The whole team is with you. We practice as a team, we play as a team, and we win or lose as a team. No one player causes us to lose anymore than one player causes us to win."

"Yes, ma'am," Casey said, managing a smile, wondering if Coach Murphy was telling the truth. Did it matter, though, if Coach Murphy said what you needed to hear?

"Attagirl," Coach Murphy said, laughing, slapping Casey's shoulder. "Don't ever think about quitting on me. We'll have such a feast someday we'll both weigh two hundred pounds like Alysa."

Casey laughed, knowing the storm had passed and she hadn't been blown away.

"Would you ask Bonnie to come in please?" Coach Murphy asked.

"Yes, ma'am." Casey went to the locker room. It was empty except for Bonnie and Lisa. They were lacing shoes and trading insults. They ragged Casey about the bite marks on her butt shaped exactly like Coach Murphy's mouth.

"Your turn, Bonnie," Casey said, jerking a thumb toward Coach Murphy's office.

The smile faded from Bonnie's face. "What did I do now?" she asked, throwing her hands in the air.

Casey slipped on a tee shirt and a pair of sweat pants and went out to the court. Coach DeFoe and the grad assistants were running practice. Players kept coming and going from the direction of Coach Murphy's office. Tobie, dressed in grey sweats, was running the stands. Tamara and Penny were running laps, too. Casey didn't know what they'd done. Bonnie came out and started practicing instead of running so she obviously hadn't done anything major.

Casey did her stretches, studying all the faces around her, looking for disgust, or even hatred, because of the Tennessee game. The faces were all familiar. She'd seen them every day for months and months, but they were unfamiliar, too,—she hadn't seen them in two days. Two days of soul-searching and change for her, and them, too, she knew. She was anxious about how they'd changed in the two days she'd been gone. Had they decided they'd be better off without her around to miss ten-footers at the buzzer?

But all the faces looked friendly, even relieved, and that made her feel guilty. It had never occurred to her that her teammates would miss her the way they'd missed Tobie. But they had. Only they'd been worried that instead of getting murdered by a suspension, she'd committed suicide by quitting. She decided Coach Murphy was right. The best thing to do was forget about the Tennessee game. That's what everyone else seemed willing to do, so that's what she'd do, too. Just pretend she'd never heard of Tennessee. And if someone mentioned it in teasing, she'd take it good-naturedly.

She timed her start so she could run with Tobie. Tobie was already good and sweaty, the front of her sweats dark with moisture. She looked like she'd been at it for a while. "How many'd you get?" she panted.

"Twenty."

Tobie curled her lip. "I got five," she said. "Hundred."

"You'll never work that off."

"I've got three years after this one," Tobie said. "If that's not enough I'll come back every year for Homecoming and run laps if I have to. I'm not leaving here owing Dr. Murphy anything."

"'Dr. Murphy' is it now?"

"That's right."

"So you're not transferring."

"Nope."

"I'm glad," Casey said, slapping Tobie's shoulder, or as close to her shoulder as she could get, considering Tobie was a foot taller.

Tobie didn't say anything.

"You know what I hate?" Casey asked. "The guilt-trip character-molding talks. I'd rather Coach Murphy would just say, 'You screwed-up. Here's your punishment.' Why does she force you to take part in your punishment process? It makes me feel like a masochist or something, taking part in my own squirming pain."

Tobie didn't say anything. She pounded ahead, across, back down the next aisle, hair flying, face impassive.

Casey did five of her laps, shot a few hoops and then worked on her jab steps and direct drive steps and pivots under the supervision of a grad assistant. Then she did some inside work with Alysa, feeding the ball to Alysa on the opposite side of where the defender was, making the ball impossible to intercept and showing Alysa where the defender was at the same time. Alysa took each pass, worked on her rear turn move and sent the ball swishing through the net.

After the inside work ended, Casey took a breather to get a guilt-trip butt-chewing from one of the grad assistants for being 'a god-damn prima donna' and disappearing for two days and causing Coach Murphy to go through a case of Mylanta-II and do everything but call out the National Guard. Then she paired off with Bonnie and worked on their teamwork against a combination press. Bonnie was a plain, rawboned black woman from Arkansas. She was also straight. Everyone knew she was sleeping with a wide receiver from the football team.

Casey felt totally flashy working out with Bonnie. They practiced silently, except for the code words they used to communicate, like 'cut' or 'down' or 'quick,' talk that didn't mean anything to anyone else, but was a familiar language to them. Their teamwork was something they both took pride in, the way they almost knew what the other was thinking, acting and reacting like mirror-images of each other. When they did screw-up and a pass went zipping into the stands, they'd stare at each other with blank expressions on their faces while a grad assistant chewed both their butts. It was like taking a step only your leg wasn't there to support you when you expected it to be and you fell flat on your face.

"Line drills!" a grad assistant shouted.

Everyone lined up along the base line, taking turns going down the court, making 'V' cuts followed by quick stops to simulate catching the ball at the half-court stripe and free throw line. The whole time the grad assistants were screaming, "Hands up! Get open! Back door! Catch and face! Quick stop! Pivot! Chin the god-damn ball! Chin-it! Chin-it! Chin-it! God-damn, you people are pathetic! If you'd learn to move without the ball you might turn out to be worth a shit!"

Tobie quit running about the time the coaches released the team to hot-dog. She came down from the stands and stood at the edge of practice, watching, not wanting to bull her way in, knowing she'd have to gradually gain reacceptance from her family after rising from the dead.

Casey finally tossed her a ball and said, "Welcome back, Lazarus."

Tobie started shooting jump shots, one after another as fast as she could shoot and retrieve the ball, acting like a starving woman who'd just been handed a steak dinner. Alysa and Weatherly did a few slamma-jammas, but Tobie didn't join in.

Casey spent the time shooting her daily fifty free throws. She made forty-six out of the fifty. She also shot twenty ten foot jumpers from the wing and nailed all twenty. She booted the ball into the stands after she finished, thinking, 'I hate this game.'

"Ellison!" a glaring grad assistant shouted. "Who do you think is going after that ball? I'm not!"

Casey trotted into the stands after the ball.

Casey got stopped by a grad assistant when she came out of the showers. The grad assistant was holding a clipboard. She studied it and bellowed, "Ellison! Report to the trainer. The crud's going around. Everyone's getting B-12 shots."

"I already had one. Yesterday morning."

"You sure? You're not just trying to hide from the needle?"

"I'm sure, Coach."

"Okay." The grad assistant made a mark on her clipboard. "Your vanishing act won you the lottery this week. Report to the trainer, anyway, for a drug test. See Coach Murphy after that." She grabbed Bonnie and bellowed, "Newby! Report to the trainer. B-12 shots for the crud."

Bonnie groaned. "Can't I take a pill instead?" she pleaded.

Casey noticed naked Tobie heading toward the showers with a mop, a bucket and a bottle of disinfectant. Tobie had a round Band-aid on her butt so she'd obviously already had her B-12 shot.

"What are you doing?" Casey asked her curiously.

"Working my way out of Dr. Murphy's doghouse," Tobie said. Her face was impassive. She went into the showers, poured disinfectant into the bucket and started mopping out the showers. Everyone ragged her for getting demoted to janitor.

Casey slipped on a tee shirt and a pair of panties and went into the trainer's room. The trainer was really a doctor. Her official title was, 'Dr. Cynthia Gilstrap, Director for Women's Sports Medicine,' but everyone just called her 'the trainer' or Cindy. She was fortyish, short, plump and had reddish-blond hair.

The trainer was holding a needle in the air and tapping it with a finger. Tamara was bent over a table, panties around her knees, bare butt shining. A blond intern, holding an orange and a hypodermic, was watching everything with wide blue eyes.

"Hold on. I'm not ready yet." Tamara took several deep breaths, screwing her face up like she was waiting for the guillotine to fall.

"What's your middle name?" the trainer asked, jamming the needle into Tamara, not looking too gleeful.

"Ouch!" Tamara shouted. "Ow! God-dammit, Cindy! I told you I wasn't ready yet!"

"You broke a finger last year and didn't blink when I set it," the trainer said, looking disgusted, pulling out the needle, dabbing alcohol on Tamara's butt and slapping on a round Band-aid.

"Ahab," Tamara hissed, pulling up her panties. She danced out, moaning and rubbing her butt.

The trainer came after Casey with a needle. Casey backed away, holding her hands in the air, saying, "Drug test, drug test," with each step.

The trainer asked Casey about any prescription drugs, steroids, the usual stuff, before handing her a plastic cup. That's what it's all about, babe. Knowing you're clean but having to do the squat-and-squirt in front of a wide-eyed blond intern to prove it. Major-college ball.

"What happens if my test comes back dirty when I know I'm clean?" she asked the trainer.

"We run it again," the trainer said, motioning Casey onto a table. "Raise your arms." The trainer slid Casey's tee shirt up, pressing warm, plump fingers into Casey's breasts. The blond intern got even more wide-eyed, looking over the trainer's shoulder.

"I didn't know you cared," Casey said.

The trainer laughed. "Your periods regular?"

"Okay-fine."

"I'm still waiting for you to tell me you went for your first Pap smear," the trainer said, her eyes and hands probing Casey. "You're old enough you need to do that regularly."

Casey studied the ceiling.

"I'm serious," the trainer said.

"And you'll go to God if I don't."

The trainer shrugged. "I'll make sure you do what's best for you. If you won't listen to me I know you'll listen to her."

"I don't want to go to a man doctor."

"Tell you what," the trainer said. "If you'll meet me at Dr. Sheldon's office on Main Street at eight Wednesday morning, I'll do the honors myself. No charge. Deal?"

"Okay-fine." Casey went back to the locker room after the breast exam/butt-chewing. There was a gridlock in front of Alysa's locker. Everyone was crowding around Alysa, peering over her shoulder at a newspaper she was holding. "What's up?" Casey asked.

"We cracked the Top Ten," Alysa rumbled. "Number Seven in one poll. Eight in the other. Bein' on National TV does wonders, even if you don't play as good as you can."

Someone fired up a boom box. An INXS song started thumping. Everyone danced around slapping hands, popping each other's sore butts with towels and crowing about being a Top Ten team.

Casey stood in the center of the group, getting jostled, everyone ruffling her hair or trying to jerk her panties down or slapping her butt or pulling her hair. She didn't know if she felt more like laughing or crying because everyone was trying so hard to show her she was part of the group, even if nobody actually came right out and said that's what they were doing.

"Y'all don't look no different to poor old Alysa," Alysa rumbled. "Better quit thinking about this foolishness and concentrate on Kansas." She flipped through the paper to the business section and rumbled, "Got to check how my stocks did today."

A grad assistant walked up. "Ellison!" she shouted at the top of her lungs, although Casey was only about ten inches away. "I thought I told you to report to Coach Murphy. Johnson! I thought I told you to report to the trainer for a B-12 shot. Let's take care of business and clear out of here. I've got a red-hot man and an ice-cold beer waiting at home. You think I want to spend all evening with you people?"

"Lordy, Lordy, poor old Alysa purely hates needles," Alysa groaned, trying to hide behind her paper.

Casey put on a pair of jeans and went into Coach Murphy's office. Coach Murphy had her head lowered. A pen was in her right hand, she was working her way through a stack of memos about a mile high. She waved Casey into a chair with her left hand.

Casey plopped down and watched Coach Murphy work, thinking how much she'd like to put an arm around Coach Murphy and nuzzle her ears and do other obscene things to her. If nothing else, Casey wished Coach Murphy would shower with the players instead of using the coach's showers so Casey could see what Coach Murphy looked like sans clothes.

When Casey wasn't feeling hot for Coach Murphy she felt like laughing because Coach Murphy was funny in a pitiful way sometimes. Like after the Colorado game when she tried to hide, but everyone saw her in a corner of the locker room, hands shaking and sucking on her bottle of Mylanta-II like a baby at her mama's breast.

Or like after the Tennessee game when she lit her daily cigarette right in front of everyone and sat there smoking, eyes closed, hands shaking as she rubbed her forehead like she had a splitting head-ache.

Being a head coach was hell. Coach Murphy worked out all her Intricate Schemes And Plans and then had to stand helpless and watch while a bunch of excitable young women put her plans into motion. Casey knew Coach Murphy sometimes felt like pulling out an assault rifle and executing an up-close head-shot right between everyone's eyes because of all the petty things she had to mess with on top of planning her Grand Schemes. Like during the plane flights when Coach Murphy would lay her head back and close her eyes only to be interrupted from dozing by a grad assistant with this problem or that problem. Like Penny didn't want to room on the road with Tamara anymore because Tamara had borrowed ten dol-lars three weeks ago and wouldn't pay it back and not only that but Tamara snored, too.

Coach Murphy would always get up and talk to everyone involved and get things smoothed out. Then she'd sit back down and try to doze again only to be interrupted again by some problem. Coach Murphy was really and truly a patient person. Nobody could put in the hours she did and go through the stress she did and fake being patient. If someone was a grump who didn't really like coaching, the hours and stress would bring the true person out sooner or later.

When Coach Murphy wasn't being gorgeous and funny in a pit-iful way, she was breaking Casey's heart. Like when the team ate meals and Coach Murphy got a piece of food stuck in her teeth and nobody would tell her because who was brave enough to tell God she had food stuck in her teeth? Or during the plane flights when she pulled out a picture of the husband and kids and sat there looking at the picture and smiling and running a thumb over everyone's face. If anyone asked when was the last time she saw her husband, she'd laugh and say, "Oh, we bumped in the night a few weeks ago."

Coach Murphy leaned back in her chair. She smiled at Casey before closing her eyes and giving them a good rub.

"It's getting to where I live in your office," Casey said.

Coach Murphy laughed. "You're scheduled to work the serving line at the Community Kitchen Sunday afternoon," she said. "With Coach DeFoe, Sabine and me. Wear something with the team logo."

"Yes, ma'am," Casey said. The last time she'd worked at the Community Kitchen she'd been assigned to serve turkey. It had been hell, fighting not to bury her face in the pile of turkey and inhale about half of it instead of serving it to needy people. This time she'd eat a big meal before she went so she wouldn't be hungry. The worst part of the Community Kitchen was the way she wanted to cry when she saw all the people in their patchwork clothes, people who acted grateful for anything they got. But maybe that was the best part, getting to help people who didn't have much, even if it did make you want to cry.

Coach Murphy moved to the blackboard in her office, picked up a piece of chalk and drew a diagram. Casey felt like purring and arching her back and sticking her tail in the air like a happy cat. She loved the one-on-one chalk-talks in Coach Murphy's office. It made her feel like a favorite kid, getting extra-special attention from a parent. Coach Murphy's eyes glistened with pleasure as she diagrammed. Chalk-talks were a lot more fun for her than doing paperwork or chewing butt.

They worked through one diagram after another, Coach Murphy asking questions, Casey answering, Coach Murphy wiping the diagram away with her hand and drawing another one. They talked in a familiar language, too.

Casey would say something like, "One-three-one to overload, weak side wing cut, high post slide," or "Simple. Five man give-and-go."

"Your job?"

"If the woman guarding me looks at the ball I cut to the basket."

"How?"

"Jab step and cut. Straight cut. Reverse pivot."

"Excellent. Against a man-to-man?"

"I look for the back door pass to Bonnie. If it's not open I can hit Bonnie high on the wing. I also look for the back door to Alysa. If it's not there I can hit Alysa at the high post and she looks for a straight cut from Weatherly. Every series is designed for a back door lay-up."

"And if you see a defense you don't recognize?"

"If I see a defense I don't recognize I have several options. I send a player through without the ball to see how the defense reacts. I reverse the ball from side-to-side. I challenge the defense by a cut or dribble move, any penetration move."

"And?"

"If I still don't recognize the defense I look to you to see what play to run. Or I burn a time-out and talk to you. Especially if the game's close and we can't afford a turnover."

"Good!"

They went through six diagrams, asking-answering-correcting-explaining. Coach Murphy looked pleased. Casey's back was arched as high into the air as it would go. Coach Murphy erased the blackboard and said, "This far along in the season, we know all our conference opponents and they know us. The better you know someone the easier it is to attack their weakness. Our first obvious weakness is a freshman point guard. That means a lot of pressure on you."

"Yes, ma'am."

"Kansas will throw complicated defenses at you to confuse you," Coach Murphy said. "That's great. The more effort they waste on trying to confuse you the better it is for us. We'll get simpler as they get more complicated. There is such a thing as over-coaching. You need to remember your composure in every situation and we'll have a feast like nobody's business."

"Yes, ma'am," Casey said. "What was that defense I didn't recognize awhile ago?"

Coach Murphy laughed. "One popular in the sixties." She walked to her desk, picked up a book and handed it to Casey. "It's in here. Find it yourself and tell me tomorrow."

"Yes, ma'am." Casey held the book in her lap. Homework. Something to occupy her time since she had a nine o'clock curfew.

Coach Murphy closed her door, moved to her desk and sat down. She said, "I want to change the room assignments on the road. I'd like for you to room with Tobie. I've watched the two of you together. She seems calmer when you're close."

"Okay-fine."

"When I first saw Tobie Daniels play I knew I was looking at the best pure ball player I'd ever seen," Coach Murphy said. She leaned back in her chair with a leathery creak. "Her high-school team won the State Championship when nobody thought they had the talent to win. They won because of Tobie. She carried them on her back, double-and-triple-teamed every game. We need her for the stretch run in the conference and in the tournament. If we can get her to produce like she's capable our team would be so much better."

"She's silky-smooth around the basket."

"I rolled in the gutter and fought the world for Tobie," Coach Murphy said, putting on her tight smile. "I've even heard there's a bounty on my hide south of the Red River." Probing, evaluating, analyzing. "I don't intend to lose her over a personality conflict. Will you spend time with her? Talk to her? Help her to think more like 'we' instead of 'me?'"

"Sure," Casey said. "I like Tobie."

Someone knocked on the door. Tobie's head poked inside. "You wanted to see me, Dr. Murphy?" Tobie asked. Her hair was damp, she was wearing jeans and barely laced Nike hi-tops and a baggy orange sweat shirt that said 'Oklahoma Tech Basketball.' Her face was impassive like it had been all afternoon.

"Have you finished your extra duties?" Coach Murphy asked.

"Yes, ma'am."

"I'd like for you to room with Casey on the road," Coach Murphy said. "Any objections?"

"I just want to play ball, Dr. Murphy," Tobie said. "Tell me what you want and I'll do it."

"That's all, Casey," Coach Murphy said. "Have a seat, Tobie." Her face was as impassive as Tobie's, making Casey glad she wasn't part of the power game they were playing because it didn't strike her as being very much fun.

Casey stood, squeezed past Tobie and left, closing the door behind her. She heard Coach Murphy say, "How are your parents this week?" Tobie said, "They suck. Mom's still leaning on me to move home and enter the Miss Texas Pageant."

Casey quit eavesdropping. She pulled twenty dollars from her pocket and dropped it in the jar that was labeled, 'Community Kitchen Donations.'

Outside the locker room she bumped into the forward from the men's basketball team who had started pestering her lately. Movie invitations, dinner invitations, invitations to his dorm room. He walked beside her, burying her with invitations and his obvious coolness.

Casey kept walking, saying, "No, no, no," with each step. The man finally quit bugging her and went into the weight room. Casey saw him start hitting on a woman working on the butterfly machine.

She couldn't understand why men were so wack. Most women figured out she was a dyke sooner or later. Other dykes figured out what she was in something under two seconds. Men rarely, if ever, figured her out. She thought it was because of ego. Men were so egotistical and so obviously cool they couldn't comprehend someone who didn't want anything to do with them.

Kim was sitting on her bed polishing her toenails when Casey got to the dorm. "The phone's been ringing mega-often," Kim said, looking up from her polishing.

Casey looked at the legal pad sitting on her bed, getting kind of a warm glow from seeing the list of names and realizing how popular she was, even if that sounded egotistical. She liked to be liked. Sharika's name was at the top of the list with twelve marks after it, meaning thirteen calls. Kristy's name with one mark. Katie's name with no marks. Katie/Carla/Darla never bugged her with calls. They'd call once, leave a name to let Casey know they were lonely for her and then leave her alone, knowing she'd come over when she had the chance. Toni Denson's name was at the bottom of the list beside two marks.

The phone started ringing. Kim sighed and rolled her eyes. Casey picked up the phone, held it until it quit ringing and then lifted the receiver and punched in Toni's number. She smiled, wondering if Sharika liked a little mystery in a lover as much as she claimed she did. The power game she was playing with Sharika was a lot more fun than the one Tobie and Coach Murphy were playing because a ten megaton climax was waiting at the end of the game she was playing with Sharika.

Toni answered on the third ring.

"This is Casey."

"Hi," Toni said, her voice soft and friendly. "I thought we might have dinner tonight so you can pour your heart out about the Tennessee game."

"No comment."

"I understand," Toni said. "The subject's off limits. Lobo Joe's in thirty minutes. My treat?"

"Meet you there." Casey hung up.

"You're gay," Kim said, looking up from her polishing again. She had an accusing look in her eyes.

"So?"

Kim didn't say anything. She went back to polishing her nails.

"Okay-fine," Casey shrugged. She left, wondering if that was the last she'd ever see of her roommate. She hoped not. She'd gotten...comfortable sharing a room with Kim.

When Casey got to Lobo Joe's, she sat in a booth with Toni and asked, "Do you ever have any doubts about your writing?"

Toni laughed and said, "Are you kidding? Whenever I write something and go back over it I think, What a piece of garbage! Who in their right mind would want to read something like this? You just have to keep plugging away and trust in yourself, trust you'll eventually get things the way you want them."

"I guess writing's a lot like basketball," Casey said.

"Uh-huh." Toni squeezed Casey's knee under the table. "I'm famished! I want to eat everything on the menu. What sounds good to you? Maybe we can get two totally different things and share."

CHAPTER 11

Casey left her dorm Thursdsay evening and drove to Sharika's apartment.

Sharika was wearing a navy blue leather skirt with maybe ten zippers, and a waist-length navy blue leather jacket. She was also wearing a white see-through blouse and no bra, with just a hint of her nipples visible through the satiny material. White lace fingerless gloves adorned her hands. White stockings, blue heels and tons of gold necklaces and bracelets and earrings completed the outfit.

Casey attacked, putting her hands on Sharika's hips, brushing her lips against Sharika's, tasting peach lip gloss, inhaling a cloud of makeup and perfume and womanly atmosphere.

"God, you look great," she sighed.

"I know," Sharika sniffed haughtily, giggling.

"Let's go to the bedroom and huff and puff and blow each other's clothes off." Casey tried to push Sharika into the apartment.

"Later," Sharika said, pushing back, stepping out and closing the door behind her.

"Where are we going?" Casey asked.

"Partying." Sharika took Casey's hand, interlocking their fingers, ignoring the white het couple in the parking lot who gawked at them and murmured. When they got to Sharika's white Corvette, Sharika opened the door for Casey, leaned across to fasten Casey's seat belt, slammed the door with a teasing smile. She tore out of the parking lot, tires screaming.

"This reminds me of the show you put on in front of Mitchell the other night," Casey said.

"I am a vain woman when it comes to my car," Sharika said. "I like people to notice me." She reached over and put a hand on Casey's thigh. Casey grabbed the hand and kissed it, sucking Sharika's fingers, running her tongue across Sharika's palm.

Sharika jerked her hand away.

"I wasn't trying to hurt you the other night when I left with Kristy," Casey said. "I'm sorry if I did."

"So her name's Kristy," Sharika said, seeming only mildly interested. "That's a pretty name."

"I'm trying to apologize," Casey said. "Not really apologize, just discuss it and tell you I wasn't trying to hurt you."

"You don't have the power to hurt me," Sharika said tartly, bobbing her head mockingly from side-to-side. "I told you you're free to have affairs. Why would I get hurt because you do?"

"I just want you to know why I did what I did."

"I know what you were doing," Sharika said. She shrugged. "I thought you might need me after the Tennessee game. You didn't so I left. Why do you want to make a big thing out of it?"

"I'm just trying to help you understand."

"I don't need your help understanding shit," Sharika said, bobbing her head again.

"Okay-fine," Casey said, imitating Sharika's head-bobbing.

They drove along a winding two-lane road. A full moon made it almost as bright as day. Casey could see farmhouses and barns and oil wells and such. During the drive they were silent, looking out the windows and ignoring each other, except for the teasing they did with fingernails and hands and Sharika's high hem, a hem that showed the tops of her stockings and a white lace garter belt that almost drove Casey wild. Sharika whipped the car through the curves gracefully, going about eighty miles an hour. She could drive.

"Are you asking me to stop seeing other women?" Casey asked after a while.

"Would you stop if I asked?"

"I'd think about it," Casey said, wondering when and where Sharika would push things to a head and deliver her ultimatum, an ultimatum Casey had heard before. Women always said they were understanding at first, but after a while they invariably decided they wanted all of you or none of you and backed you into a corner. Casey usually took the none-of-me option. She didn't like people to back her into a corner.

"If I asked you to stop, you'd leave me," Sharika said. "I'm surprised you said you'd think about it."

"I went to the tennis office the other day," Casey said. "There's no Sharika Keymah listed on the tennis team roster. I talked to some players hanging out in the office. They never heard of you."

Sharika laughed, squeezing Casey's knee, eyes flashing in the light from the dashboard. Casey said, "I'm waiting for an answer."

"Bless your heart," Sharika said.

After forty-five minutes of driving, they came to a small town. The sidewalks were rolled up, most of the stores and shops had dark windows. Casey saw a barber shop, a barbecue restaurant and a feed store. Sharika turned onto a gravel road beside the feed store, drove about half a mile, and parked in front of a small building built of blue wood and cement blocks. There were fifteen or twenty cars parked in the lot, the sound of music drifted in the air, a King Cobra sign flashed in one of the windows.

Inside the building was a dark, smoky bar, filled with maybe twenty men and twenty women. All black people. A juke box blared black music. Everyone in the bar seemed to know Sharika. Only they called her Scooter or Scoots instead of Sharika. They looked her up-and-down and bumped fists with her and said things like, "You livin' large, homegirl."

Sharika laughed, squirming onto a bar stool with an eye-popping display of shapely legs and stocking tops and a wink of garter belt when she crossed her legs. She pulled a wad of money from her purse, bought drinks for everybody and started chatting with the grey-haired man behind the bar in a language Casey didn't really understand.

Casey walked over to look at the juke box. She felt every eye in the place glued on her so she swayed her butt a little more than normal. When she got to the juke box she cocked a hip, reached back and fluffed her hair on her shoulders. If everyone wanted to look she'd give them something to look at.

The juke box had a mixture of singers. Boyz II Men, Geto Boys, Ice-T, Queen Latifah, CeCe Peniston. Casey pulled fifty cents from her pocket and picked two songs. Sharika walked up, nuzzled Casey's neck, slid a hand inside Casey's back pocket.

"This isn't a dyke bar," Casey said, tracing a fingernail between Sharika's breasts, lifting her face for a kiss. "You trying to get us killed?"

Sharika brushed her lips against Casey's. "I take my lover any-where I want," Sharika said. "What do you want to drink?"

"Contributing to the delinquency of a minor, huh?"

Casey had a malt liquor. That's all that was served other than hard liquor and she didn't do the hard stuff. The grey-haired man behind the bar was named Benny. He was a basketball fan. He pulled out a newspaper and read off Casey's latest statistics. Then he pulled out a Lady Lobos program and asked for an autograph, so he could frame it and hang it behind the bar he said.

Sharika watched with shining eyes. "I had to bring you here and show you off," she whispered.

She pulled Casey to the dance floor. They danced up-close-and-personal in front of all the straight people, Sharika brushing her lips against Casey's, wriggling all up-and-down Casey's body, giving Casey a patented probing kiss. Nobody said anything except for a few taunting kisses Casey heard coming out of the darkness around the dance floor.

After a while, the dance floor got crowded, all het couples except for Sharika and Casey dancing right in the middle of everybody, everyone bumping occasionally, enjoying the music and their bodies and the intimacy.

It totaled Casey's mind. The music, the smoke, the sweaty bodies, the malt liquor, the hot look in Sharika's eyes, dancing openly in a straight bar with an exotic-looking lover like Sharika. The juke box played a Bell, Biv, Devoe song, heavy, hypnotic, pulling Casey into the rhythm until she wanted nothing except to lose herself in Sharika's body. She probed Sharika's mouth with her tongue, grinding her crotch against Sharika, running a finger under each of her breasts, not caring because all the het couples were acting the same.

Sharika spun away, eyes teasing, doing shoulder rolls, shaking her butt, jiggling her breasts, profiling her stuff to the max. Casey pulled her close, kissed her again. Sharika whimpered, ran her fingers through Casey's hair, blew hot air into her ear, sucked cold. The taunting kisses in the darkness got louder.

"Let's go," Casey said.

"Ummm."

Sharika headed back along the winding road at eighty miles an hour.

"Why was everyone calling you Scooter?" Casey asked, resting her head on the car seat, closing her eyes, feeling so seduced and excited she wouldn't have cared if Sharika stopped and made love to her right in the middle of the road.

"A childhood nickname," Sharika said, laughing. "From the way I used to scoot around everywhere I went with a tennis racquet as big as me. I used to run around with my racquet, telling everyone how I was going to play at Thimble Town some day like the white ladies I saw on TV."

"Where's Thimble Town? I never heard of it."

"Wimbledon," Sharika said. "When I heard the man on TV saying Wimbledon I thought he was saying Thimbleton and I turned it into Thimble Town."

Casey giggled from too much seduction and malt liquor. Sharika did, too. "Child, I was corn-stalk-ignorant once upon a time," Sharika said, looking sheepish. "I didn't have my first Reese's Cup until I was in high school. You should've seen me. I took off the outside wrapper and popped it in my mouth. I didn't know it had an inside wrapper, too. A few seconds later I made a face and said, 'This candy tastes like paper.' People fell out the place laughing at me."

Casey cracked up. "You grew up around here?" she asked when she managed to stop laughing.

"Those were my people you met tonight. They've known Sharika since before she was Sharika."

"Why don't you tell me what game you're playing?"

Sharika laughed. "Think, sugar," she said, cutting her eyes at Casey.

"I can't think right now. All I want to do is make love," Casey said. She rested a hand on Sharika's thigh, loving the feel of Sharika's stockings. "You're the only black lover I've ever had."

"Do you sleep with me because I'm black?"

"I sleep with you because you're a beautiful woman," Casey said. "I think being black makes you exotic, but if I only wanted that I would've slept with you once and dumped you."

"I don't like what I'm hearing," Sharika said. "You're still just seeing me as a body. A black body. Why can't you see me as a person?"

"I do."

Sharika snorted, cutting her eyes at Casey, clicking on the stereo full blast, apparently feeling angry over something.

"What did I do?" Casey asked, feeling insecure.

Sharika didn't say anything, increasing Casey's insecurity maybe two hundred percent. "I love you," Casey said, squeezing Sharika's thigh. "We've had a fun evening. Let's not ruin it because I said something dumb. Okay? Please?"

Sharika picked up Casey's hand with two fingers, gingerly, like she was picking up a dog turd, and dropped the hand into Casey's own lap.

"Okay-fine," Casey said, turning her head to look out the window, riding silently. Seething maybe a little, too.

Fifteen miles and ten minutes later, Sharika got over her snit enough that she turned the stereo down and started pointing out landmarks. The house she grew up in was three miles down this road. The high school she went to was a mile and a half down this road.

"Drive by so I can see," Casey said, trying to work her way out of Sharika's doghouse. "We have time."

"No, child," Sharika said, and she started talking about what it was like growing up in rural Oklahoma. "There was this little country store, about a mile from my house. All the kids stopped by there after school each day, to get a candy bar and a pop. I was no different. I'd go into the store, clutching my quarter, feeling like part of the group. The people who owned the store, an old man and his wife, would follow me around, watching me to make sure I didn't steal anything. One day, the wife took me into the back and made me empty my pockets and searched me. I cried all the way home that day. I felt dirty."

Sharika slapped the steering wheel. "I got to where I hated that old man and his wife. I never stole anything from them. I've never stolen anything from anybody in my life. But they thought since I was black, I was a thief." She laughed bitterly. "I saw the white kids stealing everything they could get in their pockets, but I never said anything. I figured if the old man and his wife wanted to catch the thieves, they could watch the white kids instead of me."

"That sucks," Casey said. "Why did you keep going back?"

Sharika shrugged. "It was the only store in the area." She started talking about how she got caught when she was twelve, lying naked by the fishing pond with a white girl from the trash family down the road, kissing and touching each other. About the beating from her parents and the counseling from the Baptist preacher she'd gotten.

"I guess you came out the hard way," Casey said.

"I don't lay down with girls from trash families anymore," Sharika said. "I enjoy the best now."

"Let's find that fishing pond you were telling me about."

Sharika laughed. She started talking about a friend she'd had all through school, a tennis player named Monica Hills. Monica's first tennis racquet came from TG&Y and, girlfriend!, was she ever proud of that racquet. She took it and hit a rubber ball against the side of her parents' house for hours because there was no place else to play. Not long after, a few weeks at the most, Monica got caught shoplifting tennis balls because she was tired of hitting a rubber ball. Monica's mother beat her with a switch when the sheriff brought her home that afternoon. Her daddy turned around and beat her with his belt when he got home from work that night.

"Why you want to shame this family by thieving?" Monica's daddy had said while he beat her.

When Monica started playing high-school tennis she was ashamed because she played against rich girls in fancy tennis dresses and leather tennis shoes when she only had cutoff jeans and regular street shoes to wear. Sometimes Monica even played barefooted because she knew she'd get a whipping if she ruined her going-to-school shoes playing tennis. Monica beat the rich girls in high school even if she was playing barefooted most of the time and in cutoff jeans all the time. The day Monica got a scholarship offer from Tech she cried and cried all day long. She cried even harder when the people at Tech gave her a fancy tennis dress and a pair of leather Adidas tennis shoes like she'd always dreamed of having.

"So that's your point," Casey said. "You're the one who got caught shoplifting tennis balls. You're Monica Hills."

"No, I'm not, lover."

"You're jamming me."

"Monica Hills doesn't shoplift tennis balls anymore," Sharika whispered. "Monica Hills is dead."

"I'm sorry," Casey said, touching Sharika's arm. "I've never lost anyone close. How'd she die?"

Sharika didn't say anything, staring fixedly at the road.

"Monica was black, I'm assuming," Casey said, feeling more curious than anything else.

"Why do you assume that?" Sharika asked sharply. "Because she shoplifted tennis balls? Most kids go through a shoplifting period. I was the oddball because I never did." She cut her eyes at Casey. "Have you ever shoplifted, girlfriend?"

"Yes," Casey said guiltily. "I stole a pack of M&M's when I was ten. I got caught. I wasn't a very good thief. I walked into the store, got the M&M's, went back outside and sat on the curb and started eating them. The man in the store came out and jerked me back inside and called my mother to come get me. Mom sent me to my room when we got home. She was afraid she'd beat the tar out of me if I stayed in her sight. When Dad got home, he came into my room and talked to me for about two hours in his deep, fatherly voice. It was the most humiliating day of my life."

Sharika said, "I used to be like you. Sashaying around like my hind parts don't stink one little bit."

"I don't do that," Casey said, scrambling to catch up to the gear change.

"How about when you strutted to the juke box awhile ago at the bar?"

"Well," Casey said, feeling uncomfortable. Maybe a little embarrassed, too, because who liked to think they were acting cool only to find out everyone was jeering them on the inside?

"It won't last," Sharika said. "Life has a way of bringing you down once the jock glitter goes away. There's a real world out there. It'll eat you alive if you're not careful. There's nobody in the real world to make bad things go away, no coaches to protect you."

"I know that."

Sharika snorted. "You don't know squat, child. You're just a little baby covered with fuzzy down."

"Are you trying to say you were ashamed of me tonight? I don't buy it. Not the way your eyes were shining and everything."

Sharika didn't say anything.

"I was having fun up to now," Casey said. "Coach Murphy and Coach DeFoe and all the grad assistants spend hours trying to make me think I can walk on water. Then you come along and spend your time tearing me down."

"Your ego's plenty big, sure enough," Sharika said, bobbing her head mockingly. "I know coaches and what they're like. I know they're good at what they do. You have to look beyond that and find a balance between ego and reality. Right now all you are is a female version of a man jock, strutting around lapping up the adulation and screwing any woman who gets within half a mile."

"So what's the point?" Casey asked, fighting to control her temper. "If you think I'm so worthless, why do you want anything to do with me? I'll tell you why. Because I'm famous, because I'm a star, because I have a great body, because I'm arrogant, because I'm talented, because I'm butch, because I think you're exotic. You want me for all the reasons you say you don't like in me. Don't you? Admit it. That's all I want. For you to admit you love me because of things that make you not like me."

"Catch-22," Sharika said, laughing.

"Why are you so evasive about some things?" Casey half-shouted in frustration. "You get on my nerves sometimes, you really do."

"Clever," Sharika said cooly. "Sensuous and erotic. Feline grace and inquisitiveness. Hod-blooded." She touched Casey's cheek. "I can feel your heat through your skin, girlfriend. Just touching you makes me stronger. I feed off your fire."

"God, that's bull-shit!" Casey said. "You like my butt more than anything. If I wasn't sleeping with you, you wouldn't want anything to do with me. All I am to you is a body."

"Okay-fine."

"Okay-fine is no answer to anything."

"I hear it from you a lot," Sharika purred, her voice more buttery than normal.

"Duh."

Sharika laughed, pulling into the parking lot of her apartment, jumping out, taking Casey's hand and leading the way to her apartment. They stopped outside the door to kiss, and it was the strangest moment of Casey's life, standing outside Sharika's door, half-shot on malt liquor, half-angry, kissing, fondling, faces pressed together, an excited, taunting look in Sharika's open eyes, the lights in the apartment courtyard illuminating them perfectly, probably being watched by dirty old men through cracks in curtains.

"Let's go inside," Casey said, fumbling with the door knob, knees weak and trembly, wanting Sharika so badly she was about to explode, perfectly willing to forgive all the cutting words and asshole attitude.

Sharika stepped back, through her door, slamming it in Casey's face. Casey heard the dead bolt turn. Casey pounded, hissed, "Sharika, baby, let me in."

Sharika didn't answer. Casey heard scratching on the inside of the door. "What are you doing?" Casey asked.

"I want you, lover."

"Oh, God, I want you, too, I love you. Let me in." Casey rattled the door knob.

"I want you helpless," Sharika said, scratching the door again. "Like a bug in a spider web, all wrapped up and bug-eyed, watching the spider crawl toward her, knowing she's going to be eaten, help-less to do anything about it. At the end, right before she's eaten, not caring, trapped, weak, wanting to be eaten so her misery will end, knowing the spider hates sharing her bug with other spiders."

"So this is it," Casey said in disgust. "Your ultimatum. I knew it was coming, but tell me, Sharika, is this a mature way to discuss my...ah...transgressions? Okay-fine, maybe I'm not always a good girl, but I don't run around on you all that much, Sharika, honest I don't. I love you. I don't want to lose you. Do you believe me?"

"I believe you love me," Sharika said softly.

"Will you let me in now?"

"No."

"Is this really happening?" Casey kicked the door. "Let me in and I'll show you misery. Why are you withholding sex to try and dom-inate me? You know what that makes you?"

"I'm not always a good girl," Sharika said, giggling inside the door. "Crawl away, little bug," she whispered, scratching the door. "Now's your chance. If you stay the spider'll get you." More scratching. "Flushing Meadow. Thimble Town."

"What are you saying? Let me in so we can talk. Here I was all ready to forgive you and everything and then you pull this on me."

"You need to worry about being forgiven instead of the other way around," Sharika whispered.

"What have I done?"

Silence.

"Okay-fine," Casey said. "So I know what I've done, but I've never tried to hide it or been dishonest with you. Have I, Sharika? Can you honestly say I've ever lied to you?"

Silence.

Casey pounded and rattled and kicked.

Silence.

Casey crawled home, wondering at what point their positions had reversed. When the night started she'd been in the driver's seat, fending off Sharika's pursuit. But all of a sudden, somewhere along the line, things had changed and now Sharika was in the driver's seat, fending off Casey's pursuit.

Talk about getting on your nerves.

She decided maybe Sharika wasn't such a sweet little femme after all.

* * *

119

Katie/Carla/Darla came flying down the sidewalk on their ten speeds. They were wearing mirrored goggles and earmuffs and jeans and bright red nylon jackets and riding helmets and knee pads. Their backpacks were strapped across their shoulders. They wheeled circles around Casey, ragging on her, taunting looks on their faces.

Casey stood with her books pressed to her chest watching them, feeling strange at the three of herself she saw reflected in their mirrored goggles. Three of her and three of them.

Love times three.

It was so surrealistic.

Katie/Carla/Darla slammed on their brakes and skidded to a stop in front of her, three abreast, one foot on a pedal, one on the ground, elbows leaned on their handlebars, eyes dancing all over Casey's body, making low-class cracks about what Casey looked like when she climaxed. Like the way she tilted her head back and arched her back and clawed at the sheets and practically did the splits and the perfect O her mouth made when she screamed. Stuff Casey had heard from them before.

Casey told them they better shut up because she knew what they looked like when they climaxed, too, like the vein in Katie's temple that throbbed and trembled when she climaxed, and the way Carla/Darla both sobbed, "Oh, shit, oh, shit," over and over.

They all three said, "Like, so," and each insisted she was doubtless the most beautiful creature in the world when she climaxed. Casey told them there was a lot of doubt in her mind about any woman being beautiful when she climaxed, although maybe there was a woman somewhere who was beautiful when she climaxed, but Casey had yet to meet her.

Two men walked by, caught the last part of what Casey said and tried to butt in by saying they thought all women were beautiful when they climaxed. Katie told them to take a flying suck at a rolling donut because no man knew a thing about climaxing, not anymore than a volcano knew about erupting, anyway, and women were the only ones who knew about making love and feelings, while all men knew about was a Neanderthal-like breeding instinct which was a toe-tuh-lee wack instinct to have considering the overpopulated state of the world.

The two men walked away, slapping their heads and babbling to each other about how mouthy women were getting to be.

After the men left, Katie said, "Casey's been, like, neglecting us.

We buzzed and asked the a.m. before last and, like, haven't been serviced."

Casey told them she had a couple of hours before practice and she'd come over and see them, although she wouldn't call it 'servicing,' as long as they kept their cracks about who looked like what when she climaxed to themselves.

"We're, like, doing the splish-splash," Katie said airily. "We don't have the ticks for you."

They turned and wheeled away, feet churning, knees pumping, nonsense jabber filling the air around them, every man within a mile watching them and making kissing sounds.

Casey more or less decided every female in the world was a game-playing bimbo and they weren't really worth the bother it took to keep them mentally pacified.

She went to her dorm, grabbed her swimsuit and headed to the campus pool. It was a great pool, enclosed by a glass building, Olympic-sized, three diving boards, lounges sitting all around. The place was packed like usual. Katie/Carla/Darla were screaming and splashing in one corner of the pool. All three were wearing string bikinis.

Casey went to the ten meter board, did a jackknife and swam the length of the pool twice, one way a breaststroke, the second time the backstroke. Then she swam to the opposite corner from Katie/Carla/Darla and rested her elbows on the edge of the pool, bobbing in the water, showing she could play games, too. She eyed Katie/Carla/Darla, noticed them eyeing her.

The three bimbos dog-paddled over in a minute, eyes red-rimmed from splashing water in each other's faces, hair in dripping strings. Casey said, "God, I love the way a wet woman smells."

Katie/Carla/Darla gathered in a circle around her, ragging her about displaying her conceit by doing a jackknife and swimming the pool twice, making it sound as wrong as the juke-box-strutting scene although they didn't know anything about the juke-box-strutting scene.

"I'm tired of everyone saying I'm conceited," Casey said. "I'm not, and even if I am I have a right to be. I've worked hard since I moved here and I've had a lot of success. I bet if you took a picture of me and a picture of the President around the pool, more people would recognize me."

Katie/Carla/Darla snickered, rolling their eyes. Carla slipped between Casey's legs, wrapping Casey's legs around her hips, tickling Casey's thighs. Katie/Darla got on each side and squeezed water from Casey's hair, massaging her shoulders as they did. Casey closed her eyes and enjoyed the attention, not caring if most of the people at the pool probably knew who she was because she was famous, and who cared if the fame wouldn't last? She had it now and she was going to enjoy it.

"Don't, like, think you're out of the frying pan," Katie said.

"What do you mean?" Casey asked, opening her eyes.

"Duh," Carla said, cocking her head, hanging her mouth open.

"I love you," Casey said, touching Carla's face. "Your mannerisms are so cute." Carla sighed, looking down and smiling bashfully, tickling some more on Casey's thighs.

"You're a slut," Katie said, giving Carla a dirty look. "We, like, did the James Bond spy scene and peeped a sight we don't, like, like. We peeped Casey with more lovers than we can, like, count, you know."

"Have you three been following me around again?" Casey asked. Katie/Carla/Darla all three rolled their eyes.

"Toni Denson," Darla said. "Kristy Neapope. Sharika Keymah. Katie Catcher. Carla and Darla Davis. Shall I, like, continue?"

"Using the, like, vernacular," Katie said. "It chaps our collective asses that you real name is Cheat-sey."

"Whore-sey," Carla murmured, turning huge, soft brown eyes on Casey. "It, like, hurts," she added in a softer murmur.

"I admit I'm not always a good girl," Casey said, feeling uncomfortable, like her swimsuit had all of a sudden shrunk two sizes. "But do you honestly think I have that many lovers? Where would I get the time or energy?" She touched Carla's face again. "You believe me don't you, Carla? You know I don't mean to hurt you."

Katie/Carla/Darla ignored her and swung into a debate about love and philosophy and Plato and Woody Allen. It was more or less bizarre. The debate got pretty hot between Carla and Darla when Carla insisted there was no difference between love and self-indulgence. Love was like a Hershey bar with almonds. A woman sure didn't need a Hershey bar with almonds, but she had one every so often purely because of self-indulgence.

Darla pulled at her hair with both hands and shouted that was toe-tuh-lee wack because she could exist without a Hershey bar with almonds, but she sure couldn't exist without love. Everyone cracked up and shouted about the twelve Hershey bars with almonds Darla ate a week, and if love was removed from the world Darla would survive, but if Hershey bars with almonds were taken away, Darla would put her head in an oven.

"You're all full of cocoa," Casey said. "Love is a feeling and Hershey bars with almonds are something you eat. You can't compare the two."

"What we're, like, trying to say is this," Katie said. "Do you, like, like being viewed as a Hershey bar with almonds everyone takes a bite out of so nobody can enjoy the whole thing? If that's so, you should know we have different expectations concerning our mistress."

"Are you getting serious on me?" Casey asked.

Katie/Carla/Darla gave her level unblinking looks. Katie and Darla swam off.

Casey touched Carla's face. "You know I love you, Carla, baby, don't you? You know I'm sorry if I've hurt you. Can you forgive me? Why don't we go to dinner after basketball practice? My treat."

"You love someone besides us, don't you?" Carla murmured.

"Yes, but I love you, too."

"I can't believe that," Carla said. She made a soft, whimpering sound, her eyes filling with tears. She swam off after Katie and Darla.

"Duh," Casey said, wondering if it was the full moon making everyone act so goofy. God, she felt like shit. Sharika and Katie and Darla were all three hellcats who gave as good as they got, but Carla was different. Carla was like a day old kitten. Nobody could hurt Carla without feeling like shit...but Casey went to bed with Carla whenever they had the chance and let Carla know she was Casey's favorite and treated her that way. What more did Carla want? She couldn't be all that upset because Casey wasn't always a good girl.

Or could she?

How would Casey feel if she walked into a room and saw Carla and Sharika in bed together?

"Time for practice," Casey said, deciding she didn't have the time for serious thinking right then. She hoisted herself out of the pool.

Casey licked her lips, savoring the heavy female taste. Carla had maybe the sweetest flavor of any lover Casey had ever had. She finished buttoning her blouse, then ran her fingers through Carla's hair.

The full moon was framed beautifully in the rear window of Casey's car, the beams of light reflecting off the rippling water of Lake Osage.

Carla burst into tears.

"Like, duh," Casey mumbled, wondering why every woman in the world cried when they were in her back seat. She didn't think her back seat was an unpleasant place to be, not like the back seat of Tobie's car. The back seat of Tobie's car was crammed with so much stuff, books and clothes and rumpled McDonald's sacks and empty soda cans, that it was depressing just to look at it.

"This was wrong," Carla wailed, dabbing at her eyes with a sleeve. "It's the first time I've been, like, an unfaithful slut."

"Bull-shit," Casey said, taking Carla in her arms. "All we did was make love. Katie and Darla don't care about that."

"Dog, like, doo-doo," Carla said. "None of us are supposed to sneak off to do things. We're supposed to do things in the apartment or it's cheating. That's what we decided."

"Oh," Casey said, trying to decipher the moral intricacies of group sex.

"I have to tell them what I did," Carla whimpered. "They'll punish me. They'll blindfold me and handcuff me and tickle me all over with feather dusters until I wet myself from laughing." She brightened a little, as if thinking of her punishment was a happy thought.

"Will they do that to me?" Casey asked, more or less hopefully.

Carla shivered. "I hate to think about what they'll do to you."

"Oh," Casey said, feeling a little disappointed.

"We can't, like, do this again," Carla said. "I can't lose Katie and Darla. I wouldn't know what to do without them." She burst into tears again.

"I think I'll buy a new car," Casey mumbled, starting to feel a little guilty. If Carla felt like she'd cheated on Katie and Darla, then Casey must have cheated on them, too. It seemed like it was getting to where every time she even looked at another woman she was cheating on someone somewhere in the universe.

CHAPTER 12

The Tech-ettes flew into Kansas City, Missouri, got onto a bus for the forty mile drive to Lawrence, Kansas and walked into a raucous, rocking-and-rolling arena to play the Number Fifteen University of Kansas Lady Jayhawks.

Casey was jazzed, looking at all the National Championship banners hanging from the ceiling, knowing some of the all-time greats like Danny Manning had played there, realizing the crowd was knowledgeable and appreciated good basketball.

She lit the place up.

It was one of those feast nights when everything she put up went in. Everyone else kept giving her the ball and then just stood back to watch. Five three-pointers. Four two-pointers. Four free throws. Twenty-seven points. Six assists. Three steals. Three rebounds.

The crowd gave her a standing ovation when Coach Murphy took her out with fifteen seconds remaining. She ran to the bench, bashing forearms, feeling slaps on her butt, hearing the standing ovation, screaming, "Yeah, yeah, yeah!" over and over, getting a hug and the You-Done-Good towel from Coach Murphy.

She gave the towel to Tobie because Tobie hadn't gotten any playing time but she'd had a good attitude, sitting on the bench and clapping and cheering with her impassive face. Tobie gave the towel to Coach Murphy. Coach Murphy gave it to the team.

Lady Lobos 88, Lady Jayhawks 79.

They got back on the bus, rode the one hundred seventy miles to Columbia, Missouri and checked into their hotel. Tobie headed to the bathroom first thing when they got to their room. Casey took a scented candle from her suitcase, lit it and put it on the nightstand. She turned out all the lights and turned on the radio. She undressed and walked into the bathroom.

Tobie was in the bathtub, arms and legs splayed over half the bathroom, shaving her legs. She tried to cover her breasts with a washcloth, which seemed stupid since everyone on the team had seen everyone else naked at least a million times in the showers.

"You've got a bit much to cover with a washcloth," Casey said. "You might try a towel."

"Don't you love having a roommate?" Tobie snapped, glaring up at Casey. "All the privacy you get to take care of bathroom business. You better not do what I think you're going to do or I might throw up. I want Lisa back. She never invaded my privacy like this."

"Relax," Casey said, unwrapping a plastic cup, kneeling beside the tub.

"What's this?" Tobie asked, brandishing her pink Daisy like it was a sword or something. "What are you doing to me?"

"Are you paranoid or what?" Casey dipped the cup in the water, wetting Tobie's hair. Tobie watched suspiciously, jerking every time Casey moved. Casey said, "I wish you'd stop acting like this. It breaks my heart to see any woman as afraid as you are."

"Fuck you," Tobie snapped, since she was such a mellow, agreeable person.

Casey opened Tobie's shampoo, and washed Tobie's hair. Tobie's hair was long and thick, dark yellow when it was dry, turning a reddish-gold color when it was wet. Casey couldn't help noticing Tobie's muffin was the same color as her hair.

"What'd I do to deserve this?" Tobie asked, finally relaxing.

"By just being you." Casey rinsed Tobie's hair, picked up the washcloth covering half of Tobie's left breast, soaped it, and massaged Tobie's body. All five miles of it.

"Is this part of my brainwashing?" Tobie asked, closing her eyes, squirming pleasurably beneath the washcloth. "Did Dr. Murphy tell you to give me the royal treatment?"

"How long since you've had some loving?"

"Isn't that kind of personal?" Tobie snapped, frowning.

"Nope."

"Not that long since you've had some," Tobie said, looking jealous. "I've heard if it moves you jump it. I've heard no dyke on campus can get any loving because you have it all tied up. That's what Alysa says."

"It's not true," Casey said. "I'm in everyone's doghouse so I'm kind of wandering around doing more wishing than anything else." She put her bar of Coast back in its plastic box. You didn't have to do much traveling before you learned to take your own soap on road trips. Hotel soap would give you alligator skin in no time.

They moved to the bedroom.

Casey pushed Tobie facedown on the bed, took a bottle of lotion from her bag and gave Tobie a good rubdown, massaging her toes, feet, working her way up the mile long legs. Tobie sighed, closing her eyes, smacking her lips like a contented kid.

"God, you have gorgeous legs," Casey sighed enviously. And maybe a little lustfully.

"You were a machine tonight," Tobie said. "A god-damn scoring machine. You played as good a game as any guard I've ever seen."

"That's what it takes," Casey said. "Be a machine, babe, don't think, don't feel, just play ball."

"Tell Dr. Murphy thanks. I really needed something like this," Tobie murmured.

"All Coach Murphy asked me to do was be your friend," Casey said. "I was your friend before, if you remember."

"You know my suspension isn't finished," Tobie said. "Dr. Murphy's leaving me behind when the team goes to Texas State. She says it's for my own good. She says the people at State would lynch me if she took me there."

"That's no lie."

"It's still a suspension," Tobie said. "If I'm on the traveling squad I should go everywhere the team goes."

"What really happened between you and the State center that night?"

"She's from Dallas," Tobie said. "We played against each other in high school. There's a long history between us."

"Have you two fought before?"

"You could say that."

"Are you ex-lovers? Or did she steal a lover from you in the past? Is it something like that?"

Tobie didn't say anything.

"I'm waiting."

"We were lovers," Tobie said. "Are you happy?"

"Okay-fine." Casey flipped Tobie over so she could continue the massage, starting with Tobie's shoulders, working down to her plump, firm breasts, across her satiny stomach, past the appetizing mole on Tobie's right hip.

"I'm so afraid of failing," Tobie said, eyes still closed, looking

127

half-asleep. "You don't know what's it like with all the hype I went through. All the pressure it causes. People calling my house at all hours, three in the morning even. Reporters screaming, 'Tobie where are you going to college, Tobie tell me so I can be the first to print it.' Coaches came and lined up outside my house, screaming about their basketball teams, all the championships they'd win with me, 'Tobie come here, Tobie come there, Tobie my school's the best, Tobie that school's lying because my school's the best.' Everyone hounded me until I wanted to explode.

"Dr. Murphy was the only one who was different. She came to my house in jeans and a sweat shirt. She sat at the kitchen table and drank coffee and joked with my parents and didn't say a word about basketball. When she left she gave me a card and said I could call her if I needed help with anything or just to talk. That's when I decided on Tech. But once I got there, she's hounded me worse than anyone else has in my life: 'Tobie this, Tobie that, Tobie you need to spend more time in the weight room if you want to be anything, Tobie you only hit sixty-eight percent of your free throws when Ellison hits ninety-three percent, why aren't you more like Ellison, more of a gym rat like she is, she does more than you with less natural talent than you have, and why is that, why don't you put in the work she does?'"

"Be a machine, babe, be a machine," Casey said, although she was feeling a burn. She kneaded Tobie's quadriceps.

"Maybe they don't say that," Tobie said. "I don't know. Maybe I just take what they say and translate it in my mind into words I can understand. Don't worry about it. You're the freshman stud on the team and everyone knows it."

"I like to think I am, but I'm starting to see I'm only a cog. The best cog they have right now, but still only a cog."

Tobie said, "I don't understand. Why all the games with my mind? If Dr. Murphy would just put me in and give me the ball I'd play my ass off."

"But somebody has to be in control," Casey said. "Somebody has to have the power. In this case it's Coach Murphy. Can't you see what a controlling person she is? She has to have things done her way or she can't accomplish what she wants. We can't accomplish what we want."

"Maybe so," Tobie said, stretching, adjusting her head on the pillow. "But that doesn't make it easier to swallow."

Casey slipped off the bed, tucked the sheet and blanket around Tobie's chin, said, "Go to sleep, you big blond pussycat."

Tobie giggled. "I'm a big blond tiger," she murmured drowsily.

"Pussycat." Casey gave Tobie a peck on the mouth, blew out the candle and went to bed.

Casey," Tobie called sleepily in a few minutes. "Why didn't you make love to me? I thought you were going to. Don't you think I'm beautiful?"

"You're gorgeous. But we're friends."

"I need a friend," Tobie said softly, and then she went to sleep.

Casey went to sleep, and thought she dreamed about Sharika, but she wasn't sure. And even if she had been sure, she didn't want to admit it to herself.

Thirty-six hours later they left Missouri with their first conference loss, after losing their concentration and blowing a six point lead in the final minute. They lost Weatherly in the second half to a deep thigh bruise. Nobody knew how long she'd be out.

The only bright spot to the game was Tobie. Tobie played twelve minutes in Weatherly's place, loping up-and-down the court looking relaxed and confident, dominating both ends of the floor with her pale, frail inches, scoring ten points and blocking three shots and grabbing twelve rebounds.

Other than Tobie it was a night of losses. They lost their concentration. They lost Weatherly. They lost the game. They lost the momentum they'd started to rebuild after the Tennessee game. It was like being on a ship that had taken a torpedo hit, a torpedo of doubt, and was slowly sinking and everyone was bailing water as fast as they could, but they were sinking anyway.

The grad assistants ragged everyone on the plane home, shouting how they'd lost a game they should've won because they got all puffed from reading the newspapers, and god-dammit, did Ellison leave her game in Kansas or what.

"You threw it all away!" one of the grad assistants shouted. "Thirty-nine minutes of good basketball. You threw it all away over one minute of lousy ball. One lousy minute! How many times have we told you to never let a team up once you have them down? How many god-damn times? Execution and desire, ladies! Did you have either of those the last minute?"

Coach Murphy finally called the grad assistants off with raised eyebrows. The grad assistants gathered at the back of the plane and started a pinochle game, muttering among themselves, shooting irritable glances at the players slouching in their seats with glum expressions.

It was not a lot of fun being a Lady Lobo right then.

"Be a machine, babe, be a machine," Casey said.

"Look at Dr. Murphy," Tobie said. "Next practice will be living hell."

Casey looked, saw that certain look on Coach Murphy's face and knew Tobie was telling the truth. She wasn't looking forward to the next one-on-one chalk-talk she had with Coach Murphy. She'd played like an idiot, making one bonehead play after another, turning the ball over eight times, scoring only two points, spending the whole game chasing helplessly after a frizzy-haired hummingbird freshman named Buffy Fregosi and squalling, "Help-help-help."

That's what it's all about, babe. Being a stud-ette one game, a goat the next. Not being able to figure out diddly, why everything you put up one night went in and the next night you couldn't buy a bucket when you'd felt good both nights and you shot the ball the same both nights, and you just wished Coach Murphy wouldn't look at you because every time she did the disappointment jumped out of her eyes and slapped you in the face and you wanted to crawl to her on your hands and knees and beg her to forgive you and to please, please stop sucking on her bottle of Mylanta-II because you felt like her blossoming ulcer was your fault.

Major-college ball.

"Just a famine," Casey said, resting her head on the plane seat, closing her eyes so she wouldn't have to look at Coach Murphy. "Just a famine. The feast is right around the corner."

She opened her eyes, feeling an elbow in her ribs.

"You're on," Tobie hissed, nodding toward Coach Murphy.

Coach Murphy crooked a finger. Casey moved to sit beside her, swallowing hard with every step, feeling like her eyes were the same size as serving platters, thinking how she'd rather sit in an electric chair than beside Coach Murphy, wondering what alibi she could invent to cover stupidity.

More than anything, she wanted to dig a toe in the carpet and blubber, 'Please, Coach Murphy, don't trash me in front of everybody. I'll die of shame. Can't you wait until we get home and take me into your office? I'll grovel twice as much as normal if you let me do it when we're alone.'

Coach Murphy had a miniature chalkboard in her lap. "Let's review what you should do against a zone trap," she said, sketching a diagram on her miniature chalkboard. "You'll see a good one when we go to Nebraska."

A half-giggle, half-sob of relief escaped Casey's mouth. "I'm sorry," she squeaked when Coach Murphy gave her a quizzical look. "Dinner gave me gas, I think."

"I see," Coach Murphy said, offering her bottle of Mylanta-II.

There was an article from one of the Tulsa newspapers hanging on the bulletin board in the locker room. The headline said:

FADING LADY LOBOS FINISH ROAD TRIP 1-1.

Limp Home Having Dropped Two Of Last Three

The article went on to say, *Tech is obviously struggling and is poorly coached, as evidenced by the fact that Coach Brenda Murphy is starting inconsistent freshman Casey Ellison at point guard, the most important position on a basketball team, while senior Deb Watson sits on the bench. The lack of experienced leadership at this point renders Tech poorly prepared to compete against quality teams. According to an 'informed source,' Coach Murphy has recently survived an internal power struggle to remove her from her coaching duties. She has recently interviewed for coaching positions with two other universities.*

Tobie got pulled into the show, too. The article said, *Based on the recent vicious, cruel and unprovoked beating administered by freshman center Tobie Daniels on an innocent Texas State player and the following 'bench-clearing riot,' it was obvious the type of players Coach Murphy recruits and the type of program she runs are an embarrassment to the entire state.* It said, *Based on the 'unprovoked beating' and the 'brutal' practices Coach Murphy conducted wherein players were both physically and mentally abused, Tech was obviously a program out of control. According to another 'informed source,' the NCAA is beginning a preliminary inquiry into the Tech program for fifteen rules violations ranging from cash payments to players to altering of player transcripts.*

The article closed by saying, *Because of the lack of control exhibited by Coach Murphy over her program and because of the hoodlum players she attracts in her win-at-all-costs philosophy, because of the pending NCAA inquiry, this reporter has no alternative except to side with the masses and demand the immediate resignation of Brenda Murphy.*

Coach Murphy came out of her office. Coach DeFoe and the grad assistants followed. Everyone looked grim. It was quiet enough in the locker room to hear thoughts churning. Casey wondered if the churning thoughts matched hers, hers being, If I could get my mitts on that reporter I'd sure as hell inform his source.

"I'll only address one issue in this article," Coach Murphy said. "I signed a five year contract extension last spring. I fully intend to fulfill that obligation to the university. And to you. I'm not seeking, nor do I intend to seek, another coaching position. There has been no 'internal power struggle.' I spoke to Athletic Director Martin earlier today. I assured him I have no intention of leaving. He in return assured me he is more than satisfied with the progress I've made in the three years I've been here. We have released a statement to the press denying the allegations that I'm leaving. University lawyers will respond to the other allegations at the proper time." She walked out.

The grad assistants started ragging on everyone, shouting, "They say it's slipping away from you! They say you're no good! From the way you played in Columbia it's hard to argue with them, isn't it? Get your asses out on the floor! We have a lot of work to do!"

Coach Murphy came out ten minutes into practice, carrying a cup of coffee and her clipboard. It was easy to see the white stains around the corners of her mouth, meaning she'd inhaled about a case and a half of Mylanta-II. Everyone started whispering bets about how many cigarettes she'd smoke that day. The odds favored she wouldn't be able to hold it at one.

After practice there was another newspaper article hanging on the bulletin board in the locker room. The headline said:

LADY TIGERS SAY LADY LOBOS OVERRATED

Everyone crowded around the bulletin board, reading the quotes from the Missouri players:

"Why is everyone in the Conference afraid of Tech? Sure, they're big, but they're slow. And they can't run very fast, either."

"They came in here with their swagger and their attitude and we made 'em eat it."

"Possible National Champs? Ha!"

Everyone started reading what their counterparts on the Missouri team had said. Frizzy-haired Buffy Fregosi was quoted as saying, "Everyone in the Big Seven talks about Ellison and how smooth she is. Not hardly. I outran her, I outscored her, I outplayed her on both ends of the court. She didn't show me anything. She's a dirty player, too. She kicks and scratches and throws elbows and she even bit me one time. She's nothing but an alley cat who tries to hide a lack of talent with meanness."

Casey more or less lost her grip. She trashed the towel cart. She trashed a stack of sweats, throwing and kicking shirts and pants all over the locker room. Everyone stood around watching with bulging eyes and saying, "God-damn, Lower Case, get down, babe."

"Fuck you!" Casey howled. She ran through the locker room grabbing shoes and basketballs and anything else she could get her hands on and sailing the stuff all over the locker room. Everyone was ducking and cussing and trying to grab her.

She broke away, dug her keys out of her locker and tried to run to her car so she could drive to Columbia, Missouri and kick the shit out of Buffy Fregosi, the whole time screaming, "That lying bitch! That lying low-class bitch! I didn't bite her! Then! But I want to now! I want to eat her raw now!"

Alysa and Weatherly finally managed to grab her. They carried her kicking and screaming to the showers. Alysa held her under the nozzle while Weatherly turned the water on ice cold. Alysa kept rumbling, "Save it, Lower Case. Save it for the next time we play them. You'll get another chance at her."

Casey finally calmed down about nine that night. She pulled out her books and tried to study although she was still seething a little. When the phone rang, she snatched it up and howled, "What!" She was not in a real good mood.

"This is Buffy," a woman said in a nasally Yankee voice. "Fregosi."

"I want you!" Casey shouted, losing her grip all over again. "You god-damn pip-squeak runt bitch!"

"Let me explain," Buffy said quickly. "I didn't say those things."

"Bull-shit!"

"I said," Buffy explained. "That I'd heard you're a dirty player, kicking and biting and like that. But you weren't when we played. You played hard, but you were clean. I did say you didn't show me anything, but I also said I was sure you just had an off night because the films I've seen show you're better than you played against us."

"Who told you I was a dirty player?"

"Reporters," Buffy said. "I think they're trying to stir something up between our teams, whaddaya think. I don't want any part of that shit."

"What about the other quotes? The big-but-slow-and-dumb stuff? The alley cat stuff?"

"Some people might have said those things," Buffy said. "I won't name names, but everyone was excited about beating youse guys. I swear I didn't say anything bad. I'm telling you the truth. Can we be friends?"

"Well..."

"Let's do this," Buffy said. "If you hear I said something give me a chance before you go through the roof. I'll do the same if I hear you said something. I definitely don't want any bad blood between us, whaddaya think."

"Okay," Casey said, taking a deep breath. "I guess we can be friends. I apologize for what I called you a minute ago."

Buffy laughed. She seemed like a decent woman. "I would have gone through the roof if I'd read that you said those things about me."

"That's an accurate description," Casey said.

Buffy said, "You have to remember I'm only an eighteen year old freshman. I don't know what I'm doing half the time."

Casey cracked up.

"Are you taking any math this semester?" Buffy groaned. "I'm taking geometry. It's driving me fruity."

"Tell me about it."

"I love your accent," Buffy said. "You confused the bejesus out of me during the game. You kept yelling, 'Foh-Cuttuh' when you were calling plays. I didn't know what you were saying. One of my teammates, one from Alabama, finally told me you were saying 'Four-Cutter.'"

"I'm adjusting to your accent."

"Hey, that's Brooklyn," Buffy said. She laughed. "Is Four-Cutter the play where youse guys kinda do a weave, and then both of your wings flash through the paint, get a pick, and cut to the basket? That's a good play. I stumbled around like a buffoon the first time you ran it. I'd never seen anything like it until we played youse guys."

"Nice try," Casey said guardedly, not about to divulge any secrets.

Buffy laughed again. "I can speak normally, too," she said without an accent. "I see a speech therapist twice a week. I'm majoring in radio-and-TV. I want to be a disk jockey when I grow up."

"I'm majoring in coaching."

"See you in a couple of weeks," Buffy said. "I'm really anxious to see your gym, Mitchell. Everyone says it's unbelievable."

"It is. Thanks for calling."

"Bye, Frosh."

"Bye, Frosh." Casey hung up, feeling more under control. The phone rang immediately. It was a reporter wanting to know if Casey had read what Buffy said.

"I read it," Casey said.

"Any comment?" the reporter asked, sounding gleeful.

"Sure," Casey said. "I like Buffy. She's a good player. She played an excellent game against us. I'm looking forward to the next time we play."

"That's it?"

"That's it." Casey hung up.

Toni was alone in the newspaper office. Her hair was moussed back as usual, golden and shiny. She was wearing a beige pantsuit and a red bow tie and red heels. She said, "This is a nice surprise," and squeezed Casey's shoulders affectionately. "Want something to drink? Coffee? Coke?"

"No thanks," Casey said, sitting in a chair in front of Toni's desk. "I'm here for a favor."

"Let's hear it," Toni said, moving behind her desk with a cup of coffee.

"It's about the heat Coach Murphy's getting," Casey said.

"Ah." Toni's eyes bored into Casey's over her coffee cup. She put her cup down and licked her lips. "You want me to interview you. You want to use the school paper so you can spout the company line."

"I thought maybe you could interview Coach Murphy," Casey said. "And some of the other players. The seniors especially."

"I've already sent in a request to Coach Murphy. My request was delayed until Coach Murphy works through the big-city papers. I've been cleared to interview her at eight tomorrow morning." Toni waved a hand. "The seniors on the team are old news. I've interviewed Alysa and the others so much nobody cares anymore."

"So what do you suggest?"

Toni looked thoughtful. She leaned back in her chair and pressed her fingertips together. Slender, delicate fingers. Six rings, assorted styles. Red nail polish. "I'm willing to negotiate," she said finally. "You want to use my paper as a forum for your company line. I have wants of my own."

"I don't recall this being your paper," Casey said.

"It is so far as you're concerned." Toni smiled a toothy smile. "I'm the head of women's sports. Everything in that area goes through me."

"I think a little power has gone to your head," Casey said, wondering if she felt like punching Toni out. "You're almost acting macho."

Toni's toothy smile got wider. "Flattery will get you into my bed," she cooed. "It won't get you into my paper."

"Okay-fine. What's your deal?"

"I will interview you," Toni said. "I'll let you spout the company line. You're one of the hottest things on campus right now so people want to read about you. But I want something in return for the forum I'm giving you."

"I already agreed. What do you want?"

"Tobie Daniels," Toni said, leaning forward in her chair. "If I could interview her I'd have the proverbial scoop. She's the hottest thing on campus right now. She won't talk to me. When I go to the locker room and ask for an interview she says, 'Dr. Murphy told me to cooperate with the press.' I ask her a question, like what changes she thinks should be made so the university better meets the needs of women student-athletes and vice versa. She stares at me. I ask the question again. She says, 'You know, I don't understand the question, you know.' We go through this dumb jock game for five or ten minutes and I leave without my interview."

"Tobie doesn't like interviews," Casey said. "Coach Murphy has reprimanded her in the past for not cooperating with reporters."

"Reprimanded?" Toni's ears perked up. She traced a finger around the rim of her coffee cup and looked through her lashes, a look that was tres, tres cute. "What does 'reprimand' involve? Off the record, of course."

"Coach Murphy says, 'Tobie, you will cooperate with the press. That's part of being a basketball player.' Tobie says, 'Yes, Dr. Murphy.'"

"Oh." Toni's ears unperked. "That's not really juicy." She looked through her lashes again. "Can you deliver Tobie for me?"

"I'll try. Tobie's pretty stubborn."

"Have her call me." Toni stood, smiling, rubbing her hands together. "Power-broking makes me hungry. How about lunch?"

"Coach Murphy's taking some heat," Casey said to Tobie while they were doing their stretches.

"Really?" Tobie grunted, looking disinterested.

"You're partly to blame," Casey said.

"Really?"

"You can help," Casey said. "Toni Denson wants to interview you. I promised I'd try to goad you into agreeing. As a favor to me."

"If she outs me you're both history," Tobie said. The look in her eyes meant she wasn't kidding.

"She won't."

"Okay," Tobie said. "As a favor to you."

A man in a baggy brown suit and chilli-stained tie was waiting for them when they got back from their morning run. He bought some yogurt and walked to the bench where they were sitting. He introduced himself as the reporter for a Tulsa newspaper. The same reporter who'd written the story causing Coach Murphy to take some heat. Casey instantly bristled although she tried to hide it.

"Casey Ellison? Right?" the reporter said, poking a spoonful of yogurt into his mouth. He had a bushy moustache. Some of the yogurt got stuck in his moustache.

"That's me," Casey said.

"Tobie Daniels? Right?"

Tobie stared at him with a blank expression. "Dr. Murphy told me to cooperate with the press," she said.

"Good," the man said. "What if I told you the Texas State player you assaulted is filing criminal charges against you? Any comment?"

Tobie stared at him with a blank expression. "You know, I don't understand the question, you know," she said.

The man sat on the bench. He said, "Talk to me, girls. Don't be afraid of Brenda Murphy."

Tobie stared at him with a blank expression, mouthing her yogurt real slow, doing a great impersonation of a cow chewing its cud.

"I'm not afraid of Coach Murphy," Casey said, deciding to spout the company line. "I think she's the greatest coach in the world. The greatest person in the world, too. She gives me nothing except good things and makes me want more."

"What if I told you Buffy Fregosi's going to file charges against you for biting her?" the man asked. "I've seen her arm. You took quite a plug out of her."

Casey licked her lips. "Ummm. She tasted good, too."

"Outwardly your team seems all peaches-and-cream," the man said. "I think it's a different atmosphere on the inside."

"You know," Tobie said sharply, "the Tech men's team has only won three games all year. Why don't you go hound them?"

"Who wants to read about those bums?" the man chuckled.

"I bet you get a Pulitzer out of this," Tobie said. "Or at least a promotion for selling more papers."

The man snickered, poking yogurt into his mouth.

"You're a little piss-ant of a fuck-face," Tobie said. "You're free to quote me on that. You need a haircut, too. And that tie is horrid."

They got up and left.

"He's lying," Tobie said after they crossed the street. "The State bitch called me the other day. We made an appointment for after the season. We're settling this once and for all. I'll destroy her and she'll transfer to another world."

"What if that reporter writes what you called him?"

"I'll get more laps," Tobie said. "Whooo."

"You got in some good shots. You weren't intimidated at all."

"Reporters have been hounding me since I scored ninety-three points in a junior-high game," Tobie said. "They aren't God. They just think they are."

Toni interviewed Coach Murphy and Tobie and Casey together and took pictures of all of them standing around a blackboard. Then she interviewed them separately and took pictures of them separately. Then she took a picture of Tobie that belonged on the cover of Cosmopolitan or something.

For the picture Tobie wore a pink dress and pink hose and pink heels. Her hair, thick and lush, was fluffed all over her shoulders. She posed by the duck pond, under a tree, one leg prissily extended to take a step. She was lifting a tree branch and peering under it, eyes wide, lips slightly parted, a hint of tongue showing. The duck pond and frat houses showed in the background.

She looked so gorgeous and innocent Casey felt like throwing up.

After all the interviewing and picture-taking and personal-interviewing was over, Casey met Tobie for a salad at Lobo Joe's.

"How'd it go?" Casey asked. "If you burned Coach Murphy you're history."

Tobie put on her dumb cow look.

"I'm waiting."

Tobie broke into a grin, ducking her head, looking almost bashful. "I like Toni," she murmured. "We hit it off right away."

"I was thinking you don't look frustrated anymore," Casey said, squeezing Tobie's hand. "I'm happy for you both. I hope it works out for you."

"I do, too," Tobie said, ducking her head again, blushing clear down to her toes.

The picture of Tobie standing by the duck pond in her pink dress made the front page of the college paper. The headline said:

CRUEL VICIOUS ASSASSIN!

The article included quotes from Coach Murphy and Tobie and Casey. Tobie was quoted as saying, 'I sincerely regret what happened in the Texas State game. I wish it hadn't happened. Dr. Murphy suspended me for three games. The Conference Commissioner reviewed the official's reports and did not recommend any additional punishment. I served my suspension. I'm still working off the punishment laps I was given. Why won't everyone leave me alone? Why can't we go on and quit worrying about the State game?'

On the following page was a picture of Tobie and Casey studying in Casey's dorm room above a caption that said, *Freshmen Ellison and Daniels hard at study. The modern woman student-athlete divides her time between studying and her athletic pursuits.*

There was also a picture of Coach Murphy doing paperwork at her desk above a caption that said, *Coach Murphy's responsibilities don't end when the game does. This mother of two oversees every aspect of the nationally-ranked Lady Lobos program as well as meeting the emotional needs of her student-athletes and making their journey through academia smooth and productive.*

The article finished by saying, *Contrary to recent accusations this reporter has read, accusations that stop short of nothing except yellow journalism, Coach Murphy does not run a program that causes embarrassment to this university or this state. The type of student-athlete Coach Murphy recruits are not 'hoodlums.' They are shining examples of the high-quality women modern America has to offer. This reporter for one feels a great deal of pride every time she attends a Lady Lobos game. I doubt one could find many among 'the masses' who would disagree.*

Casey stopped by Toni's office the day the article came out. Toni was doing some toe-tuh-lee serious crowing because a shorter version of her article had been picked up by some of the Tulsa and Oklahoma City newspapers.

"Maybe we didn't put a dent in their cast-iron nuts," Toni barked, pounding a fist on her desk, "but, by Goddess, we showed them we can kick!"

Casey cracked up.

"I like Tobie," Toni said. "I mean I really like her. I might be talking love."

Casey gave her a huge hug.

CHAPTER 13

They only spent a few hours sightseeing in Lincoln, Nebraska. When they got back to the hotel Casey had a message to report to Coach Murphy in room 1850. It didn't make sense. Coach Murphy was staying in a room on the third floor with the rest of the team.

"This doesn't make sense," Casey said, showing Tobie the message.

"Ours is not to question why," Tobie said. "See you later."

The door to 1850 swung open when Casey knocked. It was a nice room, a suite. It had a living room with a matching couch and love seat, two recliners, a coffee table and a huge TV. Two doors were on the far end of the room, leading to bedrooms Casey supposed. A basket of fruit and a heart-shaped box of candy and a bottle of chilling champagne sat on the coffee table. A room key was sitting beside the Dom Perignon.

"Hello?" Casey called, taking a step into the room, idly wondering if her wildest fantasy was about to come true and Coach Murphy was going to step out wearing nothing but a smile. "Coach Murphy?"

Nobody answered.

Casey walked to the love seat. There was a red piece of paper cut in the shape of a heart on the love seat. Printed on the paper was, *Happy Birthday. Enjoy. Sharika.*

The phone rang. Casey answered.

"Hi, sugar," Sharika whispered. "Do you like your present?"

"What's this all about? How did you know it was my birthday?"

"Invite someone to your room," Sharika suggested.

"Great. When can you be here? I'm dying to see you. Why haven't you been answering my calls?"

"Not me," Sharika said. "You're lovers with Tobie Daniels, aren't you?"

"So that's what this is all about," Casey said, feeling disgusted by Sharika's unfounded jealousy. "You saw our picture in the school paper, I suppose, and, naturally, since you're so god-damn hard-headed and possessive, you immediately took things the wrong way."

"Charge room service and anything else you want," Sharika said. "The tab's taken care of. I want you to enjoy one of the last times you'll lay down with someone other than me."

"I want to lay down with you. I don't know why, but I do. Where are you?"

"The spider's everywhere," Sharika whispered.

"Where do you work at?" Casey asked. "I know you work. You have to work because you're not in school."

The phone went click.

"God-damn muleheaded female," Casey muttered. She slammed the phone down and spun in a circle, expecting the spider to be standing right behind her. The spider wasn't there.

She walked through the suite. The doors on the far end of the room did lead to bedrooms, each with separate bathrooms with Jacuzzis. The place was huge. It was also deserted.

Casey went back to the living room and opened the curtains. Behind the curtains was a wall of windows and a great view if Lincoln. She opened the front door and looked into the hall. The hall was deserted except for an empty room-service tray five doors down.

She called the front desk. "Do you have a Sharika Keymah registered here?" she asked, hearing the plastic clicking sound of a computer keyboard.

"No, ma'am," the clerk said.

"Monica Hills?" Casey asked, not trusting Sharika as far as she could throw her anymore. Monica Hills might or might not be dead.

"No one by that name, either," the clerk said.

"Who do you show is registered in room eighteen-fifty?"

More plastic clicking. "C. Ellison," the clerk said.

"Thanks." Casey called her own room. Tobie answered. Casey said, "Come to room eighteen-fifty."

"What's up?"

"You'll see."

Casey called room service and ordered two Kansas City Strips 'medium with the works,' and sat on the couch to nibble a piece of candy. Tobie looked surprised when she got there. "Have a seat," Casey said, waving grandly. "Dinner will be here soon."

They sat on the couch.

"I'm having problems," Casey said.

"Really?" Tobie asked curiously, acting like she was the only woman in the world who had problems.

"With a god-damn muleheaded female," Casey said.

"Uh-oh," Tobie said, clicking her tongue, looking sympathetic, patting Casey's knee.

"Do you understand anything about women?"

"Shit!" Tobie said, rolling her eyes. "I just love them, I don't try to understand them. They're over my head. What's the problem with your woman?"

"She thinks I'm running around."

"Are you?"

"Well," Casey said, shifting on the suddenly uncomfortable couch.

"Ah," Tobie said.

"I'm not really," Casey said, feeling overwhelmed at the thought of explaining Katie and a Twin Sandwich and Kristy and Sharika to anyone. She sighed and said, "It's more like, well, it's complicated."

"This is over my head," Tobie said. "Either you're running around or you're not. It's not something you can kinda do."

"Let's change the subject," Casey said, thinking how the whole thing was over her head, too.

"If I caught Toni running around the first thing I'd do is hit her in the head," Tobie said. "The second thing I'd do is cry. Is that so hard to understand? Does that make me a muleheaded female?"

Someone knocked on the door. Casey jumped up to answer, grateful for the diversion. The room-service guy was at the door.

They shunned the table with the fancy white cloth and candles in holders and ate their steaks sitting on the couch, balancing their plates on their laps. Tobie asked, "Who's footing the bill?"

"A friend. It's a birthday present."

Tobie whistled. "Some friend," she said. "Is this the friend you run around on? You mistreat her and she still treats you like this? Sounds like love to me." She touched Casey's shoulder. "Happy birthday. I didn't get you anything. I didn't know."

"After the game we can make bed-check and come back here," Casey said, reaching out a napkin to wipe steak sauce from the corner of Tobie's mouth. "We can open the champagne then and have a mini-party. Maybe we can invite Alysa."

"Okay-fine." Tobie finished her steak and stole half of Casey's. Tobie had an appetite on par with Alysa's. Tobie glopped maybe a quart of steak sauce on Casey's steak, which Casey thought was gross.

"How do you feel about Coach Murphy this week?" Casey asked.

"I still hate her. Like last week and the week before."

"Because you think she 'broke' you."

"Nobody breaks Tobie Daniels." Tobie's face was impassive. "Dr. Murphy did take away my dignity. She made me crawl to get back on the team. She ruined things so the good schools I talked to about transferring didn't want me. They said I'm a psych-case."

"What makes you think Coach Murphy did that? I'm sure everyone heard about the fight. Maybe they decided on their own you're a psych-case. I'm not saying you are, but maybe they think you are."

"Wake up, Case," Tobie said. "Dr. Murphy plays hardball. She decided if she couldn't have me nobody could." She ate the parsley off both plates and then went to work on the orange slices, juice dripping down her chin as she sucked on them. Casey wiped Tobie's chin.

"I've been thinking a lot about Tennessee," Casey said. "Look at them. They don't have what you'd call a star player, but they beat us because they had five players hit double figures. Jovonna Moffitt broke out and scored twenty-one on us, but everyone else was in the ten-twelve-fourteen point range. Jovonna Moffitt had twenty-one points, five assists, three steals and four rebounds."

"How do you remember all that?"

"How can I forget?" Casey asked, feeling twinges of barely-suppressed guilt, residue from feeling like she'd cost them the Tennessee game. "I spent the whole afternoon chasing her around. She ate me up."

"I wouldn't know about that," Tobie said. "I didn't get to go to Tennessee."

"Didn't you watch the game on TV?"

"No."

"Do you know what you're doing?" Casey asked, changing approaches. "This is the peak of our basketball playing careers.

There's no place for us to go after college. We'll never be Michael Jordan selling shoes and McDonald's burgers for twenty million dollars a year. Why do you want to ruin the high point of your career by fighting with Coach Murphy?"

"Get out of my face," Tobie said, picking up the box of candy, squishing a piece with her finger, wrinkling her nose and picking another piece.

"If you can't see Coach Murphy's side of things, look at your own side," Casey said. "You're hurting yourself more than anyone else. Kiss her butt if that's what it takes. You think I don't kiss her butt? If she walked in the door right now and told me to drop to my knees and kiss her butt, I'd do it without even hesitating. Everyone on the team feels the same way. If it comes down to losing what I want or kissing butt, I'll kiss butt. Most people will. Coach Murphy kisses butt, too. The Alumni Association. The Athletic Director. Look at it this way: all the people in the world are just a long line of people kissing the butt of whoever is in front of them. Don't fight it. Just get in line and pucker up and kiss butt along with the rest of us."

"I said get out of my face."

"No."

"I'll hit you," Tobie said, brandishing a fist.

"Pussycat."

Tobie walked to the door. "I'm going to Europe after I graduate," she said, more or less snootily. "I can make a hundred thousand a year as a pro in Italy. I've already enrolled in an Italian class for next year so I'll be able to talk to women when I get there."

"Okay-fine," Casey said, keeping her cool, although she felt like getting on a ladder and punching Tobie out. "The rest of us can't go to Italy. Think of us. Your god-damn attitude is keeping us from going as far as we could."

Tobie left, slamming the door behind her.

Casey sighed, nibbled another piece of candy, tried to think of another approach to use with Tobie, but found her thoughts drifting to Sharika. She felt a little guilty for using Sharika's room and money. It was a great birthday present, but why hadn't Sharika surprised Casey in the room, wearing something filmy, making a pornographic experience out of eating, giving Casey a massage and making love? That would've made the present even better.

Just what game was Sharika playing? Why did she get in a snit because Casey wasn't always a good girl, and then turn around and give Casey a great room and a great meal and a wide-open chance to make love with another woman? Not just a room, either. A suite. Was Sharika trying to prove she had money? Okay-fine. Casey already knew that.

Sharika had lied about being a tennis player. Casey knew that was the truth because everyone Casey talked to in the Tech tennis department shook their heads and said they'd never heard of Sharika Keymah. So where did Sharika work since she wasn't a student? And who was the late Monica Hills? How had Sharika been in the women's showers the day they met? The women's showers were reserved for the jocks. Okay-fine. Sharika had connections inside the athletic department so she got to use the facilities.

But...how...why...why? It was maddening...and maybe a little exciting...and challenging...like a contest to see who could freak the other out the most. But it was toe-tuh-lee one-sided. Sharika was the freaker, Casey the freakee.

Casey celebrated her birthday with a solid game. Twelve points, four assists, three steals, four rebounds. She didn't see Sharika in the stands, but she knew the spider was there. She could feel its baleful gaze on her.

Tobie got nine minutes of playing time, scored fourteen points, blocked three shots, grabbed ten rebounds. She had a chance to fight late in the game, but backed away, open hands held at her shoulders, shaking her head and saying, "Composure, composure, composure," to the Nebraska player.

Coach Murphy gave Tobie the You-Done-Good towel. Tobie threw it in the trash when Coach Murphy wasn't looking.

Tech 81, Nebraska 69.

Casey had a message that said report to Coach Murphy in room 1446. She knew it was bogus because she saw Coach Murphy and Coach DeFoe in the hotel restaurant, sipping coffee and nibbling cinnamon rolls and putting the final polish on the game plan for Iowa State.

She decided she'd had enough of Sharika and started to leave with Tobie and Alysa to tour the town. She stopped before she got through the door. The lure was too strong, the fascination with the spider too strong. She was toe-tuh-lee hypnotized. But she definitely wasn't inquisitive like Sharika claimed.

"Go ahead," she told Tobie and Alysa. "I'll catch up."

She rode the elevator to the fourteenth floor. 1442, 1443, 1444, 1445. Nothing. No 1446. The rooms on the fourteenth floor ended at 1445. She knocked on 1445. A potbellied grey-haired man in a blue three-piece answered.

"Sorry, wrong room," Casey mumbled in embarrassment. She moved down the hall and knocked on 1444. No answer. The maid was cleaning 1443, nobody was inside. The door to 1442 was open, the room empty, the sheets stripped off the bed.

Casey quit knocking and went running up-and-down the hall, checking, double-checking, looking for Sharika, looking for clues like she was on an Easter Egg Hunt. Nothing. She went to the next floor up. The next floor down. Nothing. No Sharika. No more clues. No Easter eggs.

She rode the elevator downstairs and showed the message to the desk clerk. He said, "I don't know anything about the message. I can tell you we don't have a fourteen-forty-six."

"Do you have a Sharika Keymah or a Monica Hills registered here?"

The clerk punched on a computer and shook his head.

Casey turned around and around in circles in the lobby, acting like a kid searching for a lost mother in a department store. She finally went outside because she didn't know what else to do.

A long black Cadillac limousine pulled up in front of the hotel. A rear window dropped down. Sharika's laughing face appeared.

"Hi, girlfriend," Sharika purred, looking toe-tuh-lee pleased with herself.

"Hi, Easter Egg," Casey said. She walked to the limo, hands in her pockets so she wouldn't reach out and strangle Sharika.

The window went up. Casey glued her face to the window, shielding her eyes with her hands so she could see inside through the tint. It was plush inside the limo. The back seat was separated from the front by a dark window. There was a TV, a stereo, a refrigerator/bar and a telephone. It was nicer than some houses Casey had seen.

Sharika was on her back in the back seat, wearing something white and filmy, her knees lifted, her heels buried in the car seat, legs spread, everything she had to show exposed to Casey.

Casey tried the handle. The door was locked. She mouthed, "Open the door."

Sharika smiled, slipping one hand between her legs, twisting on the stereo knob with the other hand. Casey heard M.C. Hammer rapping something about not being able to touch something.

It was the craziest thing Casey had ever seen in her life. For Sharika to be doing what she was doing on Main Street U.S.A. with cars pulling up to and away from the hotel, people getting out of the cars and carrying luggage inside, a trash truck noisily emptying a dumpster in the alley beside the hotel. Everyone stared at the bug-eyed brunette with her face glued to the window of a long black Cadillac limo like a kid outside a candy store.

Casey more or less squirmed on the sidewalk. She whispered, "You're masturbating right in the middle of Ames, Iowa. Aren't you? It sure looks to me like you are."

Sharika smiled, a dreamy smile, chewing her bottom lip, the hand between her legs moving faster.

"In broad daylight," Casey whispered. "God, that's kinky." She pounded on the window. Sharika's eyes looked taunting, even through the tinted window. She picked up the phone and said something. The limo whispered away from the curb, a scrap of paper fluttering out of the back window.

Casey scampered to pick up the paper, expecting it to be a clue. A real clue. Something she could sink her teeth in, something that would tie the whole mystery together, something that would make a light come on in her head.

Written on the paper was, *Find Sarah Jane.* Nothing else. Just, *Find Sarah Jane.*

"No!" Casey screamed. "Please! It's too cryptic! I can't take anymore!" She started chasing the limo, dodging between people on the sidewalk, maybe bumping into some, maybe knocking some flying, finally cutting into the street and running in front of a blue Chrysler because she could make faster time in the street.

The man in the blue Chrysler laid on his horn. Casey kept running. The stoplight at the corner turned red. The limo stopped. Casey went to her kick. She was going to catch the limo, tear off the door or break a window with her forehead, whatever it took, and drag Sharika's half-naked-self out and boot Sharika's half-naked-self from one end of Ames, Iowa to the other.

"Monica Hills!" she screamed at the top of her lungs. "Why are you doing this to me? Please come back!" She dodged between cars stopped for the red light, reached the rear fender of the limo, pounding on it, out of breath and out of patience, everyone staring at her.

The light changed green. The limo pulled away. So close but so far...so far...Casey took off running again, down the middle of the street, knowing, god-dammit!, knowing Sharika/Monica was looking out the rear window and laughing. The light at the next corner turned red. Casey threw it into high gear. The light turned green just as she reached the limo. It pulled away.

Casey hung it up after five blocks. She staggered back onto the sidewalk. Tobie, Alysa, Bonnie, Penny and Tamara strolled out of an ice-cream store with ice-cream cones in their hands. Everyone stood there twisting and tonguing their ice-cream cones and staring curiously at Casey.

Casey was standing with her hands on her knees, sweat dripping from her face, heaving from running five blocks in high gear and screaming at the top of her lungs. She was so frustrated and embarrassed she was ready to flop down on the sidewalk and bawl like a little kid who'd had her Halloween sack taken away by a big kid.

"You know," Alysa rumbled, "back when I was a chile in Hugo, Oklahoma, I had me a dog. He was a mangy mongrel of an old hound, not worth much except maybe shooting. Lordy, I purely loved that old dog, though. Well, now, one day he took into his head a notion that he liked to chase cars. I beat that old dog and beat him, but I never could teach him to quit chasing cars. And wouldn't you know it, that old mangy dog he went and got hisself run over one day. Yes, ma'am. Squished flat as a corn pone right smack dab in the middle of the road. All because he took a notion into his head it was fun chasing cars."

Everyone cracked up.

"Thanks for the analogy," Casey said, staggering away.

"Where you going?" Tobie asked.

"To find Sarah Jane."

"Well, now," Alysa rumbled. "Chasing split-tails will get you squished just as flat as chasing cars, Lower Case. Ain't love a hurtin' thing?"

Everyone cracked up again.

Tech 88, Iowa State 74.

On the plane home one of the flight attendants brought Casey a small package wrapped in orange satiny paper and tied with a black bow. It was a Rolex watch with a delicate diamond where the twelve should've been. On the back was engraved, *For my Lady Lobo's nine-*

teenth. Love, Sharika.

Casey felt like crying, screaming, throwing the watch down and stomping on it, punching Sharika out, making love to Sharika. Maybe not. She didn't know what she felt. Yes, she did. She felt like a kid. A kid on an Easter Egg Hunt. A kid searching for a lost parent. A kid outside a candy store. A kid who'd had her Halloween sack stolen.

No, she didn't feel like a kid. She felt like a mangy mongrel dog in heat because she guessed for the first time in her life she was head-over-heels in love. Maybe Sharika didn't work after all because she couldn't have a job and still have time to figure out so many ways to torture bugs.

"You look as frustrated as I felt before I met Toni," Tobie said.

"Duh."

As soon as Casey got off the bus in front of Mitchell, she jumped in her car and drove to Sharika's. Screw bed-check, screw curfew, screw laps, screw Coach Murphy. Screw Sharika. Literally.

She pounded on Sharika's door. And pounded. And pounded.

"Who is it?" Sharika asked finally, sounding tense and scared. "I've got a gun in here."

"It's me."

"Shit, Casey, you turned my hair white."

"I didn't mean to scare you. Let me in."

"You better take yourself back to the dorm," Sharika said without opening the door. "If they run a bed-check on you, you're in trouble."

"I don't care. Let me in. I'm about to lose my mind."

"Did you have a good birthday?" Sharika whispered, scratching on the door.

"Yes. No. I don't know," Casey babbled. "I'm on my knees, Sharika, baby. Open the door and you can see. Isn't that what you want? To make me grovel?"

No answer. Only scratching.

"Wimbledon!" Casey shouted. "Flushing Meadow. You're older than I think. Your name hasn't always been Sharika. Your nickname's Scooter. Monica Hills doesn't shoplift tennis balls anymore. You have money. Find Sarah Jane. What does all that mean? Tell me."

More scratching. "You have connections at the athletic department. Use them."

"I have," Casey said. "Sharika, can I just hold you? Please? For just a few seconds? That's all I want. I miss your feel and your smell so bad."

Silence.

Sharika's mail slot creaked open. A photograph slid out. Casey snatched it up, practically inhaling it because it smelled like Sharika's perfume. Sharika whispered, "If this doesn't do it I don't want to see you again. You're too big a fool for me."

"Okay-fine. No pressure or anything."

Silence.

Casey pounded, shouted, "I've had all of this I can take!"

"You're a jock," Sharika whispered. "Jocks never quit."

"But you're a jock, too. If neither one of us quits how can either one of us win?"

"I'll win," Sharika whispered.

"Win!" Casey shouted. "Win what? What do you want?"

"I want you helpless," Sharika said. "Like a bug in a spider web."

"Oh, fuck this," Casey said. She drove back to the dorm. One of the grad assistants was standing at the lobby desk, chatting and laughing with the receptionist. Her back was to the door. Casey tiptoed toward the elevator. She pushed the button. The door opened. She stepped inside and turned around. The grad assistant was standing at the door with a huge smile on her face.

"Sweet dreams, Casey Ellison," the grad assistant said. Casey saw her checking her watch and writing something on her clipboard as the elevator doors closed.

"Kiss my ass!" Casey shouted. She rode the elevator up.

Kim was hanging her face out of their door. "Hurry," Kim hissed. "They called for you. I told them to hang on because you're in the bathroom."

Casey walked into the room and picked up the phone.

"Zing! Gotcha!" the same grad assistant who'd been downstairs said. "Second curfew violation. Do you have any experience mopping showers?"

"Don't you have anything better to do at three in the morning?"

"But I get so much pleasure from this," the grad assistant said. She angrily added, "The last woman who told me to kiss her ass got the lips slapped off her. Remember that next time." The phone went click.

Casey looked at the photograph Sharika had given her. It was a picture of two black women holding a trophy between them. Both had huge smiles on their faces, they looked tired and sweaty, they were wearing white tennis outfits with Oklahoma Tech emblems on the breasts. One of the women was definitely Sharika, but she was different. Her hair was different. It was in a long ponytail instead of the short, naturally curly style she wore now. She looked younger but not much. Maybe a year or two.

"Do you have a magnifying glass?" Casey asked, shifting the picture. There was some writing on the trophy the women were holding that she couldn't read.

"I don't think so," Kim said.

They both dug through their desks without finding a magnifying glass. Casey went down the hall, pounding on doors, waking up the whole floor, making everyone mad enough to kill. She didn't care. She couldn't go to sleep without knowing. She finally found a magnifying glass six doors down.

She went back to her room and studied the picture under a lamp and the magnifying glass. Kim asked, "What is it?" She was huddled under a blanket on her bed, looking half asleep.

"A trophy," Casey said. "A National Championship for doubles in tennis. I can't read the year."

"Oh." Kim yawned, shivering, blinking her eyes. "Did you guys win tonight?"

"How would I, like, know?"

"Huh?" Kim murmured.

"I think I'm in love."

Kim groaned. "I don't want to hear about it," she said. "It's more than I can deal with."

Casey called Sharika. The line was busy. Or maybe the phone was off the hook. Or maybe Sharika had moved in the last few minutes. Or maybe Sharika didn't even exist, she was only a figment of Casey's imagination, a figment Casey had invented because she was perverted and liked torturing herself.

But the tooth-rattling attraction for Sharika inside of her wasn't a figment of her imagination. Everywhere she looked she saw Sharika's face, the way she moved, the way the muscles in her legs flexed and relaxed when she moved, heard and re-heard the things Sharika said, cutting things, maybe, but things that made Casey feel alive...and dominated. Toe-tuh-lee dominated, intelligence-wise, personality-wise, sexually.

It was a feeling she didn't like.

The eyes. Big, brown, moist, liquid, luminous eyes that seemed to pull Casey's soul out of her body and into Sharika's so the domination could take place.

God, she wanted to quit. But she couldn't. She just could not...because of something inside her...she didn't know what the something was...but it was there...it was the same something that wouldn't let her quit the team after the Tennessee game.

Sharika was really and truly starting to get on her nerves.

That said it all except for...Casey diddled a finger back-and-forth across her lips and went, "Bluh-bluh-bluh," because she was so frustrated and...well...mind-fucked by Sharika.

CHAPTER 14

Casey finished mopping the showers, to a chorus of jeers and taunts from everybody, Tobie included. She grabbed a quick shower, dressed and headed to the tennis department with the picture of Sharika, hoping it wasn't too late to catch someone there.

"Ellison!" a grad assistant shouted. "Telephone!"

Casey made a U-turn and picked up the receiver of the pay telephone hanging against the wall. "Hello?"

"Where are you?" Kristy sounded mad and wounded. Lately she'd gotten self-confident enough to add anger and wounded feelings to their relationship—whatever their relationship was.

"Duh," Casey said.

"You forgot me, didn't you," Kristy said. "My dinner's ruined. Your birthday cake's sitting here waiting for the candles to be lit. Your presents are all wrapped. And you forget. I was going to blow my diet tonight and everything because of you and you forget all about me. I don't believe it."

"I didn't forget," Casey lied. "I had some extra work to do. I'm on the way."

"Never mind," Kristy said tearfully. "If I'm that unimportant to you, just go on with what you were doing and don't worry about me. Come by whenever you get a chance. Tomorrow or the next day maybe."

"Tomorrow or the next day maybe," Casey mimicked in a mutter. "I said I was sorry, Kristy. Okay?"

"We don't have anything to eat," Kristy said. "My dinner's ruined," she repeated, just in case Casey had missed it the first time.

"I'll bring something. What do you want?"

"Go by Burger King." Kristy was finally sounding pacified. "I'll call ahead and have them fix something special for us."

"Okay-fine." Casey looked down the hall to the tennis office, more or less longingly, turned the other way and went out to her car. She just couldn't hurt Kristy. Kristy hadn't done anything to deserve getting hurt.

Kristy was wearing a floor-length pink gown. Her hair looked great, she was wearing a pound of makeup and her contacts, her nails were polished bright pink. She was obviously going all out to make Casey's birthday special. What was a little delay in investigating Sharika when Kristy's feelings were on the line? Casey didn't need to solve the Sharika Mystery as much as Kristy needed to feel appreciated. And it wouldn't hurt Sharika to marinate for a while, she wasn't going anywhere.

Was she?

Or was all that a rationalization to avoid accepting the truth? The truth that Casey was grasping at any straw to try and escape Sharika's web, doing anything to escape the increasingly unnerving mind-fucking Sharika was subjecting her to?

"The NCAA is really conducting a full-scale investigation of Tech over a stupid newspaper article?" Kristy asked. "Can't Coach Murphy sue for libel or something?"

"Ha!" Casey laughed. "She's a public figure. She's also an employee of the State of Oklahoma. Newspapers can write what they want about her, just like she was the Governor or some other State employee."

"Oh," Kristy said, looking thoughtful.

"Flash and success do draw attention," Casey said. "See, this is how these things work. Most of the time the school and the NCAA work things out without involving the courts. Players sometimes sue the NCAA, but coaches hardly ever do. If a coach does that, she gets a reputation as a black sheep, and the NCAA will keep attacking her until she finally quits. The NCAA doesn't tolerate people who challenge their authority. So coaches and colleges present their side of things, and then the NCAA makes their decision and hands down the punishment. The college accepts the decision and serves the punishment."

"They sound like Nazis," Kristy said. "Like, if some butt-hole of a reporter raises a cloud of suspicion because he doesn't like Coach Murphy, then she's guilty in the eyes of the NCAA until she proves herself innocent."

"That's the NCAA." Casey laughed. "I had my interview today.

It was more like an interrogation."

"What'd they ask?"

"Dumb things," Casey said. "Has Coach Murphy or any of her coaches ever given me money. Do I know of anybody who has been given money. Do I know of any transcripts that have been altered. Would I be willing to retake my SAT test so they can verify I didn't cheat and wasn't coached. How many times I saw Coach Murphy while she was recruiting me, did Coach Murphy exceed the number of allowed contacts. Has Coach Murphy or any or her coaches ever beat me. Do I know of anybody who's ever been beaten. Dumb things."

"Is any of it true?"

"No way! The only money I get is the five hundred a month allowance my parents send me."

"Will there be trouble?"

"I don't know," Casey said. "All they've found so far is an ex-player who traded her complimentary tickets to an athletic store for a pair of shoes. That was four years ago. Before Coach Murphy even came here."

"How long will it take to find out? About any trouble?"

"Two weeks. A year. Ten years. Who knows with the NCAA. They do things the way they want."

Kristy reached across the table and touched Casey's hand. "Will you leave if Tech gets put on probation?" She pulled her hand back, head lowered, picked up a French fry and swirled it in a pile of ketchup. "You have that right, don't you?"

"I'll be here as long as Coach Murphy is. But if she goes to another school I'll transfer there."

Kristy touched Casey's hand again. "Is Coach Murphy out of control like everyone says?"

"Joke!" Casey said, missing the rapid-fire 'like-for sure-toe-tuh-lee wack' that followed with Katie/Carla/Darla. But there were other things about Kristy. A softness, a clinging, a needing. It was nice to be so needed like Kristy needed her. The only people Kristy ever talked to were the customers at Burger King and Casey. She didn't have a family anymore because her parents gave her the familial heave-ho when she told them she might or might not be a dyke.

"I read in the paper you're a top candidate for Big Seven Fresh-man of the Year," Kristy said. "The paper said it's between you and

Buffy Fregosi from Missouri. The reporter was all excited about the historic confrontations you and Buffy Fregosi will have in the next four years if you both stay healthy."

"I'll settle for the Conference Championship every year."

"Let me see if I can remember," Kristy said, biting her bottom lip and knitting her eyebrows. "You're averaging almost twelve points and four assists and three steals and three rebounds and thirty-six minutes playing time per game. Am I right?"

"I guess," Casey said. "I don't really keep up with that stuff. I remember if we win or lose." That wasn't much of a lie.

"I'm so proud of you," Kristy said, biting her bottom lip again and kind of sucking in her breath and giving a little squeal. She reached across the table and touched Casey's hand. "Sometimes when I'm at work, cooking French fries or something, I just start smiling to myself, remembering the last time I saw you and the fun things we did and the interesting conversations we had." She dropped her eyes. "Everyone at Burger King always says, 'Kristy, you're just always smiling and looking happy. You must be the happiest person in the world.' I always laugh on the inside because if they knew why I'm smiling they'd probably hate me." She looked up through her eyelashes, a look that was dazzling. "I smile because of you, Casey. I wish I knew somebody to tell, someone I could brag to about being your lover. But I don't, so I have to tell you."

Casey choked on her Coke. "We're lovers?"

"In my mind," Kristy said. "You've been so patient and understanding with me. You don't put any pressure on me or expect anything from me. Those are the kinds of things only lovers would do for each other."

"Okay-fine," Casey said, trying to figure out how two women who never laid a hand on each other could be lovers.

Kristy cleared the table and lit the candles on the cake and sang Happy Birthday with shining eyes. One of Kristy's presents was a painting of Casey in her basketball uniform. It was good, all bright colors and images instead of the angst-ridden dark colors and mournful, screaming faces Kristy normally painted.

"I can't take this," Casey protested. "It's worth too much. I know everything you paint is classified as Native American Art. You could sell this for a lot of money."

"I want you to have it," Kristy insisted.

"Okay-fine. Thanks," Casey said. "It's the best present I've ever gotten. I'll treasure it forever."

Kristy's second present was a delicate gold chain. Kristy slipped it around Casey's neck, kissing the top of her head while the clasp was fixed.

"It's not much, but it's all I can afford right now," Kristy whispered.

"It's beautiful," Casey said sincerely.

Kristy chattered about something, a promotion she might get at Burger King or something, Casey wasn't really sure what because she was thinking about the hunted look on Coach Murphy's face lately, the dark circles under her eyes, the white stains that stayed around the corners of her mouth constantly, the reporters crawling all over campus, the men from the NCAA office in Kansas City. Questions, questions, questions. All over nothing. It was like being a frog in biology class, everyone dying to rip your guts open and examine everything in the smallest detail when only a second ago you'd been a happy frog, hopping from one lily pad to another gobbling down bugs.

Kristy gave Casey a long hug at the door and whispered, "Do you have to go?"

"If I blow another curfew, I'll get demoted to water girl."

"I love you, Case."

"I love you, Kris. Thanks for the party and presents."

Casey drove by Mitchell on the way to the dorm, hoping she'd see a light on in the tennis office. The only light on was the one in Coach Murphy's office. Casey parked, walked to the window and peeked inside. Coach Murphy was there with Coach DeFoe, Athletic Director Martin, a university lawyer and two men from the NCAA. Everyone looked tired; they were working through a stack of papers about a mile high.

Casey had to fight not to break the window and crawl into Coach Murphy's office and punch the men out and scream for them to take their papers and their law degrees and get the hell out, and leave Coach Murphy alone because she hadn't done anything, she was one of the most honest people Casey knew.

"We have to tell her," Casey hissed, her stomach in knots.

"I don't want to. She already hates me. This will be the end for me," Tobie moaned, squeezing the arms of the chair she was sitting in so tight her knuckles were white. The color of her knuckles matched the color of her face.

"I don't want to, either," Casey said glumly. "But we have to."

Coach Murphy walked into the office, carrying a mug of coffee. She moved behind her desk, sipped her coffee and looked expectantly at Casey, and then at Tobie.

"I made a mistake," Casey began.

"Is it something I can help with?" Coach Murphy asked, looking concerned.

"It involves you, too," Casey said.

Tobie sucked in her breath, making a sharp sound. Her face turned whiter.

Casey took a deep breath, too, and bit the bullet. "It happened when we were in Nebraska," she said, trying to word things delicately. "A friend gave me a hotel room, a suite, and a free meal and a bottle of champagne for my birthday. I invited Tobie. She ate a free meal, too. But I didn't sleep in the room. I only ate there and drank the champagne and then went back to my own room. Tobie is innocent of anything. She's only involved because of me."

"Tobie, you will pay Casey back for the cost of the meal," Coach Murphy said.

"Yes, ma'am," Tobie squeaked.

"You can go."

Tobie shot to her feet and zipped out of the office.

Casey swallowed the boulder lodged in her throat.

"Who's name was this suite listed under?" Coach Murphy asked when they were alone.

"Mine," Casey squeaked. "I was also given a Rolex watch. And another friend of mine gave me a gold necklace and a portrait, a painting."

Coach Murphy looked bewildered. "It sounds like you have a lot of generous friends," she said.

"Yes, ma'am." Casey felt like crawling into a hole for adding to Coach Murphy's problems.

"Are these 'friends' connected to the university in any way?"

"One's an ex-student. The other is either an alumnus or an ex-student. I'm not sure which."

"Twenty laps for drinking alcohol," Coach Murphy said distractedly, studying her coffee cup, looking thoughtful. "We'll have to report this to the NCAA, of course," she said after a few moments. "The watch and necklace you will return immediately. Send them by insured mail so we'll have a record of the return. The giving of expensive gifts to players is not something I want happening in my program."

"Yes, ma'am."

"I want you to find out the cost of the hotel suite and the meals you and Tobie ate," Coach Murphy said, her face expressionless. "Then you can repay your friend. Do it by check so we'll have a record. Now, about the portrait. I'm assuming it's of you, so why don't we have your friend contact me. I'll ask if the portrait can be donated to the university. If it's any good, we'll display it in the lobby. After you graduate, we'll find a way to return it to you."

"Yes, ma'am," Casey said, swallowing another boulder in her throat. "Will the NCAA suspend me? Or strip away my eligibility?" She felt like crying.

Coach Murphy laughed, looking a little more relaxed. "I doubt if they'll do anything—provided you make the recompense and returns I've outlined. These are relatively minor infractions. In fact, I'm not certain they are infractions, except for the hotel suite. But there's no sense in taking chances, considering our present situation. I'll have to discuss things with university lawyers, of course, but since we've uncovered this incident ourselves and will report it ourselves, I doubt the NCAA will be very concerned."

"Thank God," Casey said as her backbone disappeared and she had to fight to stay in her chair. "I'm really sorry, Coach Murphy. I hate that I did something that could've caused you problems."

"I appreciate your honesty in coming forward. I know it took a lot of courage," Coach Murphy said. She walked around her desk and squeezed Casey's shoulder. "But from now on, don't accept presents from friends without talking to me first. The basketball program will provide everything you need."

"Yes, ma'am," Casey sighed, feeling like ten billion pounds had been lifted from her shoulders. She hopefully asked, "Do I still have to run the twenty laps?"

Coach Murphy arched her eyebrows.

"Yes, ma'am," Casey grumbled. She went to the gym, did her stretches and started running her punishment laps. She noticed Tobie, looking relieved, the color back in her face, screwing around and laughing with Alysa.

A grad assistant came out from the direction of Coach Murphy's office and shouted, "Daniels! You owe Coach Murphy twenty more laps!"

"What'd I do this time?" Tobie asked, looking bewildered.

"You know what you did!" the grad assistant shouted. "Does Nebraska and champagne mean anything to you? Booze-hound!"

Tobie hung her head in resignation and headed toward the stands. When she caught up with Casey she hissed, "Thanks, asshole."

Casey shrugged. She guessed Tobie's analysis was right.

Alysa lumbered across the court and joined in the lap-running. "I'll make my confession to Coach Murphy after practice," she rumbled, looking sheepish. "God-damn, but it sure don't seem right that one little glass of champagne should earn poor old Alysa twenty laps. I hate running laps." She glared at Casey and rumbled, "I might take it out of your hide, Lower Case."

"You'll have to wait in line," Casey told her miserably.

Bonnie, Tamara, Sabine and Jodi trotted across the court and joined the lap-running. "We divided a twelve-pack of beer in Nebraska," they explained, looking embarrassed. "Hell, there's nothing to do except drink in Nebraska."

"Ah, but ain't confession good for the soul," Alysa rumbled joyfully since misery loves company.

What was left of the team gathered in the center of the court and serenaded the seven of them with *How Dry I Am*.

Casey showed the picture to a grad assistant and a player in the tennis office. The grad assistant pointed at Sharika's picture and said, "This one I've seen before. I don't know her name. I've never seen the other one."

"What do you know about her?"

"Not much." The grad assistant shrugged, handing the picture back. "She hangs around sometimes. She played here years ago. Keeps to herself. Why don't you ask Coach Alston? She should be back in an hour or so."

Casey went outside to wait, sitting on some steps, picking up a dead leaf and tearing it into strips. It was hard not to notice Tobie and Toni in the distance, down by the duck pond. Tobie was holding something over her head, a box wrapped in gold paper and tied with a red ribbon, and skipping around and around in circles. Toni was chasing her, jumping up-and-down and trying to snatch the box Tobie was holding.

Toni threw herself at Tobie, knocking Tobie off balance. They both fell down, rolling in a pile of dead leaves, shrieks of laughter drifting across the campus to Casey, making her feel like throwing up. Fresh love was so nauseating. Not that Casey was jealous. Not much, anyway.

She heaved a huge sigh and pictured how much fun it would be to be rolling and shrieking in a pile of dead leaves with Sharika. She heaved another sigh, just generally feeling lonely and unloved and unappreciated and unwanted and more or less as blue as one human being could feel.

Katie/Carla/Darla materialized at the bottom of the steps. Carla was carrying a picnic basket. "Hi," Casey said, brightening a little. It was hard to be blue when Katie/Carla/Darla were around. They had too much energy.

"Picnic time," Katie said.

"Not now," Casey said. "I'm waiting to see someone. Why don't you sit and talk with me for a while?" She patted the step beside her.

"Like, after while," Darla said. They marched up the steps, tugged Casey to her feet and pulled her across campus to the duck pond. They spread a red and white checkered cloth on the ground and pulled stuff out of their picnic basket. Peanut butter and jelly sandwiches and sweet pickles and sliced celery and carrots and cottage cheese and a quart bottle of beer.

Casey didn't have a real good time. She was blue to begin with, and it was cloudy and windy, and the bread got dried out and everyone going by stared at four lunatic women having a picnic almost in the dead of winter. The ducks and geese kept waddling up and begging for food. They were eating more than anyone.

Casey listened to the conversation halfheartedly, leaning back on her hands, tapping her toes together, watching the cars pass, the begging ducks and geese, the people coming and going from the frat houses across the street. After the bottle of beer made the fourth go-round she changed her mind and started having a pretty good time.

"I'm running if I see a campus policeman," she said. "Sucking down beer on campus is illegal."

"Duh," Carla said, rolling her eyes. "I didn't vote for that law."

"You don't vote at all," Casey said.

"Toe-tuh-lee wack," Katie said.

Casey took another turn at the bottle of beer and went back to watching the ducks and geese and cars and people. Katie/Carla/ Darla started talking about where they were moving after graduation. One wanted Malibu and a tofu shop. One wanted Staten Island and a Kosher deli. One wanted Chicago and a hot-dog stand near Wriggly Field.

From listening, Casey learned they all three had money. Carla/ Darla were each getting a fifty thousand dollar trust fund when they graduated. Katie had already gotten a twenty-five thousand dollar trust fund when she turned twenty-one.

"Must be nice," Casey said.

"Like, yeah," Katie said.

Katie/Carla/Darla started talking about what kind of house they were going to buy whenever they moved to wherever they moved to. They decided they could buy a bitchin' house, using part of their trust funds for the down payment, and not worrying about the monthly payments because a three-income household of college grads could afford just about any monthly payment.

Casey took another sip of beer, burped, giggled. "Maybe I'll come visit you in your bitchin' house," she said. "We can play foosball or something." She giggled again, knowing what foosball games with Katie/Carla/Darla always turned in to.

Carla/Darla looked at Katie. "Now's the time," Darla said. "She's, like, had enough that she won't cause a public scene and draw attention to her inebriated state."

"This is, like, mean," Carla murmured, studying her hands.

"You lost me," Casey said.

"I've been elected spokeswoman," Katie said.

"Spokeswoman for what?" Casey asked.

"We're not all frivolity and bitchin' good sex," Katie said, her expression resembling a professor lecturing kids on the intricacies of life. "We're highly ambitious women. Our primary ambition being to build a good life for ourselves and the devil with everybody else."

"Yeah, so?" Casey said, her butt starting to pucker a little, although she didn't know why.

"People come in three types," Katie said. "One type has sex with someone expecting it to lead to a relationship eventually. One type has a relationship with someone expecting it to lead to sex eventually. The third type are dead-end people, they have sex with someone without expecting it to lead anywhere except to more sex. You,

Casey Ellison, are a dead-end person."

Casey's mouth dropped open, she couldn't do anything except sit there and feel stunned. "Are you dumping me?" she finally managed to squeak.

"Only from our bed," Katie said. "Not from our lives. We'll be friends forever."

"God, this hurts," Casey said. "Do you know how it makes me feel to have you three call me a dead-end? Maybe you're the dead-ends. You used me like a piece of meat, just because you wanted a mistress.

"Au, like, contraire," Katie said. "We included you in our lives. We became friends with you and made love with you. We exposed ourselves to you. We gave you a chance to be part of us. We did all that expecting it to lead to a long-term relationship, not just more sex. You don't want to be part of us, you'd rather look at us as unreal or weird, so we're withdrawing our offer of inclusion."

Serious-looking Carla dug in her jacket pocket and pulled out a ring case and handed it to serious-looking Darla. Darla handed it to serious-looking Katie. Katie handed it to open-mouthed Casey. Casey opened it. It was a diamond ring.

"What's this?" Casey asked.

"A symbol of what we had," Katie said. "Something for you to keep so you'll remember us forever. We're sorry things had to work out this way, but we tried."

"We bought it thinking it would be an engagement ring," Darla explained. "But it turned out to be an unengagement ring."

"Is this what you want, Carla, baby?" Casey asked. "Do you think I'm a dead-end?"

Carla studied her hands. Her head nodded, an almost imperceptible nod.

"What am I supposed to do now?" Casey asked. "This is new to me. I've never been dumped. Am I officially dismissed? Do I just get up and slink away?"

"No," Katie said. "You're welcome to stay and picnic with us. I told you we'll always be friends."

"Sure," Casey said, sounding as bitter as she felt. "And if I break down and cry, what will you do? Comfort me as a friend? Will you pat me on the head and say you didn't mean it when you called me a dead-end person? Will you hold my hand and tell me I wasn't just a body to you when that's exactly what I feel like? Or should I just sit here and eat a peanut butter sandwich and smile and chat about the weather with you when I almost feel like punching you all out?"

"I think you're being immature," Katie said, looking and sounding condescending. Darla nodded. Casey saw a tear slip down Carla's cheek.

"I'm not taking this," Casey said, handing back the ring. "A god-damn unengagement ring. What a bunch of smart-ass bull-shit! I'll remember you forever. How could I forget what was said to me today? And if that's immature, fuck it."

"Temper, temper," Katie said mildly.

"I told you she wouldn't take anything," Carla said, slapping Darla's arm. "Like, nincompoop. All it did was make her feel cheap, it would've made me feel cheap. There's, like, no need to make her feel any worse than we already have. I hate this whole thing. We haven't handled it right."

"Don't, like, pin the donkey on my tail!" Darla exclaimed, looking defensive. "It wasn't my brainstorm."

"Was so!"

"Like!"

Casey walked away, leaving Katie/Carla/Darla sitting beside the duck pond and arguing about who actually made Casey feel cheap. She looked back one time and saw them still sitting there, arguing, throwing food to the ducks and geese and passing their bottle of beer around.

Talk about feast or famine. It seemed like only a few minutes ago she was rolling in women, she had everything under control, people liked her and wanted to be with her. All gone. Because she'd maybe treated them like shit, hadn't been a good girl all the time. Whatever the reason, everyone was gone and she was all alone except for a who-can-freak-whom-more? game and an angst-ridden lover who wasn't actually a lover.

God-damn, it hurt.

"I'm not having what you'd call a real good day," she mumbled to herself because they were was nobody around to hear.

Be a machine, babe, be a machine.

Casey carried the picture into the tennis office and showed it to the tennis coach after the tennis coach got through chewing a player's butt over making a D on a multivariable calculus test.

"Yes, ma'am," the tennis player whimpered after the butt-chewing, sounding just like Tobie when she got a butt-chewing from Coach Murphy. The tennis player slunk away.

"What?" Coach Alston asked, turning her irritated face in Casey's direction. Coach Alston reminded Casey of a thirty year old John Wayne. She jabbed the picture with a finger and growled, "This is Sharika Keymah. I don't know the other woman."

"What do you know about Sharika?"

"She was here when I took over," Coach Alston said. "Kinda grandfathered on me. I let her stay because she's an ex-jock and never gets in the way. I know she makes a killing giving private lessons at a posh country club in Tulsa. I hear she has an eighteen month waiting list to get in her classes. Used to be a pro, had to retire. Blew out a knee or something. Or got too old. Sharika's not her real name." She walked across the office, poked her head into a door where a typewriter was clicking and said, "Barb, you recall Sharika Keymah's real name?"

The typewriter stopped clicking. "Uh...Sandra June. Something like that," a woman's voice answered. The clicking started again.

Coach Alston handed the picture back. "Why don't you try Mrs. Duncan," she said. "The secretary in the archives office. She's been here since the turn of the century."

Casey headed to the archives office, smelling victory. Sharika Keymah/Sarah Jane/Hypnotic Spider was about to get crushed. The bug was going to turn the tables on the black widow, and God, it was going to be sweet. Turning the tables on the spider had gone beyond a game, even beyond an obsession. It was a matter of pride now—a matter of solving the mystery or losing her mind, going running-naked-and-screaming-into-the-woods insane.

Those were the only two choices she had.

Mrs. Duncan was a hundred and ten years old. Black, grey-haired, bifocals, heavyset, wearing a print dress. She was burrowing in a file cabinet. Casey waited until she finished burrowing and turned from the cabinet with a questioning look in her eyes before saying, "I'm Casey Ellison."

Mrs. Duncan laughed, a husky, throaty laugh. "I know who you are, child," she said.

"I was wondering if you could tell me if this is a picture of Sarah Jane?"

Mrs. Duncan took the picture, tilted her head back, adjusted her glasses and smiled. She smiled at the picture for a long time. "Sarah

Jane Jefferson and Monica Hills," she finally said softly. "Lord, this brings back memories. Where did you get this picture, child?"

"From Sarah Jane. It's a game we're playing."

"Sarah Jane always did like gaming." Mrs. Duncan chuckled. She moved behind her desk and flopped into her chair. "Her name's not Sarah Jane anymore. She had it changed to Sharika Keymah last year. Or was it the year before? I can't remember. Lord, child, when you get as old as I am the years run together and you can't remember one from the other. All you remember is how old you're getting."

"Can you tell me anything about the picture?"

"Lord, yes," Mrs. Duncan said. She titled her head back and looked at the picture again. A sad look crossed her face. "Monica and her husband and three little babies were all killed in a car wreck a few years back. Down near McAlester. Some boys driving a hundred and five miles an hour broadsided them at an intersection." She stood and walked to a bookcase.

Casey followed, trying to swallow the lump in her throat, thinking about how crushed Sharika must have been when Monica Hills died. Mrs. Duncan pulled a book off the top shelf, slapped some dust off it and handed it to Casey.

"You'll find all sorts of writing in here about Sarah Jane and Monica," Mrs. Duncan said. "They were something around here at one time, the same kind of something you are now. I saw Sarah Jane just the other day. She's a sweet child. She brought me a piece of carrot cake she'd baked. She knows how I love carrot cake."

Mrs. Duncan slapped her hips and laughed. "Not hard to tell I like my food, is it," she said. "Why don't you sit yourself down here, child, and read all you want. I'll help with any questions you have." She looked at the picture again and clucked her tongue. "Sarah Jane hasn't aged a day since she was in college. There's some that say she had her a face-lift. I don't take no truck in that. Sarah Jane's a vain child, but she's not that vain."

Mrs. Duncan walked across the room and started burrowing in a closet.

The title of the book was, *Moments In Lady Lobos Athletics, Tennis*. The book was full of old pictures and old newspaper articles in miniature form. A third of the way through the book Casey found an article about Sharika. The headline said:

LADY LOBOS WIN NATIONAL DOUBLES TITLE
Jefferson Finishes Second In Singles, Turning Pro

167

The second article Casey found about Sharika was about the U.S. Open in Flushing Meadow, New York. The article said Sharika's mixed-doubles match had been delayed when a bunch of people in the stands jumped up and started shouting about why was a bumpy-skinned N-word person being allowed to play tennis with decent white people. The match was delayed until the police came and carried the people away. The same kind of disturbance happened during Sharika's doubles match.

"Like, duh," Casey said, fighting not to pound her head on the table. Sharika wasn't bumpy-skinned. All anyone had to do was touch her to learn how silky her skin was. And who else could she play doubles and mixed-doubles with except white people when she was the only black woman tennis player at the time? As if it mattered who Sharika played tennis with at any time.

The third article Casey found about Sharika was about Wimbledon. Sharika had called a press conference and said she was tired of reading 'black' every time she read about herself, like, 'Sarah Jane Jefferson, who is black,' when nobody wrote about the other women that way, nobody wrote, 'So-and-so, who is white,' when they wrote about the other women on the pro tour.

"What difference does that make?" a reporter had asked.

"Why don't I have any sponsorship from major corporations?" Sharika asked, making her point. "With the world ranking I have, why am I basically free-lancing it on the tour and paying most of my own expenses? Why do white women with a lower ranking than mine, women I've consistently beaten in two sets, have sponsorship from major corporations? Why do all the black males on the tour have major corporate sponsorship when none of them have the ranking I do?"

Mrs. Duncan came out of the closet, clutching a VCR tape in her hands. "I knew I had this somewhere," she said triumphantly. "It's an old movie of Sarah Jane." She wheeled a TV out of the closet, put the tape in the VCR and switched it on.

The tape showed Sharika playing at Wimbledon. The woman she was playing was from England, and looked like she was twice as big as Sharika. Every time Sharika hit the ball, her racquet almost jumped out of her hand from the force of the Englishwoman's volleys.

Sharika kept approaching the net, trying to use her speed and quickness, but she was no match for the other woman's strong groundstrokes. The crowd was roaring support for the English-woman, too, and whistling derisively over every good shot Sharika hit. Sharika looked exhausted. She had to call time-out to have her calf massaged by the trainer, and she looked to be in obvious pain, from a cramp, Casey supposed.

Sharika had ended up losing in a tiebreaker. Her eyes looked moist when she walked off the court, and her chin was trembling a little, but her head was held high.

"Doesn't she look tiny?" Mrs. Duncan asked sadly. "Sarah Jane played against women bigger than her her whole life. But she always had more heart than anyone she played against. Heart and speed are what took her as far as she went."

"Oh, Sarah Jane," Casey said softly, feeling a little moist-eyed herself. "Thimble Town wasn't the way you dreamed, was it?"

CHAPTER 15

Casey started weaving her web by buying a small wreath and spray painting it black. One night, right before curfew, she drove to Sharika's apartment, nailed the wreath to Sharika's door and ran.

Kim was hanging her face out of the door when Casey got back to the dorm. "Hurry," Kim said, pointing into the room. "The phone. I think it's another bed-check."

Casey walked into the room and picked up the phone.

"I got your wreath," Sharika said, chuckling. "I guess you're ready to talk."

"I'm ready to bite your nipples off."

"That's a coarse thing to say," Sharika said, sounding disgusted.

"I'm sure you've said worse things in your life," Casey said. She went on and described in pornographic detail what else she wanted to do to Sharika.

"I'm impressed by your locker room vocabulary," Sharika said.

Kim made a choking sound. Her face was bright red. "I can't deal with this!" she shouted, eyes bulging halfway out of her face. "It's ultra-perverted!" She walked out, holding her nose. The door slammed behind her.

"You got me in trouble," Casey said accusingly, not really meaning it.

"You say what?"

Casey told her about what happened with Coach Murphy over the suite and champagne and everything.

"Oh, girlfriend, I'm so sorry," Sharika said, sounding sincere. "I didn't know. Did you?"

"Shit! The NCAA has something like sixteen hundred pages of regulations. Nobody knows them all. But you can't give me anything else from now on."

"Can I see you?" Sharika asked. "This has gone far enough. We need to talk. I'll make thing up to you the best way I know how."

"Sorry. I'm leaving for Texas State in the morning. I have to go to bed and get a good night's sleep."

"Can I see you when you get back?"

"I probably won't come back alive. 'Bye, lover." Casey slammed the phone down.

It rang immediately.

"You're in," a grad assistant said, sounding disappointed.

"Zing! Gotcha!" Casey slammed the phone down. She was in a good mood. It was a lot more fun being a spider than a bug.

She went into the hall to look for Kim, thinking it was a good time for them to thrash things out. She saw Kim three doors down, huddling and whispering with two other women. All three stopped whispering when they saw Casey and looked at her with horrified expressions.

Casey turned around and went back to her room. Maybe it wasn't a good time to thrash things out after all.

Casey wobbled into her room, looked at her face in the mirror and almost threw up.

Strings in her lips, black pits where her eyes should've been, a nose like an anteater. She felt like crying, saw her chin trembling, shouted, "Don't you dare cry! Are you the hard-nosed little bitch you pretend to be? Or a wet-eyed wimp?"

Her starting position.

The day had started out fun. Beginning with the last-second full-court desperation shot Tobie made at going to Texas State while standing in front of Mitchell as the team boarded the bus. Tobie promised Coach Murphy everything except her firstborn child, face flushed, voice low, shifting from one foot to the other, hands in the pockets of her skirt, her gym bag sitting on the sidewalk beside her, intense eyes glued to Coach Murphy's face like she'd been taught.

Coach Murphy listened with an impassive face, arms crossed, a hip cocked, one foot tapping the pavement. "No," she said after Tobie finished promising. "End of discussion?"

"Yes, Dr. Murphy," Tobie whimpered. She stood outside Mitchell with her hands in her pockets and a woeful expression on her face as the bus pulled away. Everyone cracked up when she pulled a hand out of her pocket and gave the finger to the bus. Coach Murphy pretended she didn't notice, but everyone knew she had. Coach

Murphy didn't miss much.

It was a leisurely ride to Texas, the bus filled with laughter and dirty jokes and Alysa's stories about growing up in Hugo, Oklahoma with a cottontail and a possum. Casey bought a newspaper when they all stopped for lunch at a McDonald's and ate the place out of quarter pound cheeseburgers and milk shakes and apple pies. Everyone cracked up when Coach Murphy looked at the tab and slapped a hand to her heart and rolled her eyes. She didn't reach for her bottle of Mylanta-II though, so everyone knew the tab wasn't all that bad.

The newspaper was another crack up. The headline said:

BLOODY BATTLE OF THE RED RIVER, ROUND II
Tech Thugs Assault Heartland
Death Threats To Tobie Daniels Rumored

The first line of the article said, *Brenda Murphy, the unprincipled Svengali of the Night who slips across the Red River under cover of darkness and spirits away our best women athletes, returns to the scene of the crime tonight*

Reporters were blowing everything out of proportion with their purple prose and life-or-death attitude about sports. It was just a basketball game. The Tech-ettes were going to go into Heartland, slap the fuzz off the Lady Cougars and leave. What was the big deal?

The third paragraph of the article said, *This year's Tech team is a standard Brenda Murphy squad. Coach Murphy uses three boppers to clog the inside and hammer everyone who enters the paint. On the outside, she uses two water-bug guards who flit through the chaos the boppers create and inflict the scoring damage. The Tech style of play is further complemented by the large number of players Coach Murphy carries on her roster, interchangeable players she runs in-and-out of the game until the opponent is exhausted. The only difference in this year's Tech team is lightly-recruited freshman Casey Ellison, indisputably one of the fastest and strongest players in the conference, despite her relatively diminutive size. When she's on top of her game, the Tech team is virtually unstoppable. Shutting her down has to be State's primary objective tonight if they hope to win. Heralded freshman Tobie Daniels, a Dallas native, has not been a factor in Tech's success this year and has seen limited playing time.*

After she read the article, Casey passed the paper to Coach Murphy at the front of the bus. Everyone waited expectantly. Coach Murphy read the article, stood, dropped the paper onto her seat and sat back down. Everyone cracked up. Casey felt respect. Coach Murphy always did the right thing, she always did exactly what the situation called for, she always read people correctly, read them in a way Casey doubted she'd ever be able to. But she had to be able to read people correctly if she wanted to be an unprincipled Svengali of the Night someday.

They timed things so they arrived at the arena forty-five minutes before game time. They hustled through a corridor of security guards, past a bunch of hissing students and in a back door. In and out. That was the plan. The bus was leaving fifteen minutes after the game.

Casey laughed when she heard an ass-hole in the throng shout, "Hey, Ellison! Where'd you get those arms and shoulders? Didn't you use to be on the East German swim team?"

The boos started raining down on them the second they took the floor. Paper cups. Toilet paper. Ice cubes. An army of security guards came out and ringed the court. The tip was delayed fifteen minutes to clear the floor. It was announced over the public address system if anything else landed on the floor, the arena would be emptied and the game played without fans being present. That stopped the throwing but the booing got louder.

Three minutes into the game, Tech opened up a four point lead. It was a tough, physical game like the first one had been, but everyone was playing under control. Tech went on defense, Casey in the blond Number Four's face, full-court pressing. Then, just past half-court, something happened, Casey didn't know what, somebody misstepped, one or the other or both, their feet got tangled and they started stumbling. Casey took a shot in the face from an elbow somewhere in the middle of the stumbling.

She hit the deck, face numb, mind numb, pain shooting through her head, hearing whistles shrieking. She pressed a hand to her face, pulled it back, looked at it and saw nothing but blood. She freaked; she'd never seen so much blood in her life. She spit her mouthpiece out, jumped up, hands pressed to her face and ran, wildly, blindly, eyes blurred by tears, not knowing where she was going, just feeling a need to run, bleating, "Help, help, help," with every step, thinking, 'Blood! My blood! Mine!'

Coach Murphy was in her face, grabbing her shoulders, saying, "Casey, sit down. Sit down so Dr. Gilstrap can look at you."

Casey dropped to the floor. The arena was quiet except for murmuring in the stands, and Weatherly exchanging hissed cuss words with a State player, and Alysa rumbling something about someone better hit the ground running if Alysa saw them after the game. Then Casey heard someone saying, "I'm sorry, I'm sorry, I didn't mean to hurt you."

The trainer took one look at Casey, pressed a towel to her face and hustled her into the locker room. The arena was still quiet except for the murmuring.

The trainer sat Casey down in the locker room. The wide-eyed blond intern got even more wide-eyed than normal. She ran to the bathrooms, a hand pressed to her mouth, making retching sounds. The trainer went to work on Casey's face, opening a case, snapping on latex gloves, scared of AIDS. Who wasn't? Cotton. Lots of cotton, cool, moist, pressed to her cheeks, chin, mouth, sides of her nose. Bloody cotton piled in a plastic bag. A stinging in her nose, stars flashing in front of her eyes, pain shooting through her head.

"Broken nose," the trainer said, her face close to Casey's, her eyes too close to make out an expression, doing her job and concentrating on Casey like a lab subject. "Lower lip needs stitches. No cuts inside the mouth I can see. More blood than anything, I think. Teeth look okay."

Casey clutched the sides of the table, feeling dizzy.

"Stay with me," the trainer said softly.

Be a machine, babe, be a machine.

The blond intern came back, pale, sweating. "Are you okay?" the trainer asked, looking disgusted. The intern gawked at the plastic bag of bloody cotton and headed to the bathrooms again, hand pressed to her mouth.

Coach DeFoe came into the locker room, looking worried, carrying Casey's warm-up in her arms. "What's the word?" she asked.

"Her nose is broken," the trainer said. "The swelling won't go down for some time."

"Wha swedding?" Casey asked. Her mouth was numb; she couldn't breath. "I can't breet."

"Your nose is packed," the trainer said.

"Can I play?"

"No," the trainer said. "You're through for the night."

"Sorry, Case," Coach DeFoe said. She laughed, squeezing Casey's shoulder. "I know how you feel. My nose was broken three times when I was playing. By the way, you got called for the blocking

174

foul."

"Wha!"

Coach DeFoe laughed again and walked out. Casey felt coolness on her arm, a stinging, coolness again. She looked down just in time to see the trainer pulling a needle out of her arm. "Let that work," the trainer said. "We'll do your stitches in a minute."

"Otay-find," Casey said. She stood up and put on her warm-up.

"Where do you think you're going?"

"Ta wath duh game."

"Sit back down. I need to work on your lip."

"Bull-chit." Casey walked out. The first thing she looked for was the scoreboard. Tech 24, State 19. The crowd started applauding when they saw her walking to the bench. All the Lady Lobos crowded around her, trying to slap her butt and everything.

"Don tuth bee," Casey said. "I hur all ovuh."

Everyone cracked up.

Coach Murphy walked down the bench. "Is she okay?" she asked, laying a hand on Casey's shoulder, looking at the trainer. Casey's blood was dotted all over the front of her dress. Casey giggled. It seemed funny in a fuzzy way for prim Coach Murphy to have Casey's blood dotted all over the front of her dress.

"Yeth," Casey said. "I wan duh play."

The trainer shook her head.

"No," Coach Murphy said. She walked away.

Casey sat on the end of the bench. A few minutes later the pain killer kicked in. She felt herself jumping up, heard herself mumbling, "Kit dier athes," heard everyone cracking up, felt herself waving at a vendor in the stands, demanding popcorn and a Coke, felt the trainer and a grad assistant leading her away by the elbows, felt herself weaving and arguing like a Saturday night drunk trying to talk her way out of an arrest, back to the locker room, onto a cot, heard the trainer chuckling and saying, "She'll love the pair of shiners she's going to have," heard the grad assistant chuckle, "Zing! Gotcha!"

"Wha time ith it?"

"Eight-fifty. Why?"

Sharika's presents. An ice-cream cake from Baskin-Robbins. One red rose. The Rolex watch she'd given Casey, engraved with, 'Happy thirtieth, Spider. Love, Bug.' on the back and returned as a present. Everything would be delivered at nine.

"Tell me when ith nine doe I can laugh," Casey mumbled.

"What's she saying?" the trainer asked from somewhere out there, pulling a chair close, bending over Casey with a needle and thread to chain stitch her lip.

"Zing! Dotcha!" Casey said. She was still stretched out on the cot, numb from painkiller, when Tech came in for halftime. Coach Murphy and everyone asked if she was okay and then ignored her to work on the second half game plan. That's what it's all about, babe. Getting the stuffing kicked out of you, watching as the team went on and did what they had to do, concerned for you but focused on other people since you couldn't contribute.

Major-college ball.

Tech 71, State 70 in overtime.

Kristy was waiting beside her Escort when the bus got to Mitchell, chewing on her bottom lip and looking like she wanted to cry. Katie/Carla/Darla were sitting on their bikes, whispering among themselves, and looking like they wanted to cry, too. Sharika was waiting beside her Corvette, wearing her mink coat, clutching one red rose in both her hands. She was crying, her cheeks shining in the streetlights.

Casey laid a towel over her head, grabbed her gym bag, wobbled to a grad assistant's car and got a ride to the dorm. She just didn't want to see anybody. Not with a swollen face and two black eyes and a stitched lip and feeling nothing but pain every time she took a step. Nobody could help her deal with the pain. It was something inside her body, something she had to deal with by herself.

So, when she wobbled into her room and looked at her face in the mirror, she almost threw up.

Casey went into Mrs. Manders' office and whined for permission to cut class. "You'll have to go back eventually," Mrs. Manders said. She couldn't look at Casey for more than a split second at a time. She glanced, looked away, glanced again.

"Would you want to be seen in public looking like this?" Casey screwed her face up for a second, let her chin tremble.

Mrs. Manders glanced, looked away, glanced again. "I'll okay two days," she said. "I'll call your professors and ask them to drop your assignments off here so you don't have to go to their offices."

"Thanks." Casey went to the trainer's room. "I'm going to practice," she announced.

The trainer arched her eyebrows. "Hello, Dr. Ellison," she said.

"Look." Casey held out her bottle of pain pills. "Count 'em. They're all there. I didn't take even one. I feel great."

"Bull-chit," the trainer said, then shrugged. "Okay. You know better than me how much pain you can take." She fixed Casey a white facemask that had a padded cup for her nose and straps that ran all over her head and fastened in the back. It was like wearing a bra on her nose. She strapped the thing on and went to the gym, feeling like she had an octopus glued to her face.

She spent all day practicing by herself in the deserted gym, learning to breathe through her mouth, learning to shoot hoops with a facemask, her vision partially blocked. Every time her foot landed on the floor, pain shot through her face and nose. She gritted her teeth and took it.

Be a machine, babe, be a machine.

Her starting position.

Every eye was glued on her when the Lady Lobos came out for practice, especially the eyes of the other guards. She felt like a wounded deer with a pack of starving wolves snapping at her heels. Alysa walked by and rumbled, "If I was Dan'l Boone I'd skin you and make a cap out of you, Lower Case. You raccoon-looking thing."

Casey got in her face, shoving, cussing, asking Alysa if she wanted to go outside and open her mouth again, proving to everyone that she wasn't hurt, that she still had a lot of fire left.

"Don't snap at poor old Alysa, Lower Case," Alysa rumbled, stroking Casey's head like she was a little baby. "You know how much I love you."

Casey cut her eyes at Coach Murphy. Coach Murphy was watching with a question mark showing in her eyes and that certain look on her face. Casey wanted to run to her, drop to her knees and say, 'Please, Coach Murphy, don't bench me. I'm fine. I swear I am. I love you. We're friends. Give me a break just this one time. I can still get the job done.' Saying that would've kept her off the bench, but only because she would've been taken straight to the nut-house. That wasn't the way the game was played.

Coach Murphy walked over. Casey swallowed hard. "How do you feel?" Coach Murphy asked. She didn't look away. Her eyes were glued to Casey's face like usual.

"I'm a hundred percent." Casey glued her eyes to Coach Murphy's, hoping for once Coach Murphy could in fact read her mind, could read what Casey really wanted to say, the begging she wanted to do.

"Did Dr. Gilstrap clear you to practice?" Coach Murphy asked. Probing, evaluating, analyzing.

"She gave me this thing." Casey laughed, fingering her facemask, hoping she didn't sound as strained as she felt. "Who needs a nose? All a basketball player needs are legs."

Coach Murphy walked away. She said something to a grad assistant. The grad assistant headed toward the trainer's room. Casey guessed not only had she sounded strained she'd also sounded like a liar. The grad assistant was back in a few seconds, whispering something to Coach Murphy. Coach Murphy nodded and blew her whistle to start practice.

Casey ran to where the first-team was gathered, feeling like screaming, 'I made it through one day! The next day will be better. The next even better. All I have to do is hang on. You can't have my starting position!'

She looked at all the people around her. Her teammates. The arrogant faces and voices and walks conveying the belief basketball players were better than normal people and the starters were the best of the best. And that's why you pounded the weights, took the morning runs, tried to manipulate the system as much as it manipulated you, played with pain and sacrificed the needs of your body—so your economy-sized ego didn't get turned into a pile of wolf dung by the hungry wolf-women snapping at your heels. And you were all by yourself when you were beating off the hungry wolf-women, without even a stick to help you.

That's what it's all about, babe.

Major-college ball. Fight or die. Like it or not.

Tobie was stretched out on Casey's bed, chewing on a fingernail and frowning at a chemistry book. Her shoes and socks were on the floor beside the bed. She was toe-wrestling with herself.

"Why are you majoring in chemical engineering if you hate chem so much?" Casey asked.

"Hell if I know," Tobie said. "I just like the idea of being a chemical engineer."

"Okay-fine," Casey said. She was sitting at her desk, flailing away at a geometry assignment, idly wondering if Buffy Fregosi was sitting at a desk in Columbia, Missouri doing the same thing. "How do you feel about Coach Murphy this week?"

"When she left me behind for State I decided to go into her office and hit her in the head after the last game my senior year," Tobie said. "Maybe I won't now."

"Because you're getting more playing time in the double-post offense she's putting in?"

Tobie snorted. "That has nothing to do with it. She needs the new offense. This team won't go anywhere in the tournament with me on the bench."

"No conceit, huh?"

"Fact," Tobie said, stretching out a mile-long leg, tickling Casey's arm with her toes. "You know it, I know it, she knows it."

"What changed your mind then?"

"You know, I don't understand the question," Tobie said.

"What happened to all this fear-of-failure stuff?"

Tobie looked up from her book and smiled. A heartbreaking smile, framed in a mound of fluffy blond hair and topped by pale blue eyes. "I love you," she said, sounding all soft and mushy, eyes looking moist. "You've done a lot for me. I'm not admitting anything you said was right, but you took the time to talk to me and listen to what I had to say."

"Okay-fine," Casey said, feeling all warm inside.

Tobie raised up on her elbows. "That's not good enough this time."

"I love you," Casey said, maybe sounding all soft and mushy. Her eyes were definitely not moist. "I read an article in the paper about a coach at a college back east who allegedly drives players off the team, drives them right out of school, if they're lesbians."

"A man coach?"

"No, it's a woman," Casey said.

"Ah."

"Why would someone attack and degrade and humiliate everyone they think is a lesbian until the woman leaves? Why would someone recruit a player if they're only going to drive them away because of their lifestyle? The article made me so grateful to be playing for someone like Coach Murphy."

"This is over my head or something," Tobie said.

"Do you ever think about what it's like to be black?" Casey asked, doodling Sharika's name on a piece of paper. "Or a Native American? Or any other minority?"

Tobie said, "Oh, sure," and looked thoughtful. "Let's see. I'm a woman. I'm six-four and still growing. I'm blond. I'm beautiful. I have a C-minus average in my major. I wear a size fourteen shoe. I'm pigheaded. I'm short-tempered. I'm a dyke. Isn't that enough to keep my little pea-brain occupied? Have you ever tried to buy a size fourteen in a pink pump? Most shoe salespeople say, 'Try a shipyard. They might have something in a size fourteen pink frigate.'" She arched her eyebrows like Coach Murphy and added, "Haven't you looked around lately? We are a minority. How does it feel?"

"How's Toni?" Casey asked, not wanting to get caught up in a gee-it's-hard-to-be-a-dyke conversation.

Tobie giggled, ducking her head, heaving a huge sigh before sticking her face back into her chem book.

"Are you punishing me?..." It was Sharika on the phone. "...For what I put you through?"

"You know better." Casey twisted on the phone cord, watching Kim polish her toenails, listening to the sleet pecking against the window.

"For serious, don't talk about sucking and licking and inhaling...things and that kind of stuff again," Kim said. "It makes me want to Smurf my guts out." She didn't walk out and start whispering to her friends at least.

"If you're not punishing me, why won't you come over?" Sharika asked. "I admit I deserve to be punished, so why won't you tell me if that's what you're doing?"

"The streets are too slick for this poor old Southern girl to drive on," Casey said.

"I'll come and get you," Sharika said quickly.

"She's black," Kim interrupted. "Sharika's not a white person's name. She sounds black when I talk to her. Don't you know giving it up for black people is out of vogue? I never did that even when it was chic." She gave an obviously fake shiver.

"She's gorgeous," Casey retorted not covering the phone. "Huge brown eyes with thick lashes. A button nose. Dimples when she smiles. Her skin is a luscious shade of brown like a Hershey bar. Her hands and feet are miniature-sized, size four shoes. The palms of her hands and the soles of her feet are pink. What color are yours?"

Kim eyed her soles.

"Those are all body things," Sharika said. "Can't you describe me any way but physically?"

"She's smart," Casey said. "And funny. And fun to talk to and do things with. She's a good driver and a great dancer. She's well-educated and worldly. She's a considerate, talented bed partner. How am I doing?"

"Not bad," Sharika said, sounding thoughtful.

"The bottom of my feet are pink," Kim said. "What's that have to do with anything?"

"Duh," Casey said.

"Enough of this," Sharika said. "I don't buy this line about I'm so beautiful and elegant and you're ashamed to see me the way you look. I'll close my eyes. I'll turn out all the lights. It's been too long, lover."

"Are you bug-eyed and helpless, watching the spider crawl toward you?" Casey asked.

"You know I am, hunny," Sharika whispered.

"Too bad," Casey said. "You irritating, muleheaded female. You didn't cut me any slack when I was bug-eyed and helpless. I seem to remember an overcast day in Ames, Iowa and a black limo and almost getting nailed by a blue Chrysler. Do you know how long it's going to take for people to stop ragging me about chasing cars?"

"You're lying," Sharika said. "You don't know anything about Sarah Jane. You're stalling for time to keep me from flushing you."

"Okay-fine. I'm flushed." Casey slammed the phone down. She snickered, thinking how Sharika had been exposed. Sharika wasn't a spider playing a game with a bug. She was only a softhearted wimp, making Casey discover things about her past instead of talking about them. The things were too painful for her to talk about. And Sharika sure didn't think Casey was a dead-end person. If she did, she wouldn't be slowly exposing herself to Casey through a spider-and-bug game.

Kim looked up from her nails. Her eyes were wide. "Did you just breakup? I always cry when I breakup with someone."

"Joke!"

Kim sighed. "I don't understand gay people."

"Joke! We're playing games. A kind of mental foreplay. Don't you play games with your lovers?"

"Not like that." Kim cut her eyes toward Casey and then looked back at her toenails. "You really like being with other women? For serious? You don't just fake it?"

Casey cracked up.

"Dumb question, huh?" Kim asked, looking sheepish. She grabbed the phone, punched in a number, put her hand over the mouthpiece and said, "Check this out." She moved her hand, cleared her throat and said, "Kenny? Guess who wants to suck your thingy?" She slammed the phone down, looking excited and embarrassed.

"Ultra-gross!" Casey said.

Kim's face was bright red. "I want a new roommate," she blurted.

Casey sat up, feeling stunned. "I don't know what to say. I thought we were tolerating each other just fine."

"Okay-fine," Kim said, giggling, giving Casey the finger.

Casey threw a pillow at her.

"For serious," Kim said, looking inquisitive, "how do you know who goes on top and who goes on bottom?"

"For serious," Casey said, "what's a condom feel like? What's a birth control pill taste like?"

The phone rang.

Casey answered.

"I'm on my knees, lover," Sharika whispered. "Isn't that what you want? To see me grovel? I want you back. Please."

"Better not."

The phone was quiet.

"I don't like the sound of your voice," Sharika said finally. "Casey, baby, tell me we're still playing games. I'm scared."

"Flashback to yesteryear," Casey said. "To the days of your youth. Flushing Meadow, Queens, New York City. The quarterfinals of the U.S. Open. What was the weather like that day?"

"I remember it was a hundred and ninety-five degrees when I was there," Sharika said. "I remember I got screwed on a line call and lost the match. I wanted to explode."

"Why didn't you? I would have."

"I couldn't," Sharika said. "Every match I played I was the focus of attention. I kind of stood out. Black women the world over were always judged by how I conducted myself. So all I could do was smile and take what was given to me."

"I heard you had some trouble with some cross-burners."

"I won't hide behind that," Sharika said, sounding angry. "I lost because I wasn't good enough, not because someone fucked with my mind. I don't worry about it now. I've got my niche carved out and that's all I care about. The world's not going to eat me."

"How about the semifinals at Wimbledon? Did your whining get you any corporate sponsorship?"

Sharika laughed dryly. "You're a bitch, hunny," she drawled.

"Okay-fine."

"I got screwed at Wimbledon, too," Sharika said softly. "On a point I really needed. When the call went the other way I almost blew my temper. The whole match turned on that one call. My quarterfinal match had been a four hour ordeal with a forty minute rain delay in the second set. In the semifinals I was mentally exhausted and dehydrated and my body was fading on me. I knew I didn't have what it took to go to a tie breaker. The line call I thought was wrong put me there and I lost."

"Was it a bad call? Really and truly?"

"In my eyes it was," Sharika said. "I was heartbroken. I was twenty-four years old, in my prime physically and experience-wise, and I knew it was time to quit saying next year would be my year. I stuck to a tough training schedule during the winter. I went into the season dedicated, knowing with all my heart it was the year my dreams would all come true. I was going to win Thimble Town and the U.S. Open. It wasn't meant to be. That's why I was upset when you left with Kristy after the Tennessee game. I could've helped you. I knew what you were going through."

"That's why I didn't want to see you," Casey said. "You would've gotten too close."

"Girlfriend!" Sharika exclaimed, sounding awed. "A flash of personal insight. I'm proud of you."

Casey laughed dryly. "You're a bitch, hunny," she drawled. "So what was it like actually playing at Wimbledon?"

"Oh, damn!" Sharika exclaimed, sounding dreamy, remembering when she was on top. "It's like nowhere else in the world. When you see the All-England pennant fluttering in the wind, the strawberries-and-cream, the women in bright, dazzling dresses—and everyone with raincoats and umbrellas even when the sun shines—it just does something to you. It's like a big, green-checkered whirlwind that pulls the tennis world into itself. There's just so much excitement and energy—and hope. The ground under the grass is hard, like cement, and the ball skips real low off it. You have to curtsey toward the royal box when you come onto the court and before you leave, that's the tradition. Wimbledon is big on tradition. The first time I went into the players' cafeteria, I felt like a hick from the sticks. The cafeteria is near courts two and three so you can watch the matches, and I saw all the famous players there eating, Martina and Billie Jean and Chrissie. I thought I was dreaming. I couldn't believe I was actually playing there like I'd dreamed about."

Sharika cleared her throat and chuckled. "Stop this," she said. "You'll get me crying in a minute. That was a long time ago." She softly added, "I'll take you to London some year if you want. So you can see Wimbledon for yourself. I know about a restaurant there. It's small—only seven tables. It's a nice place to go and sip sangria and have an intimate dinner after the matches end. We can even fly on the Concorde if you want. I've never done that. I think it would be fun." She cleared her throat again. "Don't you know how I feel about you? If you want anything from me, you only have to ask."

"Okay-fine. It's a date—but not until after I graduate," Casey said, feeling triumphant, knowing her web was wrapped so tightly around Sharika the muleheaded female would never escape.

CHAPTER 16

"Missouri's out!" a grad assistant shouted. "Heeehawww!" she brayed. "Hey, mule-faces! Where'd you get those putrid-looking gold uniforms? If you're the Number Two team in the country then my Grandma's bridge club is Number One!"

Coach Murphy passed the ball. "Lead us out, Casey," she said.

"I understand," Casey said, locking eyes with Coach Murphy.

"Do you?" Coach Murphy asked, voice mocking, eyes probing, evaluating, analyzing.

Casey did. The first reason for picking a freshman to lead the team was The Image. The second reason was a question, a challenge: Can you be the leader I think you are? Regardless of your age? Can you repay the trust and faith I've had in you all year? Can you give us a feast when we need it the most?

A game for all of us that will also give you what you want?

Out the door, down the runway, through the gap in the stands, onto the floor of Mitchell, into the bright lights and popping flash bulbs and howling people and pompom waving cheerleaders and CBS cameras. Single file to the snarling wolf's head, slowly, majestically, the band throbbing with *Catch Us If You Can*. Another of Coach Murphy's oldies.

The Image.

The Bad Girls On The Block. The team everyone loved to hate. Twenty-one wins, four losses. Ranked Number Five in the country in both major polls. A certain Number Two regional seed in the upcoming NCAA Tournament. Travel-hardened, tournament-hardened. Under NCAA investigation. A reputation as brawlers and intimidators. Dressed in black and led by a freshman guard with two black eyes and a stitched lip and a white facemask strapped to her head.

"Double-line lay-up drill!" Casey ordered, driving half-speed to the basket, passing to Alysa, hearing the howling in the stands swelling, seeing Missouri falter slightly in their warm-ups so they could gawk.

Buffy Fregosi with her frizzy hair, her intense eyes and her taunting smile was out front putting the Lady Tigers through their paces.

The second time Casey touched the ball, she drove half-speed to the basket, faked a pass, pulled out, dribbling the ball, watching the Lady Lobos continue to run the drill without the ball, simulating catching, passing, shooting. A well-oiled machine running through familiar movements, needing only a basketball to give meaning to their movements.

Casey savored the moment while it was hers, the hot-dogging, knowing every eye in the place was glued on her, almost hearing Dad's camcorder whirring. Nobody argued, nobody questioned her, nobody stopped and asked what was happening, nobody looked to the bench in confusion wanting Coach Murphy to put the freshman in her place. On the floor she was the point guard, the general, the one everyone looked to for instructions.

It was her team on the floor.

The Leader.

She glanced at Coach Murphy, saw her standing and watching, saying nothing, a tight smile on her face, her hands in fists at her sides, eyes shining with pride at the team she was presenting to the public, husband and two kids sitting on the front row of the stands behind her. Five-feet-three-inches, one hundred ten pounds of The Ultimate Teacher. Never telling you what to do, never saying she expected you to go beyond her teachings and become a woman with a mind of your own. If you never went beyond her teachings, if you never understood without being told, she'd still love you. But she'd never approve because you'd failed to meet your potential.

"Coach Murphy's Special on six!" Casey ordered, dribbling slowly toward the sideline, hearing the crowd explode, seeing the Lady Lobos fall smoothly into a complicated pattern, spectacular to watch, a crowd pleaser. Double exchange passes, flip passes, five-woman weave in a grapevine pattern, converging on the basket from five different directions, shooting a lay-up on the sixth pass.

A drill they'd spent hours learning and perfecting, running it again and again without the ball, cussing Coach Murphy and the tedious repetitiveness until finally realizing the drill taught them the basics of Coach Murphy's offense, everything coming together and making sense when the ball was added to the drill.

Three thunderous slamma-jammas from Alysa, Weatherly and Tobie and then to the bench, jumping up-and-down, mobbing each other, bashing forearms, calling each other's names, jazzed so high their feet weren't touching the floor, seeing the scowls on Missouri's faces, knowing Missouri was thinking, 'These bitches are arrogant and they're unpleasant to play and they're good, but we beat them once. Let's do it again and go home.'

Casey locked eyes with Buffy Fregosi, and they stared at each other for long seconds until finally exchanging curt nods. Casey began walking toward the Missouri bench. Buffy walked toward the Tech bench. They met in front of the scorer's table, flash bulbs snapping all around them, the crowd howling at the hundred decibel level.

Casey knew the TV cameras were focused on them, too. The announcers were probably breathlessly saying, "Ellison and Fregosi are exchanging words in front of the scorer's table. There's no love lost between those two."

"Welcome to Mitchell," Casey said.

"It's an honor to get to play here," Buffy said. "It's everything I was told. And more."

"Good luck, Frosh."

"Good luck, Frosh."

They shook hands and then trotted back to their respective benches.

"Look at Lower Case," Alysa rumbled when Casey got back to the bench. "She's got that Kansas look in her eyes. You on this afternoon, Lower Case?"

"Upset City!" Casey shouted, being the fire Coach Murphy wanted. Unless I...unless Buffy Fregosi...NO! It wasn't the time to think about doubts, you had to be focused on one thing and only one thing. Winning. For the team. For Coach Murphy; Coach Murphy named as one of the finalists for National Coach of the Year. A win would put her over the top. Big game, bigger than the Tennessee game which had been only ego. Semper Fi. Find your groove. Nail your shots. Follow the game plan. No turnovers. Hail Mary...

"At the point, from Chatsworth..."

Through the corridor of players, bashing forearms, feeling slaps on your butt, shouting, "Yeah-yeah-yeah!" when the public address boomed, "At forward, from Dallas, Texas, number fifty-fivvveee, Tobbbieee Dannnielllsss!"

Tobie. Seventy-six inches of mercurial woman, face blazing red, eyes on fire, expression impassive, playing a low post, rapid-fire profanity and a whirling violence surrounding her in the lane, hands held up again and again, demanding the ball, lob entry pass, Tobie holding the ball high, pivoting, nailing the fade-away jumper again and again, breaking Missouri's back until they were forced to collapse to double-team the blond pussycat and make her kick the ball out...to the point guard.

And you're on, out front, miles from the whirling violence, where the sport reaches its true beauty...one-on-one with Buffy Fregosi. This is it. All the dreams and hard work on the line, the crucial game you've played a million different times in your mind on a million different playgrounds. No doubts. Composure. The ball slick, from everyone's sweat...from your fear. A kaleidoscope of crowd color and crowd movement visible through the glass backboard, but focused on one inanimate object...a small orange circle draped with a sparkling white net and set parallel with the floor. Soaring as high as you can, ignoring the Missouri hand in your face, the Missouri body soaring, pressing damp and hot against yours, the grunt of desire from a Missouri woman trying to achieve what she wants, trying to keep you from what you want, what you need...

Do you need it more than she does?

Prove it!

Bombs away, from twenty-three feet, the trees soaring in their whirling violence, climbing each other's backs. Swish! The trees slapping the backboard in frustration at not getting a chance for a rebound, at having the game go over their heads, dropping back to the floor in a pack, open hands held at their shoulders, showing the referees they weren't really pounding the crap out of each other.

An eruption of movement, bodies from both teams flowing down the court, seemingly disorganized but everyone knowing precisely where they were going and trying to beat the opponent to that spot, the guards attacking each other like sharks in a feeding frenzy to slow ball movement, disrupt offensive patterns, shouts and hand signals everywhere, calling offensive plays, relaying defensive sets. Coach Murphy shouting above the crowd roar, "Casey! Lobo-Curl! Run it until they stop it! Your light's green! You're the one, babe, you're the one!" The Missouri coach shouting, "Buffy! You've got to contain Ellison! She'll kill us unless you put a leash on her! You're the one, babe, you're the one!"

Fast...so fast you don't have time to think, only time to react, to succeed or fail with your instincts.

Everyone in Mitchell, the Lady Lobos included, were on their feet at the end of the game, howling at the top of their lungs, counting down the last ten seconds. Casey had the ball at the end, standing inside the wolf's mouth, running out the clock, the ball tucked under her arm, while Buffy stood five feet in front of her, hands held helplessly at her sides, frustration and resignation clearly seen in her eyes as she watched some of her dreams die.

When the horn sounded, Casey fired the ball into the student section and then everyone mobbed her. Bodies were flying, everyone was pounding everyone else and screaming and rolling on the floor. The people in the stands spilled past the security guards and onto the floor. It was wild.

Casey turned around and bumped into Kristy. Casey hugged her. "I have to see you," Kristy said.

"You're looking at me."

"You know what I mean."

"I'll try," Casey said. "But if the team goes out to party I'm going with them."

"Oh." Kristy looked at her hands.

"Look," Casey said. "We haven't settled on a place to party. How about your loft? It's big enough for everyone."

Kristy's eyes lit up. She bit her bottom lip and nodded. "Like, okay-fine," she said. "I'll go home right now and start getting things ready."

Casey turned around and bumped into Katie/Carla/Darla. They started clicking their tongues and pressing soft fingers to her face, eyes concerned-looking, faces soft. Casey invited them to the party even if she was still about two-thirds mad and hurt because they'd unilaterally flushed her.

"Where's the bash, like, at?" Katie asked.

Casey told them the address. "Kristy Neapope's loft," Carla said.

"We've, like, spied on the dyke," Darla explained.

Casey saw Sharika fighting her way through the mob. She turned and pushed her way to the locker room, students and fans pounding on her back the whole time. She ran through the mob of reporters outside the locker room, past the security guards keeping everyone out, and into the locker room. She heard crying and cussing and shoe-throwing coming through the wall from the Missouri locker room, and Buffy Fregosi sobbing, "She took my head off! She went to another level and I couldn't keep up!"

"This time, Buffy, this time," Casey said softly. She wanted to go and comfort all the Missouri players, but she was probably the last person in the world they wanted to see. It was Missouri's turn to cry, Tech's turn to celebrate.

She snuck into Coach Murphy's office, stole the key to the Coke machine, opened it and started tossing Cokes and Sprites to everyone when they came trickling in. Everyone shook the cans and started squirting soda all over everyone.

When Coach Murphy came into the locker room, the players grabbed a huge jug of Gatorade and dumped it on her head. She gasped, her hair came out of its bun, she stood there dripping wet, dress ruined, a puddle of Gatorade collecting at her feet, that certain look on her face.

Everyone froze.

Coach Murphy cracked up and the celebration kicked into high gear. Someone fired up a boom box, an L7 song started blaring, everyone was whooping and dancing and popping each other with towels.

Tech 101, Mizzou 89.

Weatherly jumped onto a bench, shouting for everyone to shut up so she could announce the team awards. Everyone gathered around, jeering, laughing, squirting soda all around.

Tobie got the 'Golden Glove Boxing Award.'

Casey got the 'Face In The Elbow Award.'

Alysa got the 'Most Long-winded Award.' For her stories about Hugo, Oklahoma or her farts in the showers nobody knew.

Coach Murphy got the 'Largest Stockholder In Mylanta-II Award.'

Then they got serious. Coach Murphy jumped up on a bench. "I have an announcement," she said. "Kelli will be leaving us next year. She's completed her graduate work and has accepted an assistant coaching job at Southern Missouri State."

Everyone screamed, "Zing-gotcha zing-gotcha!" The grad assistant with red hair gave everyone her meanest look before she cracked up.

"Continuing along that line," Coach Murphy said. "Alysa won't be leaving us next year. I've offered her a position as a grad assistant. She has accepted."

Everyone started cheering and pounding on Alysa. Alysa was crying and wiping at her eyes. "Poor old Alysa ain't gonna let you scrawny white girls get away with nothing next year," she rumbled.

Coach Murphy held up a hand. "One more thing and then I'll leave you alone," she said. "We have received notice from the NCAA that they're dropping their investigation, citing a lack of substantive evidence of any violations on our part. The formal announcement will be made within the next several weeks."

Everyone cheered.

Coach Murphy held up a hand again. "The newspaper involved in this, under pressure from university lawyers, has agreed to print a retraction of their story, along with an apology to the university, the coaching staff and all the players." Her eyes glinted, she smiled with wicked delight. "The reporter who started all this has been removed from covering women's athletic and has been reassigned. He's now working in the Arctic Circle, reporting on the breeding habits of lemmings."

The celebrating got real serious. And louder.

Casey went to Coach Murphy and got a soggy hug and a You-Done-Good towel, the returning Amazon kneeling before her Queen to receive her reward, drained, wounded, flushed with victory.

"I love you," Casey murmured, feeling unsure of herself, unsure of what the response would be.

"I love you," Coach Murphy said, touching Casey's cheek, eyes soft, motherly. "You're a special young woman."

"Hearing you say that means more to me than anything in the world."

"I felt the same about my college coach."

"We're having a party," Casey said. "Will you come?"

"Some people would say it's unethical for a coach to party with her players," Coach Murphy said.

"It would mean a lot to the team."

"I'll try," Coach Murphy said. "My husband's in town and we have our circle of friends, but we'll see what we can do."

A grad assistant shouted something about whoever ripped-off Coach Murphy's keys and opened the Coke machine owed at least a thousand laps because the Cokes had to come out of Coach Murphy's budget. Another grad assistant shouted, "Watch out! We're cutting the reporters loose! Most of them are males!"

The door slammed open. A pack of reporters and TV cameras boiled into the locker room, surrounding Coach Murphy, shouting questions about the NCAA investigation and what was she doing to keep it from distracting the team, taking pictures of Coach Murphy, shoving microphones into her face. Toni Denson, ace reporter, was right in the middle of the pack, elbowing and shoving and shouting questions and poking her recorder everywhere.

Gatordade-soaked Coach Murphy stood in the middle of all the popping flashbulbs and glaring TV lights and pointed microphones and said, "If you want to know anything about this team, don't talk to me. Talk to the women who have made this year special. This is their moment."

Casey got interviewed by at least twenty reporters, everyone calling her the 'Mad Bomber,' everyone asking how it felt to set a new conference record for points scored in a season by a freshman. She sat in front of her locker in her damp uniform, answering questions until everyone was through with her. Six three-pointers. Four two-pointers. Five free throws. Thirty-one points. Eight assists. Four steals. Two rebounds.

Five days until the Big Seven Freshman of the Year balloting. Publicity was what it took to win. That's what it's all about, babe. Answering dumb questions in a damp uniform when you'd rather grab a shower, suck down a beer and spend time with someone special away from the glitter.

Major-college ball.

The party was toe-tuh-lee raucous. They hit Kristy's loft with beer and chips and dips and sliced pepperoni and cheeses and a blaring boom box. Players, grad assistants, boyfriends, girlfriends, groupies, some women by themselves eyeing all the men, some women by themselves eyeing all the women, everyone sucking down beer, pigging-out, dancing, howling.

"It's going to get louder," Casey said to Kristy.

"The hardware store's closed," Kristy said. "There's nobody around to hear."

Katie/Carla/Darla were wearing matching see-through white blouses and no bras and matching white miniskirts and white heels.

No hose, Carla with her unshaven legs and pits slapping everyone in the face, all three pantie-less under their skirts if Casey knew them.

Tobie was dancing with Toni Denson, eyes glued to each other's faces, their fresh love in nauseating full bloom. Tobie had the You-Done-Good towel she'd gotten for scoring twenty-two against Missouri knotted around her wrist, flaunting it in front of everybody, a toe-tuh-lee cocky expression on her face. Starting down a road Casey was familiar with.

Everyone crowded to the door when Coach Murphy came in. She looked gorgeous in tight blue jeans and a pink turtleneck and grey cowgirl boots. She was with her husband and Coach DeFoe and two other couples. Coach DeFoe didn't have a husband or a lover or anyone in her life. She was married to basketball. Coach Murphy's husband was a handsome man, big, with brown hair and little grey at his temples. He was several years older than Coach Murphy.

Coach Murphy took a beer and went around chatting and hugging and congratulating. She was holding her husband's hand the whole time, looking up at him with shining eyes every so often. She had a bad case of it for her husband. Everyone started screaming, "Speech, speech!" after a while.

Coach Murphy's husband grabbed her around the waist, her laughing and clutching at his arms, and lifted her onto the coffee table. Someone turned the music down and they all crowded around the table. Coach Murphy's husband looked up at her with shining eyes. He had a pretty bad case of it, too.

"First," Coach Murphy said, "I'm glad to see none of you underage freshmen and sophomores are drinking." Everyone cheered. Casey hid her beer behind her back, noticing Tobie did the same. "No driving when you leave here," Coach Murphy said. "Call a cab or walk or sleep here." Everyone cheered again. Casey supposed Coach Murphy could say everyone was getting executed in the morning and they'd all cheer.

Coach Murphy paused to look around the room, making eye contact with all her players, winking at this one, smiling at this one, just looking at this one. Everyone looked back, completely hypnotized, in love, willing to pick up a gun and go to war if Coach Murphy was leading them.

"The first one always tastes the sweetest," Coach Murphy said.

Everyone went nuts, bashing forearms, howling.

"You're a group of fighters," Coach Murphy said, making a sour face. "I can't take that out of you without breaking your spirit so I guess I have to learn to live with the fights."

Everyone screamed, "Let's rock-and-roll!"

"I have never been associated with a team more irritating," Coach Murphy said. "You people foul too much, you shoot free throws like you're blind and you always seem to be out of position defensively. But you have a knack for reaching down and finding what it takes to win. That's something I can't take credit for, it has nothing to do with coaching."

"Everyone screamed, "Great desire!"

"I'd like to thank my grad assistants," Coach Murphy said. "They've done an outstanding job this year." Everyone screamed, "No! God-dammit! No! God-dammit!" Coach Murphy looked at Coach DeFoe. "I'd especially like to thank Coach DeFoe. I don't know what we would've done without her this year. I love you, Maxie."

Coach DeFoe blushed and dropped her head. Everyone pounded her on the back. "Laps," she said, trying to look vicious. "Laps for all of you."

"When I accepted this job three years ago," Coach Murphy said, looking down at her husband with moist eyes. "When John gave up a prestigious New York-to-London turn-around so we could move back home, I had three goals. One, to win the Big Seven Championship. Two, to make the NCAA Tournament. Three, to win the National Championship." A pause. "We made the NCAA last year." Another pause. "We won the Big Seven today."

Everyone went nuts.

"The National Championship is on our fingertips!" Coach Murphy shouted.

Everyone went bonkers, bashing forearms, shouting, "Lady Vols! Lady Vols! We want you!"

Coach Murphy jumped off the coffee table. Her husband grabbed her, kissed her and swept her out the door. Coach DeFoe and the other two couples followed.

Katie/Carla/Darla grabbed the boom box, jammed a Concrete Blonde tape into it, cranked it and started hopping in the middle of the loft, chattering between themselves, knees flying high, arms waving, heads flopping back-and-forth on their shoulders, glimpses of bare flesh showing under their dresses each time their legs lifted.

Tobie and Toni started hopping with Katie/Carla/Darla, laughing, trying to figure them out, peeking up their dresses. Tobie and Toni both kept saying, "What? What did you say? What does that, like, mean?"

Casey grabbed Kristy. Kristy was sweating and running around emptying ash trays and throwing empty beer cans in the trash and passing around food trays and making sure everyone was having a good time. Her face was flushed, her eyes excited-looking.

"Looks like you're having fun," Casey said.

"This is great," Kristy said. "I've met so many nice people. Thanks for bringing everyone here." She dropped her eyes and bit her bottom lip. "I met a man," she said, nodding toward a groupie with dark hair in a corner. "He comes into Burger King sometimes." She giggled. "He's Dakota, isn't that funny? The Dakota and my people used to be fierce enemies." She paused before squealing, "He thinks I'm cool because the basketball team is partying at my place! He asked me out and I accepted. Do you mind?"

Casey hugged her. "If that's what you want, I'm happy for you."

"I don't know what I want," Kristy said. "All I know is how grateful I am to you. You've shown me what a relationship with a woman is like. Now he'll show me what one with a man is like so I can make my decision. I've already decided maybe I'm bisexual so the sex isn't all that important, I guess. Do you hate me for that?"

"No, I don't hate you," Casey said, laughing.

"I thought lesbians hate everyone who isn't a lesbian."

"Don't worry," Casey said. "We'll be friends for life. Call me after your date and tell me how it went."

"I will," Kristy promised. She leaned close and whispered, "I'm seeing my family tomorrow. They thought things over and they want me back. I'm so relieved."

"I can imagine." Casey gave her another hug before Kristy buzzed away, emptying more ashtrays, cutting bashful glances at the man in the corner.

Casey found the phone under a stack of coats and carried it into the bathtub. The bathtub was dry and smelled like Lysol and Soft-scrub. Kristy always cleaned it and dried it out after she used it. She was obsessive-compulsive about cleaning. Casey pulled the shower curtain closed, propped an arm under her head and kicked her feet up on the end of the tub.

"You have the prettiest big brown eyes," she said when Sharika answered. "I don't care if that's a body thing or not. It's the truth."

"Where are you?"

"In the tub."

"Ummm," Sharika said. "I'm sitting in front of a fire, scratching Myrtle's chin and thinking about you."

"And after Monica Hills died?"

"I know you're at a party," Sharika said. "Why didn't you invite me? I'm all dolled-up, wearing my best dress, waiting for an invitation."

"Squirm, baby, squirm."

Sharika cleared her throat. "You're digging deep," she finally said.

"You asked for it."

"I know," Sharika said. A pause. "Monica never cared about turning pro. She just wanted to teach first grade and have a home and a family. She had all that until it was taken away from her by a good ole boy who thought it was funny to run from the police. And nothing was done to the man who murdered her. A jury found him not guilty of vehicular homicide. He was convicted of reckless driving and fined five hundred dollars."

"Please tell me that's not true."

"Oh, Casey, I miss her so much," Sharika said. "She was such a special person. When she died it took something out of me. Something I could never replace. Monica was the one who always kept my feet on the ground, like I tried to do with you. We used to talk on the phone two or three times a week, and after I'd lost a match, like after I lost at Wimbledon, she'd say something like, 'Girlfriend, who taught you to play tennis like that? I sure never did!' I'd picture her standing in her kitchen, balancing a baby on her hip, and it would make things seem better, just from hearing her voice and listening to her laugh."

"It's probably an understatement to say you two were close."

"We leaned on each other the way you lean on your teammates," Sharika said. "How would you feel if your basketball team won a National Championship and not long after everyone but you was killed in a car wreck?"

"I hope I never have to feel that."

"I drifted around for a few years after Monica died," Sharika said. "Playing in tournaments, playing poorly, sleeping around, drinking too much, ignoring my training, pretending to myself my body wasn't falling apart right in front of my eyes. After I lost a knee in Spain, I retired and came home with my leg in a cast and my dreams in shreds. Once my knee healed I had to live with my parents for six months until I finally got the pro job at a country club. I've been there ever since. No jock glitter. No fame. No trophies. The only glory I've gotten was two years ago when one of my girls won State. That's it. You know everything about me now. Except where I'm going from here. I don't know that myself. All I know is I'm staring thirtysomething square in the face and I'm alone." Sharika laughed, a sad laugh. "Ain't life a bitch? If I had me a beer I'd cry in it because I'm so god-damn pitiful."

"I don't think you're pitiful," Casey said, wondering if she was about to start crying in her beer, decided she probably was the way her vision was blurring. "I think you're tough in a way I'll never be."

"You're the tough one," Sharika, said, sounding like her own vision was blurring. "When I went up in smoke it wasn't at home."

"Do you really understand me?" Casey asked. "Do you understand the threshold our team is standing on?"

"I've heard the cheers, I've stood on the same threshold," Sharika said. A pause and then softly, "Do you understand me?"

"Not completely," Casey said. "I don't think it's inside of me to ever understand you completely, all the things you've gone through in your life, all the obstacles you've had to overcome."

"I want to see you," Sharika said. "Right now. Let me prove I understand you."

"Okay-fine. I'll be in front of the downtown hardware store in ten minutes. If you're not there I'm not waiting. I'm getting naked with one of the gorgeous babes hanging around here."

"I won't be there," Sharika said. "Not on those terms. Not when you're holding other women over my head. You've won. You've proven to me I'm nothing but a body you can replace in a minute. I'd hoped you would change. I doubt you ever will."

"That was an attempt at humor," Casey said. "There's nobody else, Scooter. There hasn't been for a long time. I didn't call to gloat. I haven't done anything to gloat over. I called to wave the white flag. What else do you need me to say? That I have changed and I want to prove it to you? That I'm all soft and mushy over you? That..."

Casey heard the cat squall, the phone hit the floor, a door slam. She put on her coat and left the party, walking down the steps, standing under a streetlight in front of the hardware store. She thought about what she'd do with Sharika. Probably nothing special. Maybe go to dinner. Or maybe a movie. Or maybe go back to the party. Or maybe they'd go to campus and take a long walk down by the duck pond. That sounded good. The duck pond was a romantic spot, the perfect place to spend time with someone you felt soft and mushy about.

Or maybe they'd do all those things...or maybe...Casey didn't know what they'd do. She didn't have any say in the matter, she was just a bug, a bug all wrapped up. They were both bugs, they'd reduced each other to bugs, they'd decide together what they wanted to do.

Whatever they did it would be one-on-one, where love reached its highest beauty, Casey supposed.

She heard screaming tires and a roaring engine, saw a white Corvette flashing down the deserted street, sliding to a stop under the streetlight, Sharika jumping out, running around the car, her eyes so hot it almost burned to look at them.

AUTHOR'S NOTE

This book is obviously a work of fiction; as such it is unrealistic in places. The size of the crowds the heroines in this book play in front of are rare in women's basketball. I remember the National Championship game in New Orleans in 1991. The arena was not even sold out for the game. The 1992 National Championship game in Los Angeles had very low attendance for an event of such magnitude. Why? Because the game was played at nine in the morning, local time, to accommodate television demands for an acceptable east coast playing time. This is the way female athletes are treated by the national media.

But here's something to laugh at: The women's National Semifinals are played on a Saturday every year. The women then turn around and play their Championship game the next day, on Sunday. The men's National Semifinals are also played on Saturday. But the men don't play for the Championship until Monday evening. Why? The official line is the men are too tired after Saturday's games to turn around and play again the next day. Poor, pitiful little boys. Maybe when they grow up they'll be as hardy as women.

But the lack of fan attendance—and low television ratings—for women's basketball is nothing to laugh at. In 1991-92, the University of West Virginia had a team that won a school-record 17 straight games, led the Atlantic 10 conference, had a point guard who was among the leading scorers in the country and was ranked fifteenth in the country. Their average attendance was 591 fans per game when they didn't play as part of a men's doubleheader. Tickets for a women's game at West Virginia cost two dollars.

I can't understand this. In my home town, a ticket to the local university's games cost three dollars. A soft drink costs a dollar and a bag of popcorn costs a dollar. If you take your girlfriend to a game and treat her to the works, it costs ten bucks for two hours of pure excitement watching superbly conditioned women straining and sweating against each other. Sounds like a great way to spend a Saturday or Sunday afternoon to me. But I have been to some games where I estimated the crowd at maybe fifty people.

There are exceptions to this, of course. The University of Texas averages somewhere around eight thousand people per game. Texas charges the same price for a ticket as the men's team, too. The University of Tennessee also draws well, as do many teams in the Southeastern and Southwestern United States, traditional hotbeds for sports of all types. It is not uncommon for the Tennessee women to outdraw the Tennessee men. But then Tennessee has several National Championships to its credit. Southwest Missouri State, coming off a final Four appearance in 1991-'92 led the country in attendance for 1992-'93. The first advance sellout in the history of women's basketball occurred in '92-93 when Number 1 Vanderbilt played Number 2 Tennessee in a game that drew considerable national attention. The Stanford-Connecticut game was also an advance sell-out in '92-'93. So the future looks good for women's basketball.

Fifteen years ago, a road trip for women meant everybody loaded into the coach's car or van and drove to where they were playing. They slept crammed together in the bare minimum of motel rooms they could tolerate. They ate as cheaply as they could. The coach paid for everything, which meant before a coach scheduled a road game she had to make sure she could afford it personally. The university didn't allocate her enough money for road trips.

Nowadays, women frequently fly to road games and they eat better and have better hotel accommodations and nicer uniforms to wear. This generosity on the part of the universities is mostly the result of legal action taken by brave women. This generosity also causes endless bitching on the part of the coaches of men's sports because they have to reduce their budgets to share with the women. Coaches of men's sports say why should women get any money since none of the women's programs are self-supporting.

Who's fault is it if women's athletic programs aren't self-supporting? Don't we have to look to ourselves? Who will support women's athletics if we don't do it ourselves?

Women student-athletes are without a doubt students first and athletes second. Unlike men, who see a college scholarship as a chance to gain experience for a professional career, women see college scholarships as a chance to get an education, an education many would have to forgo if it were not for sports. When you watch a women's basketball game, you are truly watching female students who play the game to pay for their education, and because of a pure love for the sport. They don't play the game for the mind-boggling riches that await many males in the professional ranks.

As in most things when women compete directly with men on an even basis, women prove superior: The graduation rates for women athletes are substantially higher than those of men. At Georgia Tech, for instance, seventy-three percent of white female athletes graduate, compared to fifty-nine percent of white male athletes. This kind of female superiority is common at most universities. The disparity between the sexes increases when the two 'glamor' sports for each are compared. At Louisiana State University, only twenty-seven percent of the 1984 football recruits received degrees. It is not uncommon to find a women's basketball program with a one-hundred percent graduation rate. I think these figures speak volumes about the dedication and drive women can display if they are given even the slightest chance to succeed.

The most irritating thing for me personally about women's basketball, other than the lack of fan attendance, is the presence of male coaches. Sure, fifteen years ago perhaps there weren't many female coaches with experience, so colleges had to rely on men. But that has changed. Qualified women coaches abound, and it irritates me considerably to see a middle-aged, potbellied man coaching a team of women. I'm not saying all men coaches should be immediately fired. But when one does retire or move on, it makes me furious to see a university replace a male coach with another male coach, when many qualified women have applied for the same job. I have drawn a wicked satisfaction the last several years from the fact that a team coached by a man has not won the National Championship. I tell myself that no man can motivate a team of women to the level it takes to win the National Championship the way a woman coach can. College women need a mentor. Not a Daddy.

There are currently no women head coaches of a men's basketball team in this country, although the University of Kentucky does have an assistant coach on its men's team who is female. Are men telling us that men can handle women, but women can't handle men? Is that sexist bull-shit or am I six-feet tall and beautiful and rich (I'm not)? I want, no, I demand women coaches for women athletes. Why should women's athletics provide a career path for men when men's athletics don't provide a career path for women? I won't stop bitching about this to anyone who will listen until it comes true or I die. I suspect I'll die first.

While doing research for this book, I virtually lived in basketball arenas. I saw many great women athletes in person, and many great performances by these women, sometimes in a losing effort, but they always gave all they had to give. The characters in this book are composites of the women I studied. This novel was written in tribute to them. It is my humble effort to bring some recognition to them for their efforts and their dedication.

Kristen Garrett

Kristen Garrett attended college on a partial academic scholarship, supplemented by working nights as a waitress, and eventually earned a Masters degree. Since graduation she has worked as an educator for sixteen years. She likes guinea pigs and wild squirrels and pizza and driving fast. Kristen presently lives in the mountains of the Southeastern United States. This is her second novel.